Gigi,
You are such a
blessing to me! ♡ God Bless,

Mc Dowell

Lesley

By Lesley Ann McDaniel

ISLANDS OF INTRIGUE: SAN JUANS

ໜ^{Christian Romantic Suspense}

The Unrelenting Tide – Lynnette Bonner
BOOK ONE

Tide Will Tell – Lesley Ann McDaniel
BOOK TWO

Deceptive Tide – Janalyn Voigt
BOOK THREE
Coming Summer, 2015

Other books by Lesley Ann McDaniel

Montana Hearts series
⊱Christian Romance⊰

Lights, Cowboy, Action
BOOK ONE

Big Sky Bachelor
BOOK TWO

Rocky Mountain Romance
BOOK THREE

Madison Falls series
⊱Christian Romantic Suspense⊰

Saving Grace
BOOK ONE

Find out more at lesleyannmcdaniel.com

Tide Will Tell
ISLANDS OF INTRIGUE: SAN JUANS, Book 2

Cover design by Lynnette Bonner of Indie Cover Design
www.indiecoverdesign.com
  images ©
    www.dreamstime.com, File: #M_1248748
    www.fotolia.com, File: #23488527_XL
    www.peopleimages.com, File: #ID48633

Scripture taken from *The Message*. Copyright © 1993, 1994, 1995, 1996, 2000, 2001, 2002. Used by permission of NavPress Publishing Group.

ISBN: 978-1499669244

Tide Will Tell is a work of fiction. References to real people, events, establishments, organizations, or locales are intended only to provide a sense of authenticity and are used fictitiously. All other characters, incidents, and dialogue are drawn from the author's imagination.

Printed in the U.S.A.

Psalm 138:7

When I walk into the thick of trouble,
keep me alive in the angry turmoil.
With one hand
strike my foes,
With your other hand
save me.
Finish what you started in me, God.
Your love is eternal—don't quit on me now.

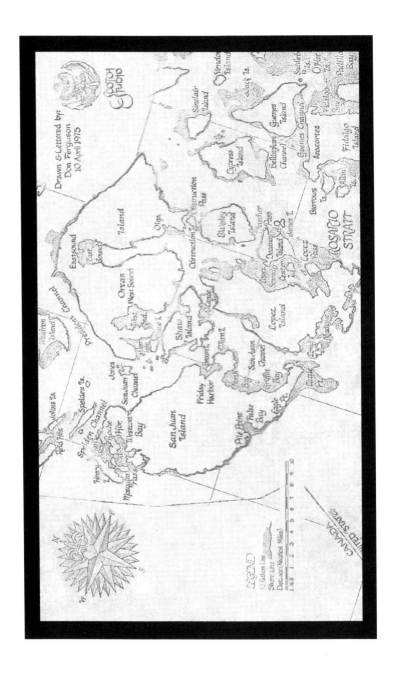

# Chapter 1

An assault of whirring, clicking cameras met Kate Jennings' limo the instant it exited the ferry. Despite the darkened car windows that concealed her, she slunk lower into the backseat, reassuring herself that the huge sunglasses she'd bought at the airport would adequately mask her features. Chase had warned that a few reporters might greet her on the island, but she hadn't expected this kind of frenzy.

Panic surged. The last thing she needed was to have her face flashed all over the news. Why hadn't she thought this through?

Massive lights and mics on poles swayed like a nightmarish forest, moving along with the vehicle as it rolled forward and eased around a curve in the road. Couldn't the driver just gun it? For a split second, she regretted coming here. What had she been thinking, agreeing to marry someone with whom the media had such an insatiable fascination?

"Kate! Look this way." A deep voice carried above the others even through the rolled-up windows of the car. "Aren't you scared of him? Come on, admit it!"

Scared? A shiver clambered down her spine at the implication. Shuddering, she lowered her chin and brought her hands to her cheeks. The only thing she had to be scared of was having a clear image of her face land on the evening news or the front page of a major newspaper. The suggestion that she should be afraid of Chase was comical in contrast to the disaster these troublemakers outside her car could initiate without even realizing it.

"Did he do it, Kate?" A man with a microphone jogged alongside the car, shouting. "What's he told you?"

A dull ache thumped at her temples. As the driver managed at last to pick up speed and pull away from the pressing crowd, Kate spoke, more to herself than to him. "It's a circus out there."

"Yes, ma'am."

She looked at his eyes in the rearview mirror. "Has it always been like this…since…you know?"

"Only at first." The car veered out onto the road and the commotion faded into the distance. "It had all but died down. You coming out here put fresh wind in their sails. They're here now because of you."

"Because of *me?*" A sick feeling churned in the pit of her stomach. "That's ridiculous. I didn't do anything."

"No, ma'am." His tone remained non-committal.

"And how do they even know about me?"

"It's a small community, ma'am. People talk, and…" His apologetic gaze met hers for just a moment. "It's made the national news."

"Right." She knew that. But they'd been so careful. "You haven't seen any close-ups of my face, have you?"

"Only shots taken from a distance, ma'am. The press has honored Mr. Cole's request for your privacy."

So far, anyway. The adrenaline completed its trek through her system, leaving her drained and trembling. "They can't get near the house, can they?"

"Mr. Cole's property is gated. The media knows not to trespass."

"Good." Twisting around, she took a reassuring glance through the rear window. "I just want to be left alone."

"You've come to the right place." He looked at her in the mirror, his eyes smiling slightly. "Shaw Island's residents are known for keeping a low profile."

"Perfect." Removing the glasses, she rubbed the bridge of her nose. "I want to keep my profile so low not even a snake will take notice."

He chuckled lightly and focused on the road ahead.

Forcing a calm breath, Kate placed the glasses in her Chloe handbag and smoothed the crisp cream linen skirt Chase had bought for her in California. She admired the stylish peach top and matching pumps that were so unlike anything she ever would have picked out for herself. How lucky could she get, having Chase now to direct her sense of style.

Pressing into the plush seat, she took in the passing beauty of the island. Since she'd hardly given any thought at all to what it would be like to live in the Pacific Northwest, its magnificence came as a pleasant surprise.

The sun danced happily through trees that appeared a vivid emerald even through the tinted glass. Coming from a place that felt grimy and overpopulated, the abundance of pure nature here could easily overwhelm.

Chase had told her that the ten square miles that made up Shaw Island held a population of only a little over two hundred people, most of whom liked to keep to themselves. With no real tourist amenities and a business district that amounted to a general store and a post office, it sounded like the epitome of lush seclusion.

It was truly a world away from the Tenderloin in San Francisco, earning it points in its favor right off the bat. Of course, California had its share of plusses, but staying there had not been an option.

Guilt cramped her stomach at the thought of

the mess she had made of her life, and of the people she'd abandoned. *Poor Dakota.* She gulped back tears at the thought of his innocent face. Her leaving must have broken his heart.

She lowered her lids as if ending one scene in a movie to begin another. There were enough other people who cared about Dakota and would see to his needs. She had to believe that. Her eyelids lifted, but tears threatened. If Dakota were capable of fully comprehending the situation, he would know that leaving had been her only choice. Either leave or wind up dead.

Still, it weighed on her that she hadn't been able to say goodbye or to offer any sort of explanation. Now she just had to close the door on the past and appreciate that fate had intervened, bringing Chase into her life at just the right time.

Glancing down at the impossibly huge diamond on her finger, she brightened. Chase was everything she could ever want. Handsome, smart, funny. So what if he was thirty years older than her? That was a bonus in her book. Not to mention that he was *rich*. Rich beyond belief, with no problem lavishing his wealth on her in every way imaginable.

True, there was the issue of his recent past that had put him—and by association *her*— in the limelight, but that was just a natural byproduct of his being so wealthy. The public would always be hungry for scandal, whether real or imagined. As long as she took care to maintain her new look—especially keeping the dark roots at bay— and didn't let the cameras get too close, she could ride this out with ease. This was child's play compared to what she had already survived.

Gazing out the window, she watched a sailboat glide across the gray-green bay. That reminded her of another bonus. Chase owned a yacht. A *yacht!* She could scarcely believe it. She tipped her head back, picturing long days luxuriating on the deck of his...*their* boat, without a care in the world. Her troubles were truly over. Well, *almost* at least.

She rolled the tension out of her shoulders. Yes, the notoriety was easy to overlook when everything else about the man was just so perfect. Some women would have a problem with a fiancé who traveled half the time for business, but not Kate. She would enjoy having time to herself in his secluded house on this practically private island. This place was a gift.

As the summer sun sparkled through the trees, reality held her in its grasp. *Finally.* Her new home. And now she had nothing to do for the next week but plan the wedding. *I'm amazingly lucky.*

The road followed the gentle curve of the bay, then straightened and moved inland. Now trees and green fields swathed them on both sides. Kate sighed. This island felt like a dream. Nothing bad could happen to her here. The paparazzi would soon tire of trying to scare up a story. She and Chase would get on with their lives in this stunning paradise where no evil could touch them. Life would be good.

The car slowed, and Kate's stomach buckled. They had to be nearly there.

As they took a severe right off the main road, a thicket of trees next to the passenger side of the car fluttered in the afternoon breeze, its branches reaching out as if trying to disengage from the tangle. A smile reached Kate's lips as she thought of Audrey Jr., the man-eating plant in *The Little Shop of Horrors*, one of her favorite old movies.

As she leaned closer to the window and pictured the shrubbery crying out 'Feed me, Seymour!', a dark form emerged from the foliage and lurched at the limo. She jerked back, her mind freezing as she caught a fleeting glimpse of a face, or rather the place where a face should be, inside the hood of an oversized black sweat jacket.

In the split second it took her to choke down a scream, the figure retreated back into the dense stand of trees. *Gone*.

Chapter 2

Settling into a cushioned deck chair, Josh took a sip of root beer and tried to relax. Shaw Island was every bit as inviting as Jessica had promised, but if he had realized he was going to feel so out of place at her home this weekend, he wouldn't have accepted the invitation.

Jessica's twelve or so other friends who had come to the island to unwind after finals were a pretty rowdy bunch, especially—as Josh had noted upon his own arrival that afternoon—when they'd had one or two Mojitos to kick off the celebration. He'd instantly regretted his decision to come, but had figured if it got too bad he could always leave. He had never, even in his days before accepting the Lord, understood the appeal of getting drunk.

Still, he had to admit that the opportunity to see this house eased his apprehension. From everything he'd read and heard, Jess' family had more money than they knew what to do with, and it was fun to see how the other half lived. While Josh felt content with his own starving-student status for the time being, he'd admired the soaring architecture, expensive artwork, and the impressive collection of Native American artifacts. He had to wonder what it would feel like to not have to worry about money. To just fix the car radio when it broke, or get a new battery. Or a whole new car, for that matter.

Jess had given him the grand tour before bringing him out to join the others. Even though it was a warm June afternoon, he'd been drawn to the built-in stone fire pit. Could be it felt safer than either of the deck's other focal points—the hot tub or the bar. Unless he went for a second root beer, he wouldn't be enjoying either of those features, but he appreciated the opulence and the view of the bay.

women crave safety not men

The guy sitting to his left—a business major whom Josh had seen around campus but had never officially met—handed him a piece of accordion pleated paper. Taking it, Josh did his best to get into the spirit of Jessica's idea of an ice breaker—a rousing game of *Consequences*.

"Okay, everybody." Settling on a stool with her back to the bar, Jessica flicked her long honey colored hair over her shoulder. Her oversized t-shirt and super-short cut-off jeans were a far cry from her usual high fashion sorority girl garb, and only served to intensify Josh's discomfort. "The next thing you write is 'the consequence was…'"

Josh would not be uncomfortable but others so bored around

He thought for a second, then wrote '*the consequence was…the planet exploded*' on his paper and folded it over to cover what he had just written. He then passed the paper to Kim on his right. Taking it, she twirled a strand of her ginger-colored hair and smiled coyly.

The smile he returned was more polite than promising. Like the game, Kim's attempt at flirtation was harmless enough. If he managed to lighten up a little, he might even manage to enjoy himself this weekend.

"Okay, the last thing you write..." Jessica paused to sip from an icy lime-slice-and-mint-sprig-embellished glass. "...is 'and the world said...'."

As instructed, Josh wrote the first thing that came to mind, which was of course a movie reference. *'and the world said...slow fade to black.'* A roller coaster feeling in the pit of his gut accompanied the reminder of how much money still stood between him and film school in the fall. So much for lightening up.

"Hey, Josh." Jessica called over to him. "You're up. Read what you've got."

He unfolded the paper and obliged. "The mysterious and fetching Dolores Del Marco met the charismatic Simon Fritz at the zoo. He bought her an alabaster statue and said to her 'what's your shoe size?'. She said to him 'I live in Canada', and the consequence was they honeymooned in the South of France, and the world said 'slow fade to black'."

Josh is having emotional stomach issues just like Kate (a woman) more likely

22

Everyone laughed harder than the story or this game warranted, but Josh smiled along at the innocent fun.

"You really should act in those films you make, you know." Kim gave him a wink as she unfolded her own paper. Leaning over, she spoke through the soft scent of rum and lime. "You've got all the right stuff to make the ladies swoon."

The realization that people were looking their way jarred him. "I think it's your turn."

Giggling, Kim flattened her paper to read.

Josh had always managed to ignore Kim's flirting, although he had noticed it escalating since she'd broken up with her boyfriend several months ago. It didn't matter. They'd both graduated from the U and they'd be going their separate ways soon. While he didn't want to encourage her, neither did he feel the need to dissuade her, as long as her advances remained benign. As far as he was concerned, she was just another nice girl who'd had too many things handed to her. Like most of Jessica's crowd, she could use the dose of reality that would probably hit once they were no longer being bankrolled by their parents.

Josh said a silent prayer of thanks that his own parents, who were by no means wealthy, had instilled morals and a healthy work ethic in him. How he'd wound up on the fringes of Jessica's elite crowd, he still wasn't quite sure.

Kim had the group in stitches over her reading. "…and the consequence was that the planet exploded." She reached over and rumpled Josh's hair. "Good one, sci-fi boy." She continued. "And the world said 'what else would you expect from a Neanderthal?'"

Reaching up to smooth his hair back into place, Josh smiled good-naturedly. This game might actually be fun without the alcoholic augmentation.

"Stu!" Jessica tossed an irritated look at Stuart, who had separated himself from the group and was engaged in a gleeful conversation on his phone. "It's your turn."

Stuart responded with an annoyed sneer and continued what appeared to be a playful conversation with some female on the other end of the line.

Being a connoisseur of character, Josh had put some effort into figuring this guy out. He had to be in his late twenties, but from the sound of things, he fully intended to keep doing nothing with his life but party, collect female admirers, and enjoy the occasional ski trip. Watching him now, Josh wondered what would happen if the guy got the rug pulled out from under him.

Never one to tolerate an obvious affront, Jessica took a sheet of paper from the bar, scrawled something on it, and walked over to Stuart. She waved it in his face until he grabbed it out of her hand. Jessica turned on her heel and marched back to where she'd been perched. She missed seeing Stuart fold up the paper and defiantly toss it in her direction.

"When is your other guest arriving?" Staci, a no-nonsense theatre major who had assisted Josh on a couple of his student films, slipped onto the barstool next to Jessica's.

Jessica rolled her eyes. "Don't ask me. All of *my* friends are already here."

Josh looked out at the water. He had no idea who they were talking about, and he really didn't care. He enjoyed getting to know people, but the thought of slipping away from the group to have some time alone suddenly seemed really appealing. With the alcohol flowing freely and so many guests to keep her occupied, Jessica probably wouldn't even notice.

Having ended his call, Stuart rejoined the group with his customary swagger. He opened up the paper on which he'd written the ending of a story like he was the town crier unfurling a scroll.

He cleared his throat, then read. "The doting and onerous Petunia met the smelly Conrad at the Sundance Film Festival."

He stopped, giving Josh a knowing glance. Who else would have come up with a film reference?

Stuart went on. "He gave her a diploma and said to her 'ever race at NASCAR?'. She said to him 'There's no oxygen on the moon', and the consequence was they ate chocolate macaroons, and the world said 'God, grant me the serenity to accept the things I cannot change, the courage to change the things I can, and wisdom to know the difference.'."

"Gee, Stu." Jessica folded her reed-like arms. "Can't tell you've been through rehab."

"Good." He lifted his glass in her direction. "Then I've achieved my goal."

Staci grabbed the pad of paper from the bar. "Are we playing another round?"

"Maybe later." Standing, Jessica started to pull off her shirt. "I'm getting in the tub."

Alarmed at the unveiling of a hot pink bikini top under the shirt, Josh stood and wandered over to the deck rail.

"Hey, Josh." Sitting on the edge of the sizeable hot tub, Jessica dipped her hand in. "Are you tubbing? The water's perfect."

Affecting a polite smile, and taking care to keep his gaze focused no lower than her chin, he shook his head. "I'm really not big on hot tubs."

"Oh, right." She flicked her hair again, nearly whipping the guy sitting next to her across the face. "It's that *water* thing." She swung her legs over the edge. "Well, we'll leave you a spot in case you change your mind."

Trying to overlook the subtle jab masquerading as sympathy, Josh turned to gaze out at the water between the islands. The day was clear and beautiful but, typical of the Pacific Northwest in June, a heavy storm front would be moving in tomorrow. Best to enjoy the outdoors here while the weather held.

"Is this your first time at Jessica's house?"

Josh jolted a little at the proximity of Kim's voice. He hadn't noticed that she'd gotten up and followed him.

"Yep. First time." Not wanting to be rude, he leaned on the railing and observed a ferry pulling into the terminal on Orcas Island. "I've never accepted an invitation before because I've always had to study or work on the weekends."

"Too bad." She leaned on the railing next to him, not quite close enough to touch his arm. "We've had some amazing times here. Like the best Halloween party ever." Kim shifted to subtly face him as she drew her arm over the expanse of wooded area below them, which led down to the water. "They created a whole haunted forest."

"I'm sure that was something." Josh forced a smile, but he was glad he'd missed it. A forest full of spooks held no appeal.

"And of course, her New Year's Eve parties are legendary. Gallons of champagne and enough food to feed an army. Last year, a bunch of us got to go out on the yacht with Sam." She pointed to the dock which was partially visible through the trees, a ways down the shoreline. "You have to

27

take one of the dinghies out to where it's deep enough to drop anchor in the bay. See?"

Turning his head slightly to take in the sight of a gleaming white vessel sitting regally offshore, Josh grunted an affirmation.

"They did a fireworks display out there in the channel." She tipped her head away from the dock, out toward the stretch of water between Shaw and Orcas. "We were practically underneath it. Maybe you'll accept her invite this year. Ring in the New Year with style."

Josh wasn't sure at the moment which part held less appeal—being out on the water, witnessing the effect of the 'gallons of champagne' on the other guests, or the obvious safety hazard of parking a boat so close to the launching pad of the fireworks. He'd always preferred to ring in the new year with a few close friends and a couple of pizzas.

"Hey, guys." Jessica waved an arm to get everyone's attention. "I have a great idea. Let's go out on the kayaks. It's a perfect day for it."

"Sounds like fun." Kim turned to Josh. "Want to go?"

Josh glanced down at a rack of brightly colored boats next to the dock. The thought of being out on the water in one of those made his palms sweat. Taking some time to himself held more appeal. "No, I think I'll go get settled in my room."

She nodded. "Maybe a bike ride around the island later?"

"Maybe. That sounds like fun."

Kim smiled, apparently encouraged.

Josh drew in a long breath. He'd been so conscientious about guarding his heart. *Lord, let me navigate this minefield in a way that glorifies You.*

As everyone else prepared to go down to the water, Josh made his own plan. He'd stay out here for a little bit, then take the opportunity to get a closer look at some of the artwork inside the house. After that, he'd see about reconnecting with the group.

No point in acting like a complete loner this weekend.

 *Chapter* 3

As the car picked up speed again, Kate twisted around. There was no sign of anyone near the road.

She whirled back to question the driver. Surely he had seen the man lunge at the car from out of the roadside bramble, and would offer some explanation. But his eyes in the mirror focused on the road ahead. She swallowed her concern. If the driver didn't seem alarmed, it must have been nothing. Just a kid from the island, maybe. Or another reporter hoping to get her attention. That would explain the hood. But the lack of a face?

A cold shiver ran up her arms. *Ridiculous.* Maybe it was a mask she had seen, or the face was too shadowed by the hood to disclose its features. Or, more likely, she had just imagined the whole thing. Exhaustion ruled and reigned, not only from the long trip up from California but from the ordeal she'd been through over the past few months. Could be she was seeing things.

Shaking off her uneasiness, she looked ahead and her heart raced for a different reason. The driver slowed in approach to an ornate metal gate. He stopped and reached up to the visor to touch a tiny remote. As the gate slid open and the car glided through, Kate wrung her hands. Why was she so nervous?

Excited-nervous. That was it. *Not scared-nervous.* Her emotions had always been so scrambled that she had a hard time identifying them. Time to start getting a handle on that.

She pulled in a deep breath and looked through the windshield at the tree-lined drive ahead. As the car leisurely rounded a curve, the flora thinned like a curtain parting.

Mamma Mia. Chase had told her all about his house—*their* house—but nothing could have prepared her for this. She let out a gasp, to the apparent amusement of the driver, who responded with a light chuckle.

"This is it, Miss Jennings." He eased the car around the sprawling circular drive, stopping at the foot of a wide walkway. "Welcome home."

Slowly, she lifted her gaze.

Wow. She'd never lived in a place that had actual landscaping, but it had probably taken massive hours and mega bucks to make this yard look so perfectly natural. Even the house itself seemed so harmonious with nature, it could have sprouted out of the ground.

The walkway made a gradual incline toward a set of huge stone steps which ascended to the stage-like, flowerpot-dotted wraparound porch. Three stories of elegant natural wood, stone, and glass competed for height with the evergreens which formed a protective half-circle around it. Large stone chimneys emerged on either end of the roof. And windows? They were everywhere. This house went on for days.

A lump suddenly appeared in Kate's throat. What had she done to deserve this?

Barely eight weeks ago she'd been holed up in a filthy motel room, afraid to go outside for fear of being shot or worse. Tears welled at the memory. If she hadn't met Chase when she had, who knows what would have happened.

But now here she was, in this magnificent place, about to be reunited with the love of her life.

The driver had gotten out and walked around to her side of the car. He opened the door and held out a hand to her. Taking it, she swung both feet to the ground and stood, instantly regretting that morning's decision to wear the three-inch heels just because Chase had once commented that they made her legs look a mile long. It could very well take the rest of her natural life to adjust to walking in these things.

She forced a calm breath, appeased by the smell of pine trees and clean air. So different from the city. The only sound to break the silence was the soft twittering of a few birds. She could definitely get used to this.

The massive double doors at the front of the house swung open and Chase appeared, smiling broadly. He stepped out onto the porch, looking even more handsome than she remembered. His chiseled features—still tanned from the California sun—and silver-streaked hair made him look more like a matinee idol than a businessman. Kate smiled. There was nothing at all wrong with being attracted to good looks, at any age. Older men admired and appreciated younger women— couldn't the reverse be equally acceptable?

Smoothing her hair, she scolded herself. Why hadn't she thought to check her make-up before getting out of the car? She was still so unaccustomed to wearing it and felt a little conspicuous, not trusting it to remain natural looking on her face.

As Chase descended the stairs, she moved to meet him. Gliding gracefully up the path, her body seemed to get ahead of her feet. Her right knee twisted painfully and sent her nearly pummeling into one of the tidy green bushes lining the walkway. She quickly righted herself, embarrassment flushing her skin.

What a klutz. She was going to ruin everything if she wasn't more careful. *Darn heels.* She made a mental note to go back to flats and work her way up from there.

"Darling." Chase reached her in an instant and placed his hands on her upper arms. "Are you all right?"

A demure nod was all she could muster. "My foot fell asleep." She shook the offending appendage for good measure.

Beaming, he gave her a warm hug, then tipped her chin up with his index finger and pressed a kiss to her forehead.

A shadow of disappointment crossed through her. She had hoped for a more passionate welcome, but this was no doubt too public a place for that. Why had she been so foolish as to expect more?

Chase called to the driver. "Take Miss Jennings' things to the guesthouse."

The guesthouse? She frowned. She wasn't exactly a *guest*.

He caught the question in her eyes. "I thought it would be more romantic for you to have your own space until the wedding. I mean..." He ran his fingers through her hair. "You did make it crystal clear in San Francisco that you wanted to wait."

She pulled in a breath. It was so sweet of him not to pressure her. She loved him, but the thought of getting physically intimate with him was...what? Not exactly *un*appealing, but something she felt better about waiting for. She couldn't explain it. Not even to herself.

"Thank you, Chase." She smiled up at him. "I appreciate your thoughtfulness."

"Come into the house." Squeezing her shoulder tightly, he guided her up the front steps. "I assume you've had lunch?"

"Yes…" Had she? Willing her knee to take pity on her, she cautioned a step. An alarming pain shot through her leg, throwing emphasis on the incline of the pathway. It didn't help that the slim skirt was more confining than she was used to.

"Hurry, darling." Chase seemed oblivious to her struggle. "There are some people inside I want you to meet."

"Oh, really?" Her stomach dipped. "Who?" She tried not to let her voice betray her anxiety, but it came out sounding pinched.

A mischievous grin played on his lips. "Let's just leave it as a surprise."

The ringing of his cell phone drew his hand to his jacket pocket and his attention from her. "Sam. Talk to me." He spoke into his phone, then held up a hand and stepped ahead of her, indicating his need to take the call in private. His tone turned urgent as he climbed to the porch and vanished around the corner of the house.

Left alone on the steps, she huffed out disbelief. She had only been here for five minutes. Couldn't he let a call go to voicemail just once?

As she leaned on the pillar next to her, she kicked off her shoes and rubbed her sore knee. Scanning the sloping rock and flora garden on either side of the walkway, she scolded herself. It would do her no good to get angry at Chase on her first day. Besides, he clearly thought it appropriate to leave her to explore on her own.

Excitement pushed aside the anger. This was her house!

She glanced toward the corner where Chase had disappeared, but there was no sign of him. Dipping down to pick up her shoes, she faced the front door. Her nerves strained at the thought of running into the people inside, whoever they were, but restlessness stirred. This was her home too now, and she was dying to take a look around.

She stepped forward and gave the door a gentle nudge. Surprised by the weight of it, she pressed her palm to the wood and eased her head inside as it opened.

Instantly, the air left her lungs.

Chapter 4

Whoa. This place was something. The interior had the same natural feel as the outside, with exposed beams and lots of Native American-style art on the walls.

As Kate slipped inside, her feet felt soothed against the shiny hard wood floor. Stopping to listen intently, she took comfort in the silence. She was definitely not up to meeting anyone just yet.

A humongous staircase swooped up to the second story, with a railing that extended halfway around the upper portion of the foyer. To the left of the stairs, Kate saw an entryway into what she assumed must be the living room. As she moved gingerly toward it, the full impact of the room ahead took her breath away.

"Wow," she mouthed. At the far end of the practically-train-station-sized living room was a soaring wall of glass with an astonishing view of a deck with a fire pit and a hot tub, the tops of trees as the land abruptly sloped downward, then expansive water, and another island beyond. On the wall to her left rose a majestic stone fireplace.

She smiled lightly as she pictured herself snuggling with Chase on the champagne colored leather sofa positioned in front of it.

A display of what looked like hand woven baskets in various shapes and sizes filled one wall, interspersed with pieces of clay pottery.

Unbelievable. Looking around, she felt so rich. The decor wasn't exactly her style, but that was okay. She could get used to it.

Next to the fireplace, another doorway beckoned, and she padded toward it.

Seriously? This was the kind of dining room you see in movies, with a long table leading to yet another soaring window with the same view as the living room. As Kate's gaze moved upward, she held her breath. Situated above the table was the most unique and beautiful chandelier she had ever seen.

Quietly, she stepped into the room, not taking her eyes off the colorful formation overhead.

Squiggles of glass formed a beautiful cluster, its tendrils extending like vines attached to the ceiling. The colors echoed those of the view from the window behind it—blues like the water and sky, greens from the foliage, and brown from the woods—streaked with subtle highlights of fiery red, orange, and purple.

There was something about it that seemed to glow, even though the chandelier itself wasn't illuminated. It was magical. And mesmerizing.

Overtaken by an urge to touch it, Kate glanced over her shoulder. No one was around, but she'd have to be quick.

She set her shoes down next to one of the upholstered dining chairs and hiked her slim skirt up just enough to allow for the necessary mobility. Being careful not to slip on the highly polished wood, she hoisted herself up onto the table. Once on her knees, she reached up, but it was still too high. *Stupid cathedral ceiling.* Never one to give up, she checked once again over her shoulder. Taking care not to further aggravate her injury, she pulled herself to her feet.

Standing face-to-glass with the bottom tendrils, she slowly extended her fingers. It was so delicate, she was almost afraid to touch it. From up close, she could see that the tendrils weren't just random shapes as they'd appeared from a distance. They actually resembled tiny seahorses. She let out a giggle of delight, then placed her raised fingers over her lips. She scolded her blasted habit of acting like a child at the most inappropriate times, even though she knew it was because so many of the joys of childhood had eluded her. Maybe it wasn't so terrible that she latched onto moments like this when she could.

Confident now that she wouldn't utter another sound that might alert anyone in the house to her presence, she removed her fingers from her lips and inched them toward the smooth glass. Close up, she could detect the trick that had made the glass seem so luminescent. Tiny flecks throughout the glass that looked like real gold caught the light as it danced in through the window. Kate clicked her tongue at the discovery, as if she had unveiled a magician's secret. This was even better. It was an artist's secret.

She extended her fingers and was just about to touch the tail of the bottommost seahorse when a slight sound behind her sent her head whipping around. To her dismay, a guy about her age stood in the doorway, round eyes fixed on her.

A gasp caught in her throat.

"Uh..." He seemed to struggle for words. "Did you lose something up there?"

Her brow creased. "No...I...I'm coming back down. I...just wanted to get a better view."

"I see." He smiled and the room lit up. "So, how's the view?"

She wanted to respond, but her tongue had been momentarily tangled, not so much because she'd been caught doing something ridiculous, but because this guy was drop dead gorgeous. Dark hair, strong features, and deep brown eyes that could melt her like chocolate if she didn't turn away soon.

Amusement danced in his eyes, making them all the more impossible to turn away *from*. He moved toward the table. "Would you like a hand getting down?"

Would she? She froze. How was she supposed to gracefully lower herself with an injured knee and a reed-thin skirt?

Fingers fidgeting, she twisted her engagement ring so that the diamond rested inside her palm. *Protecting the stone*. Why *else* would she have done that?

As she attempted a smooth dip down to a kneeling position, he raised his hand to her. Reflexively, she reached for it, her gaze locking with his. Suddenly, her legs turned to pudding, causing her knee to make an encore performance of its earlier twisting maneuver. Yelping in pain, she collapsed forward, both knees thunking on the hard surface.

She realized, to her horror, that she was now face to face with Mr. Gorgeous. He had caught her by the elbows, effectively stopping her from tumbling all the way to the floor. She quickly pulled herself free with so much force that she fell backward, landing in the center of the table on her backside with her knees bent gawkily in front of her.

He stared at her, wide-eyed. "Are you okay?"

"Yeah." Painfully straightening her legs, she smoothed down her skirt as best she could manage. "I'm just peachy."

Eyes softening, he held out a strong hand. "Let me help you. For real this time."

She paused, studying the sincerity in his gaze.

Judging him to be devoid of ulterior motives, she scooted forward enough to take his hand.

He helped her to her feet, then—to his credit—dropped her hand and took a polite step back.

"I don't think we've met." Acting as though she hadn't just made a supreme fool of herself, he offered his hand again, this time more formally. "I'm Josh Collins."

Once again, she quickly assessed him. He seemed nice enough. Not at all like he was coming on to her, thank goodness. She shook his hand. "Kate Jennings."

"Nice to meet you, Kate." His shake felt firm and confident. "I don't remember ever seeing you at U Dub. You must be one of Jessica's friends from the island."

Jessica? She tipped him a look. "Oh...I just...got here." Why couldn't she form a coherent sentence?

"Hmmm." Taking a slight step back, he playfully studied her. "Don't tell me you're one of Stuart's friends?"

Who on earth was Stuart? She allowed a small smile and shook her head, unable to cut short the fun he seemed to be having.

"Let me think..." Snapping his fingers next to his ear, he looked up toward the high ceiling. "...Kate...Kate.... Nope. It's not ringing a bell. I remember Stu mentioning a Candy, and a Shelby, and a Madison, but never a Kate."

She raised a good-natured eyebrow. "This Stuart sounds like a real ladies' man."

"He's got a solid rep, that's for sure." His forehead creased, accentuating his handsome features. "So, I'm confused. If you're not a friend of Jessica's, and you're not one of Stu's hangers-on, then who—"

"Joshua, my boy." Chase's abrupt entrance commanded the room and brought Kate swiftly around. "You must have arrived while I was in my office earlier."

"Yes sir." Josh raised his hand to meet Chase's.

As the men exchanged a greeting, Kate gave herself a subtle inspection to make sure everything was back in place. Realizing she was still shoeless, she quickly slipped her feet into the pumps and shifted demurely to Chase's side.

Chase placed a firm hand on the small of her back, still speaking to Josh. "I see you've met my fiancée."

An endearing blush washed over Josh's cheeks as he caught her eye then looked away. An inexplicable mix of embarrassment and disappointment welled in Kate's throat. Josh hadn't realized she was an engaged woman. Why did it bother her that Chase had made it known so abruptly?

Chapter 5

Met his fiancée?

Had Josh heard right? Heat crept up his face. He hadn't even known Mr. Cole was dating, much less engaged. It had probably made the news, but Josh had been buried in finals for the last few weeks. Still, it was strange that Jessica hadn't mentioned it.

"Oh." He fumbled for a response. "I guess so." Something wasn't right here. Why would any woman want to marry a guy who had been a suspect in his previous wife's disappearance?

He caught Kate surreptitiously twisting an enormous block of ice to the top of her ring finger. Their eyes met and hers quickly flicked away.

He cast his own gaze down, thoughtfully. *Ah. Money.* That must be it.

Mr. Cole had his hand pressed against her back in what seemed like an unnecessarily possessive manner. He smiled amiably at Josh while speaking to Kate. "Joshua here is one of our houseguests."

"Oh?" Kate gave Josh a pencil-thin smile.

Gone was the fun-loving girl from just a minute ago.

He tried not to let his thoughts show on his face. "Thank you for having me, sir."

"Jessica's friends are always welcome in our home."

Kate tilted her head at her fiancé, tiny lines forming between her eyebrows. She opened her mouth to speak, but Mr. Cole didn't give her a chance.

"Will you be joining us on the island all summer?"

"No, sir." All *summer*? Josh crossed and uncrossed his arms. Why had he even come for the weekend? So many strange things had happened in this family. "I'm just here for a little break before I start my summer job."

"Oh." Mr. Cole nodded. "So, you won't be staying for the wedding, then?"

"I hadn't planned on it." Josh watched Kate wind a hank of her pretty blonde hair around her finger. Why did she seem so uncomfortable? "Actually, I wasn't aware there was going to be one."

"Well, perhaps you'll consider coming back up next weekend. It's going to be a nice event."

Next weekend? Josh shifted his weight from foot to foot, not wanting to look at Kate. Did she realize how peculiar this situation was? "I'll certainly consider it."

The awkward silence that followed gave Josh the distinct impression that he was the one third of the population of the room that made three a crowd. He was about to excuse himself when the boisterous sound of Jessica's friends coming in from the deck to the living room drew everyone's attention.

Mr. Cole gave them a smile that didn't quite reach his eyes. "Well, this seems like a good time for introductions." He held out an after-you hand to Kate. "Shall we?"

Kate's lip quivered, then she offered up a tight smile and started for the doorway. Mr. Cole gave Josh a fatherly pat on the shoulder and they fell into step behind her.

Kate seemed to hesitate at the entrance to the living room, and Josh couldn't say he blamed her. It would be intimidating to meet this crowd even under the best of circumstances.

Mr. Cole positioned himself on Kate's left, with a hand firmly placed on each of her shoulders, as if he was preparing to present her as his own personal achievement. Josh eased in on her other side, hoping to lend some sort of silent support. He sensed that she felt even more out of place here than he did.

"Excuse me, everyone." Mr. Cole's deep voice cut through the high pitched chatter. All eyes turned to him then landed in judgment on Kate as the group fell silent.

She stiffened almost imperceptibly.

"I'd like you all to meet my fiancée." Mr. Cole sounded more like he was announcing a new stock option at a business meeting than introducing his future wife.

Josh cleared his throat. This felt weird. Maybe he should just take off after dinner.

In typical Jessica fashion, she flipped her hair over her shoulder and turned to stare out the window, while taking a long sip of her Mojito. Josh subtly rolled his eyes. She and her friends had been fun to hang out with at school, and he had certainly felt for her with the terrible year she'd had, but he'd started to see a side of her that he found totally unappealing.

"Jessica." Crossing to her, Mr. Cole reached out for her arm.

Slowly, she looked up and smiled sweetly, then rose and allowed him to guide her to where Kate still stood next to Josh. Mr. Cole settled his hand domineeringly on Kate's back, forcing her to take a step closer to Jessica.

"Jessica," he said. "Meet Kate."

Josh frowned. Kate was just *now* meeting Jessica? This just kept getting stranger.

"So…." Jessica drew her glass to her lips and subtly sized up her future stepmother. "This is the famous *Kate*."

Whoa. Give the girl a little alcohol and she could win a competition with the contents of her glass over who was icier.

Josh was about to say something, anything, to break the tension when the French doors from the patio swung open and Stuart stepped in with a drink in his hand and a girl on each arm.

"Stuart," Mr. Cole called to him. "Come and meet Kate."

The creases between Kate's eyebrows had deepened in the last ten minutes. At this rate, she'd have to hire a make-up artist to putty them in for her wedding pictures.

Through a poorly, if at all, concealed smirk, Stuart quickly assessed her from across the room, then raised his glass to his lips as he spoke. "Nice to meet you, *Mommy*."

Ouch. Stuart was never one to be tactful, but this was totally over the top. And why was Mr. Cole letting him—both his kids—treat Kate with such disrespect? This just didn't add up. The group tittered, and Kate's eyes narrowed. She glanced down, and Josh could see her puzzling over Stuart's comment.

Suddenly, it dawned on him why she had seemed so confused earlier. She hadn't even known who Jessica and Stuart were. Was that possible? Hadn't Mr. Cole told her about them? Josh considered. The Coles had been all over the news in the last year. Where had Kate been living, in a cave?

Josh leaned in so that only Kate could hear.

"Don't worry. None of these other people are related to him."

"Oh." An endearing combination of relief and gratitude eased the strain on her face. "Thank goodness."

Chapter 6

Relieved to finally be on her own and away from Jessica and her rowdy friends, Kate fumbled with her new key. She fumed. Her vision of living a peaceful life as the lady of the manor had slipped into something far less appealing.

Reasonably, she had assumed Chase would walk her down to show her where she'd be staying, but he'd gotten another phone call and had promised to check in on her later. It was just as well. The way she felt right now, she might just pick a fight with him, which was the last thing she needed to do straight off the bat.

She hated feeling irritated with Chase, especially when she'd looked so forward to seeing him. But how could he neglect to tell her about Jessica and Stuart? And why, when he allowed her to find out, had he done it so publicly? Didn't he realize how humiliated she would feel?

The lock clicked and she slipped the key into her purse. And why was she staying in the guesthouse while the actual *guests* got to stay in her house?

The reminder of the 'actual guests' brought with it a not entirely unwelcome vision of Josh, which she tried unsuccessfully to shoo from her mind. She felt undeniably drawn to him, but that was normal, right? He was a nice guy who had the added advantage of being disarmingly great looking. But, it didn't take a genius to figure he was probably Jessica's boyfriend, so why did the thought of him leaving after the weekend send her spirit plummeting even lower?

Grumbling to herself, she walked through the front door, then stopped cold. This place was heavenly. The far wall in front of her was made almost entirely of glass, just like in the main house but on a more comfortable scale. It seemed both homes were designed to be an audience for the breathtaking view of the crystalline water.

How ungrateful could she get? This house was most likely a million dollar property all on its own. It just seemed puny in comparison to the main house, that was all.

As she stepped toward the window, her tender knee folded under her weight. She let out a moan, clutching her leg. *Stupid knee.* If she wasn't more careful, she'd need a cane to make it down the aisle.

She ditched her shoes—good riddance—and moved reverently forward. This place wasn't huge by any means, but it felt sumptuous, with an open-plan design intended to throw all the focus on the outdoor spectacle. It would be like living in a movie theatre with nature as the featured attraction.

She wandered toward the windows and stone fireplace, then into the nice-sized dining area with the kitchen beyond.

Remembering a time when she had loved to dabble in the kitchen, before her life had become all about scrounging to survive, she wanted to cry. After years of sharing a sparse condo kitchenette with a herd of cockroaches and a transitory string of roommates who showed little if any respect for one another's food stashes, she stood in awe of the gourmet kitchen.

Cookbook shelves lined one side of a trapezoid-shaped island. Turning her head sideways, she read some of the spines. Most of them focused on Pacific Northwest cuisine, which could come in handy if she decided to tackle something other than microwaved instant oatmeal. She should learn how to cook for real now that she was going to be a wife.

A pretty basket filled with assorted teas sat out on the island countertop, daring her to indulge. Behind the basket, a silver tea kettle awaited its call to duty on the smooth black stovetop. Moving around the island, she filled the kettle at the sink, then turned on the burner and set it back down. She grabbed a bag of something called Market Spice, breathed in the to-die-for cinnamony aroma, and plunked it into a waiting mug.

Now what? Might as well unpack while her tea water heated. She'd lived out of her ratty old backpack for far too long and was ready to take a swing at settling in, even if this home was only transitory. Now to find where the driver had left her things.

She looped back toward the foyer, where she'd noticed a doorway off to the left of the entrance. As she walked down a short hall, she noted a bedroom and a bathroom along the way to a set of double doors at the end.

Feeling as if she were breaking and entering, she opened the double doors. *Good grief.* If the guesthouse master bedroom was this plush, what must the one in the main house look like?

With a bed practically the size of the entire room she'd briefly shared in San Francisco with two other girls, and an easy chair next to its own corner fireplace, this room could please a queen. It even had a private deck with the same stunning view as the living room. She pictured herself sitting out there leisurely finalizing wedding plans.

Her suitcase rested on one of those expensive-looking hotel luggage stands. After an obligatory check to the inner pocket to make sure the zippered pouch she'd grown to hate was still safely tucked away, she made a snap decision to leave it there. In due time, she would decide what to do about it—tell Chase, maybe?

No. Chase would insist on reporting it, and the last thing on earth she wanted to do was talk to the police. After the way she'd been treated—by the officers who had come to her house the time her mom had called them on her stepdad, then by the police who'd degraded the kids on the street.... And that detective in San Diego. She closed her eyes against a shudder. No. She definitely didn't trust the police.

Maybe she'd think twice about confiding in Chase. In the meantime, the pouch would be safe in her suitcase.

After rezipping the inner pocket, she opened the main compartment. She removed her wedding planning binder, ran her hand across its smooth pearl white cover, and placed it on the bed. She quickly unpacked all the new clothing items she'd acquired on that shopping trip with Chase, which took up a tiny fraction of the humongous walk-in closet. Going back out to the suitcase, she contemplated. She tugged at a grey sleeve of the one remaining clothing item in her case, then quickly pulled on her *It Came From Outer Space* sweatshirt over her blouse. It felt like a hug from an old friend. So much had changed so quickly over the last few months, and right now a small thing like her ratty old favorite sweatshirt which she'd had since high school was more comforting than anything she could imagine.

Well, almost anything.

Carefully, she reached into the outside pocket of her suitcase and took out a small stack of photos. Perching on the edge of the bed, she flipped through them, one by one, smiling at each. It felt a little OCD, but she didn't care. This was it—what was left of her childhood.

She lingered on the last one, like always. She was long past tearing up when she looked at the shot of herself with her mom, but a brew of bittersweet emotions still stirred.

It had been taken her sophomore year, just a few weeks before everything in her life had fallen apart. Looking at this picture, it felt as though nothing had changed, and she was standing in the front yard of their house next to her mom, wearing the vintage embroidered blouse that had been one of her favorite thrift store finds.

She swallowed hard to prevent her throat from closing. What had happened to that blouse, along with the rest of her things when she'd left San Diego? She pictured the other girls living in the condo claiming her things, like a pack of cheetahs ripping the meat off a gazelle. The thought made her stomach turn.

Maybe it hadn't happened that way. She had tried for months to comfort herself with the thought that Shari and little Iowa had protected her meager belongings from the others. When they'd realized she was gone for good, they would have divided her things between the two of them. She hoped, if that had been the case, that they would find comfort in good memories of her whenever they wore something that had belonged to her. She looked again at the picture. The vintage blouse would be too big for Iowa, but it would bring out the green in Shari's eyes. That thought always made Kate smile.

Wiping a tear away, she placed the 'mom' side of the photo against her lips. She'd tried not to think about her parents since she left. Did they even still live in the same house? She couldn't care less about her stepdad, but would she ever get to see her mom again?

Her eyes pinched shut. Maybe she wasn't quite past tearing up, after all.

A sharp whistling sound dragged her from her thoughts. *The tea kettle.* Keeping the stack of photos in her hand, she grabbed the wedding binder and headed for the kitchen. She had to stop being so jumpy. Probably the residual effect of seeing that creepy guy in the black sweat jacket earlier.

Stop it, Kate. That was probably just some islander crossing the street, not realizing a car was turning in front of him. Forget that it was a warm cloudless day, not the type of day people who *weren't* up to no-good chose to don a black sweat jacket and pull the hood down over their face.

Reaching the kitchen, she lifted the sputtering

and spewing kettle. Just like her to overfill it.

After making her tea, she mopped up the puddle that had accumulated on the floor in front of the stove then grabbed her photos from the counter. She'd have to put them away someplace safe—she couldn't let anyone see that she used to have dark hair and a funky style, back when everyone knew her as 'Kathy'. More and more, she appreciated the importance of keeping her past hidden.

Her past. Images flashed through her head like a nightmarish slideshow. Escaping the horrors of living with her stepdad only to trade them for the dangers of San Diego street life. And later, watching from the viewing chamber as Joe performed surgery at the clinic.

She stopped herself, blinking hard to drive out that awful image. Too bad she hadn't discovered the truth sooner. Before she became an unwitting accomplice. And now a thief too—no better than Joe. Joe wasn't a surgeon, any more than he was a miracle worker or a messiah or anything else but a con man and a thief and a….

Oh, poor Karen.

The shaking in her hands started again. She'd been doing such a good job of washing out that memory. Rinsing it from her reality.

Her hands rubbed at her face as if she could physically drive all thoughts of Karen out of her memory bank. *Start fresh.* Whatever it took.

Willing her hands to steady, she picked up her mug then headed out to the deck that was just off the living room. Glancing down, she enjoyed that this view was even more intimate than the one from the big house, because this house sat a little lower, and closer to the water. Settling into a plush deck chair, she looked out at the sunlight dancing on the water, and at the soft green islands beyond. This was exactly what she needed to wash away her concerns.

The water seemed alive. Not just the water itself, but the birds flying, and something—fish?—jumping. Yet for all the movement around her, this place was remarkably quiet. Just the joyful chant of the birds and the lapping sound of the water hitting the rocks below her. She really had come to paradise.

Taking a satisfying sip of her tea, she gazed out at land directly across the water, and realized it was the Shaw Island ferry landing. She could actually see the ferries coming and going from here. Even if she became a recluse at Chase's house, the view gave her an unexpected link to the outside world.

Leaning forward, she looked down off the deck at a steep stone incline that led practically straight down to the rocky shore. A chill ran down her spine.

She sat back, trying not to panic. What was she doing in a house in the woods with no one around her? At least in San Francisco, she'd had the reassurance of the constant presence of witnesses should anything happen. If Joe found her here, what would stop him from doing the unthinkable?

She mentally shook herself. *Don't be ridiculous, Kate.* If Joe was going to find her, he would have done it by now. Wouldn't he?

She really needed to stop thinking this way. She'd been careful. Even traveled to a different state. How could she not be safe?

Returning in her mind to that day at the clinic, Kate scolded herself. Why had she gone back to check on Karen when she'd heard her yelling at Joe? If she had just kept walking, she wouldn't be afraid for her life now.

She choked back the anguish that came from her next thought. She *had* gone back. And become a witness to Karen's murder. Then she had made herself an accomplice by doing nothing about it.

Not that she could have stopped Joe, but she could have reported what she'd seen to the police. A brutal stabbing. A woman murdered in cold blood right in front of her. And because she'd been too scared to report it, Joe had gone free.

Her eyes lowered to the water where a long dock jutted out just a few yards from the bottom of her deck stairs. A couple of small boats bobbed next to the dock. Out a little further, a larger boat sat unmoving in the bay.

She strained to see it through the trees. Could

that be Chase's yacht? She remembered now that he had told her the water was too shallow off this dock and that he kept it moored at the yacht club in Friday Harbor unless someone was using it. She squinted to see if there were any signs of life on the deck. Seeing no one, she read the name on the side. *Magnificent Obsession.*

She smiled. *That's right.* Chase had told her that Sam, his business partner whom she had yet to meet, had come up with the name. Maybe he was a movie buff like her.

A movement grabbed the corner of her eye in the trees below. Snapping her head to the left, she saw nothing unusual, but the certainty that something was wrong lingered. She leaned, ever so slightly, toward the railing.

Nothing. It must have been a squirrel, or a bird. She sat back and closed her eyes.

Suddenly, an odd smell set off her internal alarm system. She bolted out of her seat.

Something inside the house was burning.

Chapter 7

Kate panicked. Had she remembered to turn off the stove?

She dashed back inside, and saw a thin wisp of white smoke trailing up from the burner. It would be so like her to start a fire her first day there.

She reached out to make sure the knob was turned all the way to 'off', but pulled her hand back when she felt heat rising from the stovetop. It was off…why was it still hot?

What now? Even with all the trouble she'd had in her life, she'd never been good at keeping a cool head.

Think. Power source. Fuse box! She dashed from room to room looking for a grey metal panel. Why did they always hide these things? She hoped against hope that rich people didn't have their houses built with fuse box doors that blended in with the wall so as not to clash with their décor.

Unsuccessful, she ran back to the kitchen. The smoke had gotten thicker, and she wondered if the stove might actually explode.

At a loss, she ran outside, her knee giving her

a painful warning not to move too quickly. Not only that, but her feet were bare. *Smart, Kate.*

She needed help, but what was she supposed to do—call 9-1-1 and have the fire truck come to announce her ineptitude? How would it even get through the locked gate?

True fear started to set in as she proceeded painfully up the stone path toward the big house. She didn't want Chase to know what she'd done, and above all she didn't want his kids to know. Jessica would think Kate was a complete idiot, and she'd probably be right.

A rustling noise from the direction of the front yard pulled her attention, and she slowed her steps. Through the trees, she made out the form of the one person who might show her some compassion.

"Josh!"

He lifted his head, and his eyes lit up. "Hey—"

"Come on! I need your help!" Wildly waving her arms, she shifted her momentum to start back in the direction from which she'd come. If they wasted time, the guesthouse might wind up as a pile of very expensive ashes.

He quickly caught up to her. "What's wrong?"

"My stove is smoking." She tried to disregard the handsome features beneath the concern on his face. "I can't find the fuse box."

"Did you look outside?" He started around the side of the house, looking over his shoulder for her answer.

"Oh, well…no." Slowing to appease her knee, she watched him disappear into the thick foliage that surrounded her house.

She hobbled back to the front door and entered the house, rounding the corner from the foyer just as Josh opened the back door and entered the kitchen.

"Whoa." She halted. "That was unlocked?"

Barely looking up, he gave her a nod as he headed for the stove.

It alarmed her for a moment that the door had been unsecured all this time and she hadn't bothered to check. A string of unwelcome memories trailed after that thought. Barricading herself in her room and praying her drunken stepdad wouldn't try to get to her. Cowering in public restrooms, hoping not to be discovered by security so she could sleep in peace. Her surroundings had improved by leaps and bounds, but this was no time to let down her guard.

Inside, the smell lingered but had lessened, and the air appeared clear. Josh approached the stove looking a whole lot less fearful than she herself felt.

"Is it still hot?" She ventured toward him, hoping she hadn't made a complete fool of herself for no good reason.

"A little."

She kept her distance as he confidently

checked the stove like he did this every day. He expertly removed the control panel along the front of the cook top.

Leaning a little closer, her confidence in him rose by the second.

"Oh, I see what's going on." He glanced at her and pointed at the part of the stove he had exposed. "This thing has water in it. Check it out."

She stepped forward. He was right. The area inside looked like a robot's guts, and was partially filled with water.

He reached for a roll of paper towels and started soaking up the wayward moisture. "Did something overflow?"

She hesitated to admit it. "I guess I overfilled my tea kettle."

"Oh. Well, the seal here isn't in place, so no wonder the water got in. My guess is that this has been a problem for a while, so it's not anything you did."

"Oh…but, why was it smoking?"

He cocked a contemplative eyebrow. "Was the smoke white or grey?"

"White."

"I bet it was steam, which would make sense considering how hot this water still is."

"Oh." Her pulse began to normalize. "And the burning smell?"

He shrugged. "Looks like the water shorted out a wire. See how the insulation is melting?

Good thing you caught it when you did."

A shudder ran through her as she took the soaked towels from him and located the trash can under the sink. "You sound like you know what you're talking about."

"Sort of." He tossed her a half-smile. "My uncle's a contractor and I work for him in the summer. You'd be amazed at the problems that can crop up in a house, so I've gotten some practical experience. You'll have to get the wiring fixed before you use the stove again, but I can fix this seal if you want."

"Would you?" She crossed back to him and perched on the stool on the opposite side of the island.

"No problem."

They shared a smile, and her face heated. What was that all about?

He started to return to his work, but got sidetracked by something on the counter. "Hey, is this you? You look so different."

She followed his gaze, and her pulse took off running again. She never left her photos out where other people could see them. How could she have been so careless? Horrified, she grabbed them. "It's…from a long time ago."

He shifted his attention back to the stove. "When was that taken? High school?"

She nodded, embarrassed now by her abrupt action.

If he was offended he didn't show it. "Looks like California. L.A?"

She hesitated, not wanting to reveal too much about herself. "Sure." *Sacramento, really.* A small lie of about four hundred miles, but what did it matter?

"No kidding? What part? I grew up in Orange County."

"Really?" *Great.* Not wanting to risk getting caught in her own web of lies, she changed the subject. "Look, I really appreciate your helping me, but you don't have to hang around."

"I'll be done in just a minute." He continued to work. "So, is that your mom?"

She held the photos in her lap with trembling hands. "Yes." What was she saying? She was so flustered now she couldn't think.

"Is she coming up for the wedding?" The question seemed conversational, not like he was prying.

"No, not exactly." She casually slipped the photos between two of the cookbooks next to her knees as a temporary hiding place. "Sorry to be dramatic. I just don't think I look good in pictures."

His glance said he understood they were changing the subject. "You know, *most* people don't like the way they looked in high school. *I* was a typical nerd. Totally into chess and movies."

"Really?" She perked up, delighted by the

normal turn in the conversation. "Me too."

"You play chess?"

"No. I mean I love movies. I never could get into chess."

"I could have guessed the movie part." He nodded at her shirt. "That's a classic."

She glanced down at her sweatshirt, realizing with a start that she was dressed like a total slob. "I just threw this on because…"

"Because you wanted to be comfortable?" He smiled that nice smile. "Are you a fan of the film?"

She studied his face. The fact that he called it a 'film' gave her a clue that he wasn't making fun of her. "I've seen it a few times. I got the shirt at a film festival I worked at in Sacramento a million years ago." Her heart filled with that odd sense of security at the reminder that she'd been wearing her two most cherished clothing items—this shirt and her favorite pair of jeans—that day she'd had to flee. Thank goodness Joe was okay with her wearing casual attire under her lab coat, or she would have lost those too.

"Very cool." Josh nodded.

She started to feel a little less self-conscious about her appearance. "Have you seen it? The movie, I mean."

"Seen it? I own it. I love those fifties sci-fi flicks. That's my all-time favorite genre."

"For real? Mine too." She scooted forward. "Have you seen *The Ugly Swamp Thing That Ate the*

World?"

He nodded, laughing. "I tracked it down on video. I paid way too much for it, but you know how brutal eBay can be." He held up a defensive hand. "Yes, I admit to still owning a VCR. Some of those masterpieces aren't out on Blu-ray, even if I could afford to keep up with technology."

She laughed, not wanting to confess that she hadn't ever watched a movie on Blu-ray. They were lucky at the condo in San Diego to have access to Joe's old VCR that he had 'forgotten' to return to a video store years before. It was on its last leg, but it still worked. Hearing that Josh actually owned one intentionally made that seem less pitiful.

"You'll appreciate this." She picked up her phone and clicked into the settings. She held it up as a warbly, synthesized tune played. "Who would have thought the theme from *The Ugly Swamp Thing* would be made into a ringtone."

"You know," he shook his head. "I think you're the first girl I've talked to who's ever even heard of that film."

"Are you kidding?" She put her phone away. "I could watch those movies all the time."

"Good to know. I always have to go alone or drag along one of my friends who'd rather see something first run."

"Really? I'd go in a heartbeat. Where do you live?"

"Seattle. U district." He straightened, allowing his hands to still.

"Well, if you see an old sci-fi flick playing, you should call me. I'm just a boat ride away. We could grab some burgers and make a night of it." The thought eased her into a new level of comfort. This could turn into something resembling a normal life, with friends and everything.

He looked pleased, then his expression dropped. "That's probably not a good idea."

"Why not?"

He returned his focus to the stove. "Because you'll be married."

She frowned, her stomach tightening. "Just because I'm getting married doesn't mean I can't have friends."

"Sure, but not single guy friends."

"Why not?"

"Trust me." He glanced up at her without lifting his head. "It's just not a good idea."

Her heart sank. Chase always talked about wanting to take her to the opera and the symphony. She'd never even consider asking him to go to an old sci-fi flick. She really didn't see the harm in two friends sharing a mutual interest.

"Done." He put the cover back on the stove. "If you want, I can see about getting someone out here to look at the wiring." He leaned in, lowering his voice conspiratorially. "Just between you and me."

"I'd appreciate that." She smiled, relaxing some. "I'd rather not let Chase in on how stupid I can be."

"It wasn't stupid." Looking up, he cocked a reassuring eyebrow. "And it wasn't even your fault." He returned the smile, in a way that made her want to melt like the insulation on that wire.

As they started for the door, she tried to keep her bewildering and somewhat intrusive response to his presence out of her voice. "So, you're really into movies, huh?"

"I'll be going to film school next fall, if I can swing it financially. I'm counting on putting away as much as I can this summer working for my uncle."

"Film school? That's great. You want to make movies?"

"Documentaries. That pretty much ensures I'll be broke my whole life, but money isn't everything."

Her lips pursed. *Money* might not be everything, but the food, shelter, and safety it could provide sure were. "Maybe you should find a wealthy benefactor."

"Great idea." He took the couple of steps up to the small entryway and turned to face her. "Know anyone with money to burn?"

"Why not Chase? He'd back you."

"Right." He nodded, rolling in his lips as he reached for the doorknob. "I think I'd need you to convince him of that."

"I'm sure Jessica will put in a good word for you."

"Uh huh." He seemed slightly amused by the suggestion as he opened the door and stepped out.

"Why not?" She leaned on the doorframe. "Isn't she your girlfriend?"

He sputtered a little laugh. "Where did you get that idea? We ran in the same crowd at school, but we really don't have all that much in common."

"Oh…" Lifting her hand in a wave, she watched as he walked back up the path toward the house.

So, he wasn't Jessica's boyfriend. *Secret relief.* Must be because Josh deserved someone nice, and from what she'd seen so far of Jessica, that wouldn't be her. Still, if he was a boyfriend, he'd be around a lot, and that might be…comforting. It was good to have someone she could relate to.

She leaned against the doorframe and smiled. And maybe talk into going to a movie sometime.

Chapter 8

"You're so lucky to be getting married." Kim chirped from the window end of the dinner table. All the girls nodded agreement.

Josh winced. 'Lucky' wasn't exactly the word he would choose. Not under these peculiar circumstances.

Next to Josh, Kate leaned forward and smiled a response to Kim. She'd barely uttered a word throughout the meal, but had appeared to relax a little after Mr. Cole had excused himself to take a call. It was funny. She seemed like such a different person when he wasn't around.

"Do you have your dress yet?"

Unsure which of the girls had fired off that question, Josh flaked off a piece of Ahi tuna steak and put it in his mouth. His patience with talk about the wedding had worn about as thin as the wasabi butter sauce the fish had been served in.

"I ordered it from a designer in San Francisco." Kate allowed her fork to hover over her barely-touched food. "They shipped it to the Friday Harbor Bridal Salon. I'm picking it up tomorrow." She sounded self-conscious, like she'd prefer not to be the focus of everyone's attention.

The fish went down Josh's throat like a lump. He really didn't blame her.

He'd made a new plan to leave after dinner. Jessica, Stuart, and their friends were too much for him, and the situation with Mr. Cole being engaged to this young girl was beyond strange. He had known before coming here that it might feel awkward being in the home of a man who had been suspected of orchestrating his wife's disappearance, among his other notorieties, but having Kate here had really thrown him for a loop.

He glanced across the table at Jessica. She laughed and tipped back her head, swilling the last bit of wine from her glass. At school, he had thought she was fun to be around, but after witnessing her treatment of Kate this afternoon, his attitude toward her had shifted.

"Where are you having the wedding?" Another perky female voice sounded from the far end of the table.

"Here at the house." A strained politeness tinged Kate's speech. "We want it to be small without the press interfering."

"Maybe you'll have helicopters hovering overhead." Kim's eyes widened like the idea thrilled her. "It'll be so celeb-du-jour."

Josh swallowed his disgust. One thing was for sure, he wouldn't be hanging out with this crowd now that he had graduated. He wouldn't be accepting any more invitations out to Shaw Island either. Unless…. He stopped himself. Why was he intrigued by the idea of coming back?

He had to admit that under different circumstances, he would really like Kate. Not the future-Mrs.-Cole Kate, but the fun Kate he'd originally met standing on this very table.

Of course, she was obviously not a woman of faith. That had been the reason he'd avoided getting involved with any of the girls at school too. Having that in common was a nonnegotiable point. So why did he feel drawn to her in a way he hadn't experienced before? It was a draw that went beyond physical attraction and their shared love of old movies.

He took in a breath. What kind of guy was he to have these thoughts about another man's fiancée? That was the real reason he needed to just remove himself from this situation.

"Do you have a lot of people coming to the wedding?" Staci's enthusiasm, though sincere, was a bit more refined than Kim's.

"Oh, no." The words came out on a nervous quiver. "Just a few of Chase's friends."

"Dad's friends?" Stuart cocked an eyebrow. "And what about *your* friends?" His emphasis on the word 'your' implied a hope for a fresh batch of female eye candy.

"Don't be a jerk, Stu." Jessica tossed him a

look. "Maybe she doesn't *have* any friends."

Josh gave her a heated glare. Why was she acting this way?

Kate answered slowly. "I…*have* friends. They're just not in a position to come up here."

Jessica scowled. "When I get married, I want to fly everyone I know to Italy for the wedding. And I know they'll all be there."

"Of course they'll *be* there." Stuart slurred. "Who's going to turn down a free trip to Italy?"

Mr. Cole entered the room, giving Kate a warm look as he retook his seat at the head of the table. "Well. What have I missed?"

Jessica smiled with fake sweetness. "We were just discussing why your next wife has no friends."

Josh tossed a scowl across the table. Was she enjoying this?

Kate looked at Mr. Cole and shook her head as if she was trying to no-big-deal Jessica's impudence. "She's talking about our guest list for the wedding."

Mr. Cole smiled lightly. "Jessica, I'm sure Kate has friends. They're just down in California and won't be able to make it up here."

Jessica twisted her mouth and held her wine glass up to a server who hastened over to refill it. "Then, who's going to be your maid of honor?"

"Oh." Kate rolled a small red potato around her plate with her fork. "I hadn't really thought about that."

"Now that's just sad." Jessica made a show of swirling the red liquid in her glass. "A wedding without a maid of honor. No one to go with you to pick up that wedding dress tomorrow."

"Oh, but…" Kate stammered. "I won't have to go alone. Your dad is going too." She turned a pleading gaze on Mr. Cole. "Right, Chase?"

He chewed and swallowed. "Not tomorrow. I'll be in meetings all day with Sam. We're close to finishing the proposal for the new drug we're submitting to the FDA."

"But…" Kate's voice trembled. "I can't go into town by myself. What about the press?"

"Hmm." Mr. Cole seemed to consider. "I have a simple solution for that." Using the commanding tone of a man who was used to directing business subordinates, Mr. Cole spoke as he sliced into a broccoli floweret. "You'll have Jessica. She can accompany you in her capacity as your new maid of honor."

Kate and Jessica fired each other a similar look of horror, which floated over the center of the table like a storm cloud.

After a moment, Kate sputtered. "Oh, I…don't think she'd want—"

"I'm sure she'd be happy to do it." Cutting into his tuna, Mr. Cole glanced up at Jessica. "Wouldn't you, dear?"

Chewing slowly, Josh watched Jessica attempt to form an answer that would get her off the hook without blatantly defying her meal ticket father.

Realizing the hopelessness of that, she attempted a compliant smile. "Sure." She turned an ireful eye on Kate. "*Happy* to."

"Good, then that's settled. You'll go together tomorrow to pick up Kate's dress and to choose one for Jessica." Mr. Cole's gaze turned toward the wall of windows. "It's a lovely evening. I've asked for dessert to be served out on the deck."

Noisily, everyone scraped their chairs back and headed outside. Josh pushed to his feet, but didn't step away from the table.

"You coming, Josh?" Kim asked as she retrieved her half-full wine glass from her place at the table.

"In a minute." He glanced down at Kate, who had remained seated.

Kim flicked a look at Kate, then smiled at Josh before following the others out to the deck.

As Mr. Cole stood, he touched Kate's chair as if he intended to pull it back for her. Her gaze fell on her plate, which she'd barely touched. "I...I'll just be a minute."

"Of course, dear." A muffled tone sounded and Mr. Cole pulled his phone from his jacket pocket. "You don't mind, do you? I'm expecting another call from Sam." Without waiting for a response, he put the phone to his ear and headed toward the foyer.

Jessica came around the end of the table and

fairly hissed at Kate. "If you think I'm going to wear a hideous pink taffeta dress and stand next to you with a smile plastered on my face, think again."

Kate's eyes grew wide. "I...I'm not a fan of pink either."

"Good." With a departing fiery glare, Jessica stormed off.

Kate looked pale, like she'd just been doused with cold water.

Josh retook his seat next to her, mentally calculating when he'd have to leave to catch the last ferry. "You didn't eat much."

Brow furrowing, she started to pick at her food. "I guess I'm just not very hungry."

He gave her a sideways smile. "The food was good, but...." He leaned toward her, lowering his voice. "Just between you and me, I'd rather have a burger and a shake."

She looked up, surprise flashing in her eyes. She forked a small bite of tuna. "I'm with you." Her face fell as she looked at the French doors where Jessica had exited. "I didn't mean to upset her."

Josh frowned. "Of course you didn't." This was crazy. How could he possibly comfort this girl when she was voluntarily engineering a huge train wreck? The sooner he got away from all this, the better.

"I don't know if I can do it." She now gripped

her fork like she might want to stab someone with it.

He jarred. Was she seeing the folly of her plan to marry Mr. Cole? "Do…what?"

"Go shopping with Jessica." Her teeth gritted. "She's obviously not happy about me marrying her dad."

Disappointment flared. She could go through with the marriage, but she couldn't handle the shopping? "Don't worry about Jessica. She's still pretty upset about her mom. I mean, not that that's an excuse or anything."

Nodding, Kate stared at her plate.

His heart went out to her. "Besides," he heard himself continue. "I could go with you on your wedding errands tomorrow with Jessica. Kind of act as a shield." He paused, then added. "If you want me to."

She looked up, her face brightening. "I'd owe you a milkshake."

He smiled in response. "Make it chocolate, and you've got a deal."

Was he crazy? This girl was an inch away from stealing his carefully-guarded heart, and he was letting her do it. What was he thinking?

 *Chapter* 9

Kate sunk down deep into the front seat of Josh's car as he drove off the ferry onto San Juan Island. His suggestion that they could elude the press lurking outside the estate by taking his slightly dinged-up teal blue Toyota instead of the limo had seemed risky at first, but to Kate's amazement, it had worked.

As the car advanced slowly along with the rest of the ferry traffic, she peered out the window at the main street of Friday Harbor. Instead of a swarm of paparazzi, a mix of tourists and locals milled about a very cute, old-fashioned looking town.

A couple of kids zoomed past on skateboards, stirring up melancholy thoughts of Dakota. He loved pretending to roll down the street on one of his longed-for modes of wheeled transportation. To Kate, it had always seemed like a blessing in disguise that he couldn't afford a skateboard or roller blades. Lacking strength and coordination, the poor kid would have been crushed by his inability to soar the way he did in his imagination.

It was probably better that he was stuck with pretending, even though the sight of him at fifteen running and leaping garnered too many cruel comments.

Kate blinked. She had to believe that when she'd left, someone had stepped in to shield him from the harshness of the world.

Recognizing that slinking down like a fugitive was far more suspicious than just behaving like a normal person, she pulled herself up a few inches. She scanned the quaint area, which looked like the setting for a Hallmark movie. Quaint shops lined the street that, under different circumstances, she'd be itching to explore. As it was, she bit her lip and prayed that they could do what they needed to do and get back on the ferry before anybody tried to get her picture.

Optimism overtook her tongue before she could suppress it. "This town is so cute."

A harrumphing noise from the backseat reminded her that Jessica had grudgingly accompanied them, no doubt just to please Chase. Kate clamped down on her enthusiasm for the picturesque town and vowed to keep her thoughts to herself to avoid giving Jessica more opportunities to berate her. Her fragile self-esteem didn't need that right now.

"There it is." Josh curved smoothly into a parking place directly in front of a pale pink storefront with the words 'Friday Harbor Bridal' painted in elegant script on a sign above the entrance. "Wait right here." He exited the car, crossing to Kate's door in a refreshing show of chivalry.

As he opened it and reached in to help her out, Kate gave herself a mental pep talk. She could do this.

Glancing around for reassurance that no one was going to assault her with a camera or a microphone, she stepped out of the car and tested her weight on her sore leg. Confident, she took one step, then stopped and stared. There in the window of the gift shop next door was a pink flier featuring a color photo of a woman beneath the word *'MISSING'*.

Kate's heart took off at a sprint. Without reading further, she knew that the pretty blonde in the picture had to be Trina Cole, Chase's first wife.

"They've been up all over the islands for a full year." Jessica spit the words from just behind Kate. "Get used to it."

Alarmed by the comment, Kate looked down the sidewalk. A pink rectangle adorned every window on the street. Panic set in. What exactly was she up against here?

Josh joined her. "Try not to let it bug you." He opened the door to the dress shop. "At least the wedding people thought ahead."

He jutted his chin toward the window next to the open door. A single piece of scotch tape remained with a tiny bit of pink paper sticking to it. The implication was obvious. They had made a hasty and possibly passive-aggressive effort to avoid offending their high-paying customer.

She forced a wan smile and entered the shop.

Twenty minutes later, she stood in the fitting room staring at herself in the triptych of full length mirrors. Her gown, which had looked elegant and impressive in the designer's watercolor rendering, now looked more like a parachute with a chandelier perched on top.

"It's really quite exquisite, Miss Jennings." The woman who had helped her into it bent to spread the train out so Kate could experience the full effect.

"Do you think so?" Kate frowned. Maybe she just wasn't used to seeing herself dressed this way, but she felt more like she should being saying "Trick or Treat" than "I do."

"Oh, yes." Standing, the woman assured her. "The shop in San Francisco did an excellent job, and it will hardly need any alterations. You know, those are real Swarovski crystals on the bodice."

Kate nodded, as if the significance of that was actually…well, *significant*. The designer in San Francisco had looked at Kate's collection of photos clipped from bridal magazines and had come up with this design, tying together the different elements Kate had said she liked. It was a one-of-a-kind, but at the moment that distinction seemed to

Kate not to be very impressive.

"Are you ready for the viewing?" The high pitch of the woman's voice betrayed an edge of nervousness that would no doubt be quashed only when the sale was finalized.

"Viewing?" Kate hated feeling ignorant, but she'd never even set foot in a bridal salon before, much less paid attention to their standard protocol.

"Yes. You know…" The smile in the woman's eyes melted slightly as she swept an arm toward the door leading out of the small room. "Showing your friends."

"Oh. Right."

Friends. The thought of parading around in front of Jessica sent her mind into a tiny tizzy, but she wanted Josh to see the dress. She needed some reassurance that she didn't look ridiculous in it, and she had a feeling she could count on him to be honest.

She scooped up as much of the skirt as she could in her arms to facilitate walking, and followed the woman out of the room, trying futilely to keep the crystals on the bodice from jingling.

When she stepped into the viewing area, Jessica looked up from her phone, made a sound of amused disgust, and went back to typing a message. Josh stood, looking at Kate with an expression that was impossible to read.

"What do you think?" She hated the insecurity she couldn't keep from her voice.

Tapping away at her phone, Jessica uttered something that was barely discernable. "S-t-a-y-p-u-f-t."

Kate's lower lip started to quiver and she bit down on it to keep from crying.

Josh looked at her with a smile that was slight, but sincere. "It's really beautiful."

Making a snorting sound, Jessica ramped up her texting.

Josh shot Jessica a warning glance then turned his attention back to Kate. "It's your wedding." He took a step closer to her. "Do you like it?"

Did she like it? She studied her image in the mirror. Why was she even questioning? This was exactly what she had asked for. Finding an alternative would take hours, and what if she found nothing better? She didn't want to risk wasting Josh's and Jessica's time, nor that of the poor bridal shop woman. Besides, it was just a dress. No big deal.

Her shoulders slumped. "It's fine."

The woman clapped her hands, but Kate felt the hollow absence of that magical feeling she had always expected to descend over her at this moment in her life. Choosing a wedding dress was supposed to be something a woman shared with her best friends amid tears and clinking champagne glasses. This felt more like she was agreeing to try out a cable package she wasn't completely sold on.

The next half hour passed in a whirlwind as the woman marked a few alteration points with pins, and Kate changed back into her linen suit and "sensible" flats. She was then escorted into an office where she signed so many papers she felt like she was buying a house. When she finally made it out to the front of the salon, Josh stood, the only one in the room.

Relief competed with polite curiosity. "Where's Jessica?"

"Well, after picking out her maid of honor dress…" He motioned toward a slinky strapless red gown that adorned a velvet hanger on the wall. "…she went out to get a chai. She said she'd see us on the ferry."

Surveying the dress, or what there *was* of it, Kate shook her head. The plan to have Jessica as her maid of honor was a sure argument for elopement. If Josh hadn't offered to accompany them today, Kate very likely would have traded in her wedding dress for two plane tickets and a ladder.

She sighed in resignation. "That's just as well." Starting for the door, she reached into her bag for her sunglasses. "She doesn't like my dress."

"So what?" Josh swung the door open for Kate. "It's not her wedding."

"And neither do you." Kate slipped on the glasses as she stepped out onto the sidewalk. "I could tell."

He followed her outside. "Hey, it's not my wedding either."

"Fine." She glanced up and down the sidewalk, relieved to see that no photographers lurked. "I was just hoping for a little reassurance that I didn't look like a lampshade or something."

"I said the dress looked beautiful. I wasn't lying." He paused. "It's just that…"

She looked at him. "What?"

He winced. "Well… it just doesn't look like you."

"*Look* like me? What do you mean?"

"I mean, it doesn't look like your style."

A deep affront tried to settle in her chest but was crowded out by an unfamiliar warmth. "How would you know what my *style* is?"

He dipped his chin toward her, as if speaking in confidence. "I saw that picture of you, remember? You looked so different."

She shrank back. "That picture was taken a long time ago."

"Even so…" He nodded with a confidence that should have come across as arrogant, but somehow didn't. "Something tells me the girl in that picture is the *real* Kate."

She felt awkward at what seemed like a little too perceptive an observation on his part. What would he think if he knew that the "real" Kate was actually a girl named Kathy?

"Come on." Hands in his pockets, Josh tipped his head in conjunction with his forward movement up the sidewalk.

"Where are we going?"

He lifted a one-shouldered shrug. "You owe me a shake, remember?"

Glancing again at the row of flier-dotted windows, she wavered on her still-unsteady legs. "Okay, but…can we take the car?"

Josh stopped and turned, giving her that cockeyed grin that had wormed its way into her heart mostly without her knowledge and definitely without her consent. "If you still think you want to live here, you have to carve out your own place in the community."

Cautioning a step forward, she contemplated his words. Why had it seemed feasible and even desirable for her to hole up on Chase's property like some kind of outlaw? This town was charming, and no one here seemed to be paying any attention to her. Josh was right. If she had any hope of making a real life for herself, she had to show a little backbone. She could do this.

Pleased that she could walk without a hitch in her gait, she caught up to him. "So where's the ice cream?"

He smiled. "I think I saw a sign just around the corner."

Casting a quick glance up and down the street to confirm that there were no paparazzi or looky-loos staring at her, she gained confidence.

He looked over at her as they strolled. "Are you okay? You're limping a little."

She sighed. So she wasn't hiding it as well as she'd hoped. "I'm fine. I just twisted my knee yesterday wearing those stupid high heels. I'm not really used to them."

"I'm not surprised. You strike me more as the athletic shoe type."

"Meaning what, exactly?"

"You just seem like a person who would prioritize practicality over fashion."

It was hard to be insulted, considering the accuracy of his statement. She pursed her lips. "For someone who's known me for less than twenty-four hours, you seem to have a lot of opinions about me."

"Not opinions, really. Just observations." He sounded congenial, like their being together was the most ordinary thing in the world. "So, what else do you need to get done today?"

"Well…" Considering that she hadn't thought past getting the wedding dress, the question caught her off guard. "I do still need a wedding gift for Chase."

He nodded, his expression noncommittal. "Where do you want to look?"

"Well, I…" This could present a problem.

What do you buy for the man who has everything, including a yacht and access to a private jet? Her gaze darted around and landed on a couple up ahead, bent over a colorful shop window.

Lowering her shades, Kate squinted. "Oh, look. I think that's an art gallery." Removing the glasses, she quickened her steps, allowing the slight limp to protect her knee. As she got closer, her spirit lifted. The window featured a display of vibrant glass art. "It's just like Chase's...I mean *our* chandelier."

Josh chuckled as he fell in behind her. "Now that's the Kate I want to hang out with. The one who sees what she wants and goes for it."

If only she were as self-confident as he made her sound. "Thanks for the reminder, Josh." She rubbed her knee. "But promise you'll stop me if I try to climb any furniture."

He chuckled. "Promise."

Kate suppressed a grin. There was nothing flirtatious about this exchange. Just friendly banter between...well, *friends*. At least, that's what she told herself as they stepped up behind the couple.

"That's so unexpected in a town like this." The man, who looked like a young college professor on vacation, commented to the auburn-haired woman beside him.

"Oh Mark." The woman shook her head. "It's so tragic. What kind of world do we live in?"

Tragic? Kate jockeyed to see what kind of

artwork would elicit a response like that. Her heart fluttered at the realization that they weren't commenting on a piece of art. They were commenting on the flier in the window.

Her face heated. Instinct told her to turn and head for the car but now that she was close enough to one of the fliers to actually read it, she couldn't stop herself. As she absorbed the details, a creeping realization took hold. If what Chase had told her was true, she and Trina had something in common. They were both runaways.

The thought flowed through her like ice water. Had anyone made fliers with her picture on them when she went missing? Distributed them around Sacramento, asking if anyone had seen her? It had been six years, but maybe some of the fliers still remained, fading like the memories people held of her. Did total strangers gape at the washed-out, torn remnants, commenting on the tragedy of it all?

A fire lit behind her eyes as the weight of what she'd done really hit her. She had broken her mother's heart, abandoned her childhood friends. Her fate remained unknown to them, and she hadn't even given their pain a thought. How selfish could she be?

She shut her eyes. As concerned as she'd been these past weeks that Joe or someone loyal to him might recognize her face if it made the national news, it hadn't occurred to her that someone from back home might take notice as well. Would that be a good thing? She was an adult now. They couldn't force her to go back, but it might at least put their minds at ease.

And there might be a small chance that she could have a relationship with her mother again.

The auburn-haired woman made an abrupt about-face and stepped right into Kate, who had been teetering closer to the couple than she realized.

"Oh, pardon me." Alarm filled the woman's compassionate blue eyes.

Kate forced out a shaky apology. "My fault. Really." She dipped her chin and stepped back, not wanting the woman to recognize her.

"Are you all right?" Genuine concern tinged the woman's voice. "You look a little pale."

"I...I'm fine." She cast one last emotional glance at the flier, then her focus hit something behind it, inside the gallery.

"Are you sure? Because—"

"Piper." The man spoke in a stern but kind voice. "She said she was fine."

"Oh, there I go again." The woman acquiesced. "I probably should have been a counselor instead of a writer."

Barely registering the woman's words, Kate moved closer to the window to get a better look, scarcely believing she could be so lucky. It was a glass mosaic sculpture of a seahorse, done in the same color palette as Chase's chandelier.

"You're a writer?" Josh's voice sounded dimly behind her as he picked up the conversation with the couple.

The seahorse stood on a small pedestal, reverentially set apart from the rest of the display. About two feet in height, it was made up of bits of glass which had been painstakingly pieced together.

She edged in closer so that her nose practically touched the window. *Incredible.* There were gold flecks in the glass, just like in the chandelier at home. It would be a perfect match.

She swallowed hard to suppress a childish giggle.

Vaguely aware of Josh talking with the woman about the writing he did for his movies, Kate turned her head to encourage him toward the window. "Josh, look!"

Hand lifted in a wave as the couple moved on, Josh joined her.

"I found it." She pointed to the seahorse. "The perfect wedding gift for Chase." She started for the door. "Come on."

"Well, that was easy." Just as he moved to follow, a muted ring tone sounded and he reached for his pocket. He pulled out his phone and gave it a quick look. "You go on. I'll just be a minute."

Kate hurried inside to claim her treasure. What a beautiful stroke of luck. This would show

Chase that she was a keen observer of details. She smiled to herself. Soon she would be identifying arias in operas and steps in ballets. This was who she was. Not Kathy Jennings, teenage runaway, but Mrs. Chase Cole—a connoisseur of the arts.

It was all going to be okay. It had to be.

Chapter 10

Kate stood in front of the sculpture, waiting for the saleswoman to look up the price. From this proximity, Kate could see the quality of the piece. It was truly a work of art.

"I'm so sorry." Confusion creased the woman's brow. "I'm afraid this piece hasn't been appraised yet. I'll have to consult the owner as to what she intends to do."

"Oh…but I really want it. Money is no object." Had she really just said that? She sounded like a caricature of a wealthy snob.

The woman smiled in nervous reassurance. "I'm sure we can work something out, Miss Jennings."

"Jennings? *Kate* Jennings?"

Wincing, Kate tried to ignore the feminine voice behind her. The day had been going so well. If she could just complete this transaction without anyone causing a scene—

"You should be ashamed to show your face in this town."

The anger searing a hole in Kate's back made

it clear that ignoring the speaker was not going to be an option. Resigned, she turned to see a woman of about fifty, wearing a gallery name tag and a pinched expression. Her cropped grey hair stood up in tiny spikes on the top of her head, giving emphasis to her prickly disposition.

Timidity edged out Kate's confidence. "Excuse me?"

"You heard what I said." The woman glowered at her through small red glasses, then turned her vitriol on the saleswoman. "Jocelyn, you know how I feel about that sculpture."

"I'm sorry, Marion." Apprehension glistened in Jocelyn's eyes as she gave Kate an apologetic glance. Clearly trying to mitigate the situation, she looked again at Marion. "I thought you'd decided against keeping it."

"I did." Marion's jaw tightened. "But you *know* who this woman *is*."

Tears welled in Kate's eyes. She would have run if not for the fear of her knee buckling again. Her eyes darted to the window, and she saw Josh involved in what looked like an intense conversation on his phone. He was in no position to come to her rescue.

"Marion…" Jocelyn sent a look of cautious warning, the meaning of which Kate couldn't even guess.

Marion held for a beat, her nostrils flaring like a bull as she glowered at both of them. Then her jaw firmed in irrevocable decision. "I put this piece on display so it could be enjoyed." She snapped a look at Kate. "But it remains unpriced for a reason." She took a quick glance at the door as another patron entered, then lowered her voice to a menacing hiss. "If you think you're going to take her place, you've got another thing coming."

With a parting sneer, she whirled around and stomped off to a room at the back of the store, banging the door shut behind her.

"I'm so sorry." Jocelyn spoke in a soft jittery voice. "Marion owns the gallery but that's no excuse for her behavior." She glanced around, as if to assure herself that no one was close enough to overhear. "She wanted to keep this piece for her personal collection, but since she almost lost the gallery a year ago she needs every sale she can get."

"Oh." Alarmed by the woman's candor, Kate nodded. "I'm glad she didn't lose her business. But, why is she so upset with *me?*"

"Don't take it personally. It's just that…Trina Cole was her best friend."

Kate's heart raced. She hadn't even considered that Trina would have had friends on the islands. No wonder that woman resented Kate. And she probably wasn't the only one.

A bead of sweat trickled down Kate's forehead. Suddenly the thought of making a place for herself in this community seemed completely ludicrous.

By the time she exited the gallery a minute later, her knee throbbed and her stomach burned. At the rate she was going, they'd have to carry her down the aisle on a stretcher.

Seeing her, Josh clicked off his call, his face slightly ashen. "Mission accomplished?"

"Not exactly. Turns out the sculpture's not for sale." Kate frowned at his uncharacteristically cheerless demeanor. "Is something wrong?"

"That was my uncle." He slipped his phone back into his pocket. "Turns out he can't hire me this summer after all. The economy's not so great for contractors right now."

"Oh. I'm sorry to hear that." While her sentiment was sincere, she couldn't but help hope that maybe now he'd be free to stay for the wedding. "What are you going to do?"

He shrugged. "I guess it's in God's hands. If I had known sooner this was going to fall through, I would have started job hunting a month ago." He glanced up the street at the line of traffic rolling off the ferry. "It's going to be tough to find something now that everyone's done with school."

Her heart went out to him. She remembered what it had felt like to be jobless with no decent prospects. "I suppose that means you'll be heading back home now."

"Soon, but…" He tipped his head toward the corner. "I promised you ice cream."

A smile curved her lips. "Ice cream it is." Relief surged as they started to walk. She'd have to say goodbye to him sooner or later, but the longer he stayed the more time she had to adjust to being here on her own. "Hope you don't mind a leisurely pace."

"I don't mind." He gave her a critical glance. "But maybe we should have a doctor take a look at your knee."

She shook it off. "I'm fine, really. I…"

As the line of ferry traffic worked its way up the street, a blue Honda jerked to a stop adjacent to Kate and Josh, causing the driver behind it to lay on his horn. Ignoring him, the driver of the Honda leaned across the passenger seat to roll down his window, then drew a camera with a long lens up to his face.

Kate squealed. Turning her back to the car, she started to dig around in her bag for her sunglasses.

"What's the matter?" Josh eyed her.

"The press." Why hadn't she remembered to put her glasses back on?

He looked past her. "Yeah. So…?"

"I can't explain." Kate's panic escalated as a small crowd began forming and the traffic snarl grew louder and more pronounced.

"Oh my gosh!" A young woman extended a full-arm point. "That's the lady who's marrying that pharmaceutical billionaire."

Kate's stomach did a gymnastics maneuver.

Where were those glasses? She dipped her chin and put her hand up to conceal her face from the photographer as she angled her shoulder in the direction of Josh's car and took a couple of wobbly steps.

A teenage girl zipped in front of her, thwarting her advancement. "Can I interview you for my blog?" She pulled her phone out of her purse and held it up like she might snap a few photos while awaiting a response. "Please, please, please?"

Tossing a glance over her shoulder, Kate saw the photographer get out of his car. Terror surged. She had to get out of there before either the professional or Miss Can-I-Interview-You-For-my-Blog reeled off a string of close-ups of her face.

As she put her hand to her forehead, the crowd closed in on her like she was Madonna on her bodyguard's day off. Shrieks and honking drummed in her ears and the gymnastics demonstration in her belly advanced to the next event.

In true security man-style, Josh spread his arms and inserted himself between Kate and the pressing throng. She seized the opportunity to break away in the direction they'd originally been heading. So much for making it to his car. The irate driver behind the photographer yelled at him to move his car then leapt from his own vehicle and intercepted the photographer at the curb. Grateful for his unintended and expletive-filled assistance, Kate hobbled as quickly as she could down the sidewalk, her eyes zipping around for a safe refuge.

"Kate!" Josh's voice came dimly from behind as she slipped around the corner.

Partway down the street, a small building that looked like it had once been a house grabbed her attention. A sign reading 'A Scoop in Time' hung from the edge of a shingled overhang above a cute little porch. *Ice Cream.* Trying to ignore the pain in her knee, she willed herself toward it.

The bell on the door made an unnecessarily loud jangling noise as she slunk inside, an array of reassuring sweet scents filling her nose. The only other customers, a couple with a little girl, eyed her curiously as she slid behind an old fashioned coat rack next to the door. Mortified, she turned her gaze back to the window.

A moment later, Josh bolted into the shop. "Kate, what are you—"

"Shh…!" She motioned for him to join her as she peered out the window, straining to see the corner she'd come around.

Josh patiently moved next to her as directed. She held her breath, but no one on the sidewalk outside seemed to be paying any attention.

"Don't worry." He touched her shoulder. "It looks like we lost them."

Her guard melted a little. "I'm just so tired of

them taking pictures of me every time I step out in public." Her hands moved to the sides of her face. It felt good to talk about it, but she had to take care not to let her defenses down too much.

He pulled his hand away, and a wave of inexplicable disappointment rushed through her. What was the matter with her, anyway?

"Look." His voice sounded soft and kind. "This is going to blow over. People will get used to seeing you around the islands and they'll stop acting this way."

She looked up into his eyes, which were a richer shade of brown than she'd realized. Though her heart beat like a steel drum, her voice came out barely above a whisper. "Promise?"

A hint of amusement shaded his smile. "I can't exactly 'promise' anything, but if I know human nature, people around here will move on to the next big thing before too long. Besides, what's the worst that can happen? You get your picture taken a few more times and people speculate about your motive for marrying the local billionaire. In the big scheme of things, that's really not so terrible."

She looked away, not wanting to let on that the 'worst thing that could happen' was actually far worse than just that.

"Kate." Josh looked down at her, a little more perceptively than she would have liked. "Is there something you're not telling me?"

Oh no. Why did he have to be so smart?

Forcing a contrite expression, she thought fast. "Yes. I have a confession to make." Her attempt at lightheartedness came out too shaky to convince even herself. She tipped her head toward the ice cream case. "I have a secret passion for coconut."

"Oh?" One corner of his mouth lifted. "I'm a chocolate fan, myself."

"And I owe you that shake, right?" Casting another nervous glance out the window, Kate moved carefully toward the counter, where a young girl stood wiping off the glass case. She pulled a five dollar bill out of her purse and pushed it along the counter. "A chocolate shake, please." She turned to Josh, who had followed her, but was keeping a skeptical eye on her. She smiled. "I'm suddenly dying for that cone you promised, so—"

Abruptly, the man with the camera skidded past the window, giving it a quick glance as he passed. Kate grabbed the front of Josh's shirt, using him as a human shield. Peering around him, she watched the photographer stop a couple of tourists, no doubt to ask if they'd seen her, and bounce on his toes like he might spring out in any direction.

Kate looked around frantically, then snapped at the girl, who had her head inside the ice cream case. "Restroom!"

Eyes widening at the urgent outburst, the girl pointed with her scoop to a door near the back of the store. "It's a single stall, but no one's in there."

Kate pivoted on the black and white checked floor just as the little girl from the nearby table darted in front of her and nearly sent her headlong into a shiny red and white booth. She panicked. The kid was clearly headed for Kate's only reasonable hiding place.

"Whoa!" Josh looked down at the girl, who had sidelined herself by careening into his legs. "I thought this was an ice cream parlor, not a football field!"

The girl stopped to stare up at him and Kate grappled with the momentary advantage. As she attempted to regain her footing, the girl's mother swooped in and put her hands on the girl's shoulders.

"Marissa what do you say?"

The little tyke glanced up as she did a dance that clearly indicated her need to make it to the restroom was very different from Kate's. "Sowwy."

Kate's heart turned to butterbrickle. How could she cut in front of a child?

A quick glance at the window reassured her that the photographer had moved on. Crossing back to the counter for support, she held up a weak hand, indicating that the girl should go before her.

"Here you go!" Smiling brightly, the counter girl thrust a cold cup into Kate's hand.

The little girl's mother looked weary as she spoke to her daughter. "Let's go." She gestured toward the restroom. "I'm right behind you."

Kate caught sight of the photographer jogging past the window in the other direction. She shoved the shake at Josh, maneuvering so that he would once again block her from the window. At the same time, Josh stepped aside for the woman, causing Kate to accidentally move directly into her path. They did an awkward step dance as the little girl dashed around them and pushed open the women's room door with the urgency of someone running from a fire.

An unidentifiable emotion charged the mom's eyes as she angled herself sideways and tried to push between Kate and the booth.

Kate's stomach lurched. Was this another friend of Trina's, suddenly realizing who Kate was? She braced herself for another admonishment.

Instead of fixing a glare on Kate, the woman glanced over at the restroom door as it closed behind her daughter. Her look softened to one of apology and she stopped trying to get around Kate. "I'm really sorry about that."

"Oh, no big…" Josh met the woman's gaze, then gave a grunt of surprise and stepped forward.

Kate looked up. Did he know this woman? He stared, incredulity slacking his features. "Sorry. It's just… has anyone ever told you, you look like

Shania Hane?"

Kate honed her focus on the woman. It was true. The woman bore a striking resemblance to the movie star, but that was of little interest to Kate at the moment.

The man who had been sitting with the woman and child stood and joined them, settling his hands against the woman's shoulders. "She hears that a lot."

Kate breathed out, hoping that no one would mention the 'striking resemblance' she herself bore to the woman whose sunglass-concealed face had appeared on the national news more than once. She really needed to get Josh out of this conversation, to spare herself and to spare this poor woman.

"Josh!" Without thinking, she grabbed his arm and pulled him out of the woman's way. "You'll have to forgive my friend. He's a big movie buff."

"Yes," he went on, getting that light in his eyes that he seemed to get whenever he talked about film, like nothing else really mattered. "And *Genesis Expedition* was one of my favorites." He tilted his head to one side, studying her intently. "You look *just* like her."

Kate flashed him a look that seemed to go unnoticed. Didn't he realize how annoying this was?

The man sighed. "This is Devynne Lang. Devynne is the owner of The Healing Quilt, here on the island." He stepped around Devynne and stretched out his hand. "I'm Carcen."

Kate stared at his hand. What was she supposed to do? Josh was still gaping at the woman named Devynne like some kind of crazed fan.

Kate stepped forward and took the man's hand. "I'm Kate and this is my… friend… Josh." She wanted to bite back the words the second they were out. Why had she just admitted to being the woman this entire community was probably bent on hating? She bit her lip, waiting for the light to go on in their eyes.

Josh seemed to recover his senses. He snapped his mouth shut and gave himself a little shake. "Yeah, I'm Josh." His face reddened. "But…" he pointed toward Kate, "she said that already. I'll just be quiet now. Nice to meet you."

In spite of her irritation with him at the moment, Kate almost laughed. So he had a less-than-totally-cool-and-collected side to him after all.

The man just smiled and then looked down at the woman without a hint of recognition of Kate. "Need to go see to Marissa?"

"Yes." She offered them a parting smile and headed past Kate, toward the restroom.

Relief and thankfulness for the deflating of another potential disaster coursed through Kate. Once the man turned to go back to his table, Kate backhanded Josh across his bicep.

His eyes trailed after the woman, who lingered outside the closed door. He rubbed his arm, seeming to barely notice the blow.

She blew a puff of air through her lips. "That poor woman." She kept her voice low.

"Huh?" He finally focused on Kate.

Kate gave him another stern look. "Don't you realize she's probably sick of hearing that she looks like Shania Hane?"

He squinted. "I thought it was a compliment."

Her mouth twisted. "Haven't you learned anything from watching me suffer through this celebrity thing? Don't inflict that on some poor innocent woman who happens to look like a movie star."

He pointed after the woman "But—"

"But nothing. You know she isn't really her because Shania Hane died in that awful accident. Remember?"

His enthusiasm seemed to deflate. "You're right. I just got caught up in the moment. It's part of being in the film business. You know… thinking about making connections." He looked at the woman again. "It's so weird, though…"

With a loud *thwumk*, the door to the ladies' room banged open and the little girl dashed out.

"Mama!" Frustration filled her tone. "They got the signs on the doows wong! Thewe's a man in thewe and he tol' me to give you this." She thrust something into her mother's hands, ran to the door

108

marked 'men', and pushed through it before her mother could stop her.

Kate's heart began to race, and she took a step toward the front door. A man in the ladies' room? That photographer? Her defenses snapped to high alert.

The woman hurried toward the door the girl had just disappeared behind.

The man with her—Carcen—grabbed her arm and jerked her to a halt. He thrust her behind him, backing away from the table with alarming urgency. He pointed at Josh. "Both of you get outside, now! Call 9-1-1.Tell them there might be a bomb."

A bomb! Terrified, Kate turned and stumbled for the door, grabbing at chairs for support as she went. The certainty that Joe had found her and that other people had been put in danger blurred in her mind.

Bounding down the steps and onto the sidewalk, she looked around. Where was she supposed to go? If Joe had taken a bomb into the ice cream store, that meant he'd been following them—that he was watching her *now*. Why hadn't she thought it through before bolting out the front of the shop? She should have gone around the counter and escaped out the back.

Or would Joe have expected her to do that?

Confused, she jerked toward the main street and twisted her sore knee, which gave out and sent her plummeting toward the concrete.

Two powerful hands gripped her arms from behind, and terror paralyzed her. She struggled to get free, whirling around and flailing her arms in self-defense.

"Whoa." Keeping a solid grasp on one of her elbows, Josh held up his other arm to shield himself from her frenzied hits. "Calm down, Kate. It's okay."

Seeing that it was him, she melted into a puddle of embarrassment and relief. He could protect her, but was it really fair to put his life in jeopardy any more than she already had?

"Aha!" Just then, the photographer appeared in front of them, reeling off a series of shots.

Kate shrieked, throwing her hand over her face.

"Hey, Mrs. Cole..." The photographer taunted as he continued to click. "How long do you think you'll last before you disappear too?"

The words sent a tremor through her. He would have no way of knowing that the real danger in her life had nothing to do with Chase.

Josh took a powerful stride toward him. "Hey, get lost."

Kate did her best to steady her breathing, but it was no use. Joe had to have been watching her. Waiting. He had to have seen her enter the ice cream store and had taken advantage of the opportunity to get to her. Then that little girl had walked in on him. That poor little girl could have been killed, and it was all her fault.

Terror filled her. In spite of all her precautions, Joe had found her. She had to face it. She had run but she couldn't hide.

Chapter 11

Josh gave a peripheral glance at Kate as he drove down the ramp onto Shaw Island. She'd hardly said a word on the ferry, so he had taken the full hour of sitting in the car with her to ponder her behavior. Neither her overreaction to getting her picture taken nor her totally losing it over the bomb scare made any sense. Yet she seemed to think that marrying a guy whose previous wife had vanished without a trace was perfectly rational.

But the craziest thing of all was that Josh couldn't put the brakes on his attraction to her.

"Stop the car!"

Kate jumped at Jessica's piercing command from the backseat, but Josh just cringed in annoyance. He pulled over to allow the two cars behind him to pass, then shifted to 'park'. Jessica hopped out, hurried to a red sports car that sat in front of the small general store next to the ferry dock, and got in. As the car swooped around, Kim blew Josh a kiss from the driver's seat.

Josh resisted an eye roll, if just barely. Hand

on the steering wheel, he turned to Kate. "I'd check the local news to see if they're reporting anything about the bomb scare, but my radio doesn't work."

Kate shuddered. "Can we just get going?" Clutching her stomach, she slumped even further into her seat.

"In a minute." He shut off the engine. "After you tell me what's really bothering you."

"It was a *bomb*, Josh." Her eyes held the torment of confusion and indecision. "I'm going to have to just stay at Chase's…I mean *our* house. It's obviously too dangerous for me to go out."

"Dangerous?" He hadn't taken her to be a drama queen, but this was definitely an overreaction. "You honestly think someone would put a bomb in the ice cream parlor…why? To scare you away from marrying Mr. Cole?"

"Of course not…. That would be ridiculous." Her voice weakened. "But when I went into the gallery, the owner made it really clear that I'm not welcome around here."

"She did? That doesn't seem like a very smart way to do business."

"No, but she was Trina's best friend. She's obviously pretty bitter about me being here."

"I guess that's understandable." A wave of protectiveness moved through him. "But did she threaten you?"

"N…no. She just wasn't very nice to me."

"But not *dangerous*."

"I guess not." Chewing her lower lip like she might just bite right through it, she pondered. "But even if that bomb scare had nothing to do with me this time, next time—"

"Kate, you're not thinking clearly." He turned in his seat to fully face her. "Take a couple of deep breaths. Nobody wants to hurt you."

Obviously, she needed some perspective. The sheriff in Friday Harbor hadn't told them much— just asked them a few questions and had the ice cream store cordoned off with yellow tape. Ordinarily, Josh would have stuck around to observe in case he ever needed to film a scene about a police investigation, but Kate hadn't been able to stop shaking. They'd gotten on the next ferry for Shaw instead.

Now Josh longed to encourage her to open up about what was *really* scaring her. He tried to affect a more reassuring tone. "If the sheriff had thought this had anything to do with you, he wouldn't have let you leave."

Kate's eyes darted around the parking lot. "I don't trust the police."

Whoa. Where did *that* sentiment come from? He studied her. "Why not?"

With a vague headshake, she wrapped one arm around her middle and gnawed on her thumbnail.

"I know you must have a good reason for feeling that way, but all the police officers I know are really good at what they do."

She frowned, finally looking at him. "You know a *lot* of police officers?"

He shrugged. "A few. My roommate is a rookie cop."

Her eyes widened. "Seriously?"

"Yeah. Eli's wanted to be a cop since we were kids."

She nodded, taking that in. "So you've been friends for that long? Must be nice."

"It's good to have people in your life who you can always count on." He smiled. "And he's a good cop."

"Even so…" Her tone was quiet, but filled with emotion. "The police don't *know* everything."

"Kate." He tried to catch her eye. "What aren't you telling me?"

"Nothing." She looked down then away—a sure sign that she wasn't being entirely honest. "I guess those fliers just upset me more than I realized."

"Understandable. But the fliers are about Trina, not about you."

She blinked, obviously trying to fight back tears. "But that photographer almost got a good close-up of me. If I hadn't put my hands up, my face would be in every major paper in the country tomorrow." Swallowing hard, she swiped at her eyes with her finger.

He leaned over to open the glove box, glad to

see that the packet of tissues he'd acquired at some point was still there. "I don't understand why that would be so terrible."

Accepting the tissues, she rolled in her lips and looked nervously around the mostly unpopulated parking area. An old VW van appeared on the road in front of them and pulled into a parking space. As the driver's door opened, Kate held a tissue up to her face and sunk down in her seat.

Josh couldn't help a slight chuckle. "I don't think you need to worry about *her* giving you a bad time."

"Why not?" Kate pulled her head up a little to watch the woman in a formless blue dress and white head covering amble along the walkway in front of the store to the post office in the same building. "Is that a *nun?*"

"Yeah." Encouraged by her interest, Josh smiled. "There's a monastery on the island."

"Seriously?" She leaned forward, her desire to stay hidden apparently quelled by her curiosity.

"Jessica told me that the nuns used to run the store, but they sold it. You still see them around the island."

"Huh." She leaned her head back. "Well, at least I know *some* of my neighbors will show me some grace."

As he moved to restart the car, he realized that he didn't want to take her back to the house yet.

He told himself it was because he wanted to give her more time to recover from the ice cream store incident, but in all honesty he was enjoying his time with her. As he looked around the small settlement, an idea struck.

Instead of starting the car, he pocketed the keys and opened his door. "Hey, come on."

Her pretty blue eyes filled with fear. "Where are we going?

"I just want to show you that you don't have to hole up like a hermit."

Ignoring her look of uncertainty, he got out and crossed to her side of the car. By the time he opened her door, she had appeared to have at least progressed from terror to indecision. He reached out a hand and she hesitated, then accepted it. He helped her to stand, somewhat unsteadily, then started to lead her across the street.

Looking like she trusted him about as much as she did law enforcement, she slouched low into her shoulders and fell into stride next to him. "What are we doing?"

He nodded toward the country store. His observant eye from his stop yesterday on his way in was about to pay off, or so he hoped. "We never got our ice cream."

She tilted her head in realization. "What happened to your shake?"

He shrugged. "I left it on the table when you ran out of the ice cream parlor. Other things suddenly seemed more important."

Stepping onto the rustic front porch, they passed under an old wooden sign with the words 'General Store' painted in faded red letters. Josh pulled open one of the old fashioned wooden double doors and followed Kate into the small but serviceable store.

He watched her shoulders visibly ease. It would be hard to feel threatened in such a cheerful place.

"This way." Resisting the urge to place a guiding hand on the small of her back, he tipped a nod toward the rear of the store.

"This place is great." Kate regarded the island memorabilia hanging on the walls above groceries, colorful produce, wine, clothing, and even hardware which were displayed on antique tables and shelves.

As they reached the back of the building, Josh watched Kate's eyes light up. She walked up to the ice cream counter and peered into the glass case.

"Hey!" She looked up at him with the bright blue enthusiasm he'd found so appealing just the day before when they'd had their first conversation in Mr. Cole's dining room. "How did you know they'd have coconut?"

He smiled. "Sometimes things just work out."

By the time they stepped back outside with a couple of cones in their hands, Kate's mood had visibly lightened.

"This is exactly what I needed." She took a big bite of fluffy coconut and her face gave way to a look of pure delight.

"And there wasn't even one bomb threat the whole time we were in there." Taking a bite that encompassed both the chocolate and the peanut butter that formed his favorite flavor, he made an after-you gesture toward a red wooden bench in front of the store. "See. Perfectly safe."

The sideways glance she cast him as she sat let on that she didn't entirely believe him or appreciate his attempt at humor. Sure, the community wasn't exactly throwing a welcome party, but it would be a stretch to think that someone had been trying to scare her away. Something else was clearly troubling her, and Josh couldn't quite explain his desire to find out what it was.

An adorable knee-height black dog with soulful brown eyes and graying paws sauntered around the corner and made a slow beeline for them.

"Hey there, fella." Josh checked the dog's tag. "'Lucky'. Nice name."

"Hi, boy" Kate reached out to pet him. "I could use a little luck. Got any to spare?"

"It's a nice thought." Josh petted the dog, who

seemed to think that if he persisted with the warm island welcome, he'd be rewarded with a bite of ice cream. Clearly, he'd played this game before. "But I think luck is highly overrated."

She let out a little laugh. "You don't believe in luck? Why not?"

"Because everything's in God's hands." He wanted to be real with her, but he had to be careful not to overstep. "Things seem to happen randomly, but the reality is that God is always in control."

Kate looked at him skeptically. "So you're saying that God planned for them to have coconut ice cream today?"

He smiled. "I wouldn't put it past Him."

"Mm." Twisting her mouth, she returned her focus to eating her ice cream and petting the dog. "Well, all I know is, my luck changed when I met Chase."

Discouraged at her stubbornness in sticking with her worldly view, he took advantage of the conversational opening. "How did you and Mr. Cole meet, anyway?"

She hesitated. "We…uh…met in San Francisco. He came into the place where I worked."

"Oh?" Josh pretended to focus on catching a driblet of chocolate with his tongue. "And where was that?"

"I was working as a waitress." She dipped her

head, as if there was more to the job that she wasn't saying. "He came in one night and we just started talking."

He nodded without judgment, hoping she'd continue.

She wiped a bit of melted coconut off her chin. "It was love at first sight."

Josh tried not to cringe at her use of that phrase. "And did you recognize him right away?"

"Recognize him? Oh, you mean because of Trina?" Tipping her head, she attempted to get a better angle on her ice cream. "I know the story was in the paper, but I don't pay attention to the news. My world was pretty small."

Small…and apparently sheltered. How could she not have known about the story that had been headline news for the past year? He bit into his cone. "So, how long till he told you about his missing wife?"

"The second night he came into the club."

"The club. That's where you worked?"

"It was a sort of club…where we served drinks…" The blush that scaled her cheeks implied that more was served there than just drinks. She caught his eye. "It's not what you think. I didn't…" She twirled her free hand like she was tossing off a piece of clothing. "Anyway, he told me that his wife had left him for another man, but that no one knew where she was."

"And…you didn't think that was strange?"

"Maybe a little unusual. But he was honest with me about the situation. He told me that his wife had just vanished and that the police always suspect the husband if a wife goes missing. There was no evidence of foul play, but they targeted Chase anyway." She paused to take a less enthusiastic bite of ice cream. "Then when we got engaged, he warned me that the media would be on me like wolves and he was right. I guess I shouldn't be surprised that they aren't letting up." She cast a nervous glance at the couple of cars waiting to board the next ferry, and the wooded area beyond. "That's been the hard part."

Josh nodded slowly. This woman was obviously intelligent. Could she honestly have been so naïve? "So, you really think she left intentionally? That nothing happened to her?"

"I'll admit that part seems strange. Maybe something did happen to her. But I know Chase had nothing to do with it."

"How can you be so sure?"

"Because he told me. He was out of town the last day that people saw her here on the island, so he couldn't have had anything to do with it. Look, if you knew him the way I do, you'd understand that he could never hurt anybody. He's the kindest man in the world. He helped me out of a really tough bind that I was in."

Josh's imagination started to wander. A rich guy takes advantage of a woman in a vulnerable situation. He had money and he had helped her. That was obviously the basis for their relationship. But why *marry* the guy?

He tried to sound casual. "What kind of 'tough bind'?"

"I'd rather not say." The redness in her cheeks deepened. "Anyway, our romance has been a regular whirlwind."

He nodded tightly. "And *how* long has it been?"

"Eight weeks." She stared at her cone. "I know that doesn't sound like a very long time."

"No…"

"But that doesn't matter." She looked at him, her grip on her cone tightening. "Sometimes you meet someone and it's like you've known them your whole life. Know what I mean?"

"Sort of." He eyed her. He did know what she meant because he'd had that undeniable sensation about her. "Except that if you *had* known Mr. Cole your whole life, you wouldn't have found out about his two kids a week before your wedding."

Her forehead creased. "Are you making fun of me?"

"Of course not. But Mr. Cole is kind of notorious. Public opinion has been pretty much swayed against him. Not just because of this situation, but his unethical business practices."

"He's a very successful businessman."

"That may be true, but there's talk that he

greases palms to get his drugs pushed through the testing so they can get FDA approval faster. I don't think a lot of women who are well-informed would choose to get engaged to the guy."

She straightened. "You don't have to insult me."

"I don't mean to insult you. But haven't you wondered why Trina would just leave?

"He told me she was troubled."

"Even so, mothers don't usually just leave their kids."

She twisted her mouth. "Well, you've *met* her kids."

"I'm serious, Kate."

"I don't have all the answers, Josh."

"And that doesn't bother you? Don't you think you *should* have all the answers before you join this family?"

"Not when I know Chase is innocent." She stood and crossed to the railing at the edge of the walkway.

"But how do you *know* that?" He stood and followed her. "The media reported what he said, but—"

"But, what?"

"I don't know. It just doesn't add up." He paused, confirming in his heart that he had to take this opportunity to say more. Even if it made her angry, at least someone would have said it to her. "Maybe you should wait a while before you marry the guy."

She turned a gaze on him that was both dark and fiery. "Wait for *what?*"

"I don't know. For Trina to resurface." He paused, glancing past her at the bit of Blind Bay that peeked through the trees. "One way or the other."

As he returned his gaze to Kate, a cloud passed in front of the sun, stealing the brightness from the parking lot and sending a chill through him.

She glanced over at the bay, fear cutting a jagged line across her face. "What if that never happens?"

"Then at least give yourself some time to get to know Mr. Cole a little better." The cloud passed, and the sunlight returned. "Marriage is a covenant. It's not something you should rush into."

Her jaw firmed, and she took a stiff bite of her dripping cone. "I don't know anything about 'covenants'. I just know that I want to be a wife."

He frowned. "It's better to stay single than to marry the wrong person."

The little creases in her forehead returned. "Are you saying you think I'm marrying the wrong person?"

"I don't have any way of knowing that." He hated having to be so blunt with a girl he hardly knew. And the fact that he was undeniably drawn to her might be clouding his judgment. "I just get a really uneasy feeling about this. And it's more than just the age difference—"

"Okay, stop right there." The hurt in her eyes ignited in anger. "I know it might seem a little strange at first...me being closer in age to Chase's kids than to him—"

"Kate." He held up a hand. "I didn't mean to judge."

"Have *you* ever been in love?"

He jerked back, totally caught off guard by the question. "I..."

Turning her back on him, she huffed out indignation. "Because age makes no difference to true love."

"Look, it's your life and your decision." He held a beat. "And no."

She looked over her shoulder at him. "No, what?"

"You asked if I've ever been in love. The answer is no. Not really."

The fire in her eyes flickered out and was replaced by something else. Surprise? Discomfort, maybe. Josh couldn't quite read it, but he hated that she'd become silent again. He hadn't wanted to anger her, but at least she'd begun to open up.

A gentle rain started to dampen the ground in front of them, making him grateful they were under cover. He had to face it. Trying to help her was only drawing him deeper into the emotional hole into which she was not going to follow. He had to get away before he did some irreparable damage to his own heart. It would be better for both of them if he left tonight, but he wanted to make sure she'd be okay.

He drew in a breath to speak, but the door to the post office opened and the same nun they'd seen earlier stepped onto the walkway. She looked out at the light rain that had started to fall, then her gaze fixed on Kate.

"Excuse me." The nun approached, and Kate snapped her head toward her as if she'd been startled. "Aren't you the girl who's going to marry Chase Cole?"

Kate blanched as she gave Josh a look edged in fear. She looked back at the nun. "Y…yes. I am."

"Oh. I thought so." The nun folded her hands in front of her. Her eyes narrowed and she started to speak, then bit down on her words. She looked away as if reconsidering what she wanted to say to her. "Did that young man find you?"

Kate frowned. "What young man?"

"The nice one who was asking about you."

"Nice man? What did he—"

The ferry whistle blasted, making Kate visibly startle. The nun glanced over her shoulder. "Oh, it's here already." She looked back at Josh and Kate. "Please excuse me. I'm meeting someone who's going to stay the week at Our Lady of the Rock." She turned and started down toward the landing. "That's our monastery, you know."

Kate's jaw trembled and her hold on her cone loosened. "A man was…asking about me…"

Josh grabbed the cone from her hand before she dropped it. "Probably just a reporter. They're not always very subtle."

She shook her head. "No, you don't under…" The cars started to exit the ferry, and Kate snapped her focus to the parking area. "That looks like Chase's car." She took a couple of steps, stumbled, and caught herself on the railing.

"Kate, you shouldn't—"

"You don't understand." She shot Josh a look that reminded him of a scared rabbit. "I need him to keep me safe." Maneuvering around the railing and into the rain, she waved an arm to signal Chase.

"Kate!" Josh followed on her heels, not wanting her to go.

She stopped abruptly, pulling in her arm. Josh followed her gaze, wondering why she'd suddenly turned as pale as the ice cream he salvaged from her wilting grasp.

As the car passed by them, he saw the reason why. There was already someone riding in the passenger seat of Mr. Cole's car. And that 'someone' was a woman.

Chapter 12

Kate paced like a caged tiger. Her first couple of days on Shaw Island hadn't gone at all as she'd hoped. Instead of relaxing in her new home with her husband-to-be, she was all alone in the guesthouse, wringing her hands and probably wearing a path in the carpet.

Hours had passed since she and Josh had seen Chase get off the ferry with a woman in his car, and there had been no word from him. Where could he be? Shaw Island wasn't that big.

But the other question pressed on her mind—who was he with?

Halting, her gaze rested on the dark blue water past her living room windows and the twilit ferry landing on the other side of the bay. The light afternoon rain had progressed into a persistent deluge that only served to darken her mood.

She was still reeling, not only from the events of the day, but from the realization that she had hurt people she loved by running away, not just once but twice. Even if things settled down in her life, how could she ever hope to make that up to them?

Maybe her access to Chase's unlimited funds could be put to good use. She could start a foundation to help runaways. Some kind of safe house where kids could go without being afraid of being turned in to the cops. If she could make that a reality, maybe all of this suffering would be worth something.

An involuntary shiver accompanied the reminder that she'd left Dakota behind when she'd fled San Diego. She winced, pinching back tears. Was there a chance that Joe would assume Dakota knew her whereabouts? Would he take his anger out on him? Now that she knew, or thought she knew, what Joe was capable of…

A pathetic moan escaped her throat. The thought of sweet, innocent Dakota suffering because of her poor choices made her sick. She couldn't let herself think about it. People would look out for him—she had to believe that. Shari and Ben and Iowa…they would fill in for her where Dakota was concerned. They cared about him too.

A persistent rumble gurgled from her stomach. She'd been too upset to eat dinner, plus the thought of facing Jessica and her friends only made it worse.

She crossed to the kitchen to check the fridge, which was surprisingly well-stocked. Staring at what would normally be an appetizing array of snacks, she settled on bottled water and a bag of organic dried fruit.

How could her life possibly get straightened out at this point? She was a fugitive, for all intents and purposes. If she came forward with what she knew about Joe, she'd go to prison. Even if the authorities believed she didn't intend to take the money, that detective had already told her she was an accessory to Joe's crimes. Surely, she had only made things worse by running.

Nothing was going the way she'd planned, although she *had* managed to convince herself that the incident in the ice cream parlor had nothing to do with Joe. If he had found her, he wouldn't waste time planting a bomb, nor would he want to risk drawing attention to himself. There had to be some other explanation for that.

Wandering back to the living room, she braced the bottle between her elbow and her side and ripped open the bag of fruit. Then there was that odd encounter with the nun. Josh was probably right about the man she'd mentioned being a reporter. If Joe had tracked her all the way to Shaw, he wouldn't have to solicit help from a nun to make that final step.

She fingered what looked like a dried strawberry, then popped it in her mouth. Maybe it had been that photographer who had later found her in Friday Harbor. The guy who was probably still determined to get the one shot that would pay his rent for the month and get her killed if Joe saw it and recognized her. The thought made her stomach do a flip flop and she abandoned the bag and the bottle on the coffee table.

A gust of wind bellowed, forcing rain and branches against the windows and causing her to shudder.

Running her hands through her hair, she sat on one of the sofas. The more she thought about Chase, the angrier she got. He was a week away from becoming a married man again. He had no business driving around with another woman, much less staying away from home without letting Kate know his whereabouts. She had to set a better precedent. Let him know her boundaries right off the bat.

As she made a move to get her phone from her purse, her other, less courageous side took over. What did she know about being married? The only models she'd had were her mom and dad, who never seemed to communicate, and later her stepdad, who would fly into a rage at the slightest query as to his whereabouts. No, accountability hadn't been a strong suit in Kate's childhood home.

Leaning forward, she put her face in her hands.

Nothing made sense, and she was going to go crazy if she kept analyzing the situation. She looked around for something to take her mind off the waiting, and her eyes landed on her wedding binder. She opened it to her 'To Do' section at the front and ran her finger down the list of items, most of which had been checked off. She pulled the small pen from its position in the front of the book and put an X in front of 'gown fitting'.

Her eyes lit on the magazine clipping she'd almost discarded, but had slipped into the front pocket of the binder instead. She hadn't included it with the pictures she'd shown the dress designer but now, as she pulled it out, she felt comforted in an odd way. The gorgeous skirt was slim at the waist and tapered out to a full mid-calf hem. The fitted, lace bodice had a V-neck and cap sleeves. It looked like something Grace Kelly or Audrey Hepburn would have worn in the 1950s, and was a style Kate adored. Why hadn't she told the designer that was what she wanted?

Never mind. She *knew* why. It wasn't suitable for the future Mrs. Chase Cole. Too young and hip. Not classy enough. She had made the right decision.

As she slipped the picture back into its pocket, a noise from the direction of the front door threw her senses into high alert. A *scrape-thump*, like something had brushed past the outside of the house.

Her breathing stopped. An animal? No. It must be the wind. She sat completely still, listening. Had she just imagined it?

Another sound, this one a little louder. Not the wind. The crunch of footsteps!

Shoving the binder aside, she leaped to her feet. Anger mingled with adrenaline. It was fine for Chase to relegate her to the guesthouse, but hadn't he considered her safety? Then again, why should he? She hadn't told him about Joe.

The noise sounded once more, and her gaze fixed on the kitchen window. That side of the house was thick with trees and shrubbery. Perfect to conceal anyone wanting to sneak around the house.

Holding her breath, she edged her way across the room, grateful that she'd closed the kitchen curtains. She had to just peek out to reassure herself.

Reaching the window, she lifted a shaky hand. Just as she pulled back the curtain, something…or some*one* brushed past the window. Kate reeled back.

No…no…!

Her gaze traveled the wall in the direction the person—if it was a person—would be moving. Toward the back door!

Heart racing, she charged to the door, ignoring the pain caused by the rapid movement, and grabbed the knob, jiggling it to assure that it was secure. Terror and uncertainty paralyzed her. Should she stand her ground? Hide somewhere?

Panicking, she scanned the kitchen. Vivid

images she had thought she'd shut out filled her head. It had been six years, but as she grabbed a knife out of a rack on the counter she remembered crouching in the broom closet of her childhood home, gripping her mom's sewing shears.

A wave of queasiness assaulted her as she clutched the knife in front of her with trembling hands. Would she be able to use it as a weapon? All those years ago, she had known without a doubt that she would defend herself against her angry drunken stepfather if he ever came at her again. That was when she'd realized she had to leave that house for good.

The sound came again, this time distinctly closer to the door. Her entire body shook with a too-familiar will to survive.

Then the faint sound of a car engine jolted her. *Chase!*

He would protect her. Surely he would see the lights in the guesthouse and come to her before going to the main house. She stumbled back to the kitchen window and peeked out. Through the darkness, she could barely see movement from between the trees up at the circular drive. That was Chase's distinctive gait, but he was walking the other way, toward the main house. Anger flared. She desperately needed him, and he wasn't even coming to check on her.

She staggered over to where she'd left her purse on the sofa. With her free hand, she fumbled for her cell phone. Keeping an eye on the back door, she tapped Chase's number, but got only his voice mail. Why wasn't he answering?

The wind gusted again, and she could have sworn the knob on the back door rattled. Her thoughts blurred. Joe...or someone sent by Joe. There was no other reasonable explanation.

Dropping her phone on the sofa, she scurried to the front door and undid the deadbolt. Still clutching the knife, she darted outside. Wind and rain lashed at her and she could barely make out the trail that wound its way up the incline to the main house as she started to climb.

Light poured out of the distant windows of the main house, but everything else around her was black. She tried to cry out to Chase, but the wind swallowed the pathetic sound she managed. A faint *twunk* reached her ears. The front door of the main house shutting?

Now all she could hear was the wind whipping through the trees and the hammering of her heart. She tried to move faster, but her knee gave out and she toppled to the ground.

Get up, Kate!

As she pushed her palm against the stone path, she sensed someone approaching her from behind. Her head snapped around, and she caught a movement among the trees. Was someone there? Or was it just the branches swaying in the wind?

A horrifying certainty that Joe had found her

flooded her veins. Was she going to die here, on this dark path? Or worse, would he drag her away and make her pay for what she'd done to him?

Raising the knife, she opened her mouth to scream, but again the wind silenced her voice. Then she sensed that whatever or whoever was there moved away, and the feeling of being followed vanished like smoke.

She looked around, holding the knife up with one hand and her hair back from her face with the other. Had she just imagined it?

She pulled herself to her feet and stumbled the rest of the way to the house. Grabbing the railing, she dragged herself up the steps to the porch. She was desperate to find Chase, to throw herself into his arms for comfort and security. She would beg him to let her stay in this house tonight, and everything would be okay.

Twisting the door handle, she pushed against the solid wood, but it wouldn't budge. *Locked.* Of course. She pounded on the door, feeling like a fool for not having a key to her own house.

After what felt like a full minute, the lock clicked and her stomach jolted. Slowly, the door opened. She held her breath. All she saw was the dimly lit foyer. No one was there.

Alarmed, she cautioned a half step forward into the cavernous room, which seemed ominous now with just the faint light at the entryway. Rain and wind whirred outside and she shivered against the question of who had unlocked the door. And why had they just disappeared?

She took a couple more careful steps inside. Suddenly, another roar of wind so powerful it made the house shake stole her balance and pulled her from her thoughts.

"Boo." An eerie voice came from behind her, accompanied by a whoosh of wind and a resounding slam.

Kate whirled around, wielding the knife and letting loose a scream.

Chapter 13

Just as Josh stepped out of his room, the unmistakable sound of a woman's scream pierced through the howling of the wind and rain. *Kate?*

Alarmed, he hoisted his backpack onto his shoulder and hurried to the stairs. Descending, he strained to see into the dimly lit foyer below. There next to the front door, Stuart stood with his hands raised like he was under arrest. Even stranger, Kate faced him holding up a butcher knife as though she were auditioning for a remake of *Halloween*.

"What's going on?" Heart racing, Josh took the remainder of the stairs at a sprint. As he reached her side, he saw that the knife shook in her grasp. Her tousled hair dripped, and the knees of her pants looked as if she'd taken a fall in the mud. What had happened to her since he'd left her to rest at the guesthouse all those hours ago?

He fired a glare at Stuart. "What did you do?"

"Me?" Stuart shifted a defensive hand toward Kate. "I wasn't the one prowling around like a murderer."

Puzzled, Josh turned his gaze on Kate. Lowering his backpack to the floor, he reached out a careful hand for the knife. "Maybe I should take that now."

He waited till realization dawned in her eyes and she willingly allowed the handle to slip from her hand to his. Once he had confirmed that it was just a plain old kitchen knife, he took a step back and eyed them both. "Where did this thing come from, anyway?"

"From the guesthouse." She shot an accusatory glare at Stuart. "And I wasn't *prowling*. Why did you sneak up behind me?"

"Did I *scare* you?" Stuart let out a jittery laugh like he wanted to try to make a joke of this. "I heard you pounding on the door and I thought I'd have a little fun."

"Some *fun*." The edge in her voice suggested that her fear had turned to anger. "And for future reference, I'm not big on practical jokes."

Josh looked at Stuart for a response. The guy had to be close to thirty—decades past finding pleasure in intentionally scaring someone.

All Stuart managed was a disinterested shrug. No doubt all those years of entitlement had drained whatever empathy God had infused in him.

Josh tried to tamp down his irritation. "You might want to think twice before you sneak up on someone who's carrying a weapon. You almost gave Janet Leigh a run for her money." Lifting the knife, he made a quick stabbing gesture for effect.

Stuart frowned. "Janet who?"

"Never mind." Not wanting to waste any more breath on this guy, Josh turned to Kate, setting the knife down on an entry table. "Kate, what's going on?"

She leaned one hand against the table, clearly taking the weight off her hurt knee. "I was just looking for Chase."

"Oh." Stuart tittered. "Mommy was looking for Daddy."

Annoyed, Josh watched as Stuart crossed to a cabinet that stood against the wall adjacent to a dark hallway. "Is something funny, Stuart?"

Removing a bottle from the cabinet, Stuart contained his laughter and shook his head. "It's just so ironic, that's all."

"What is?" Josh couldn't keep the exasperation from his voice.

"Same blonde hair." Stuart slid a bulbous glass from a hanging rack inside the cabinet. "Same blue eyes."

Josh half-turned to Kate. "Just ignore him."

Stuart made a big show of pouring an amber liquid into the glass, then looked down at Kate through narrowing eyes. "You remind me of her." The utterance came out sounding dark and menacing.

Kate shot Josh a look of wide-eyed confusion

edged in fear.

"Of who?" Whatever patience Josh had left was rapidly disintegrating.

Stuart returned the bottle to the cabinet, took a swig from the glass, and crossed over to Kate. He leaned in so close that she recoiled, no doubt at least partially from the potency of his breath.

"You remind me…" He sneered. "…of my mother." It came out in a conspiratorial stage whisper as if he thought he was a character in a Woody Allen movie. He winked, then turned to stumble down the darkened hall.

Huffing out exasperation, Josh gestured toward her dirty slacks. "Did you hurt yourself again?"

A slight eye roll seemed to indicate that this was the least of her worries. "I'm fine. I just heard Chase come home and I…" She swept a hand across her front. "…fell in the rain, and…

"Uh huh." He tipped a nod at the knife. "And what's with the cutlery?"

She shrugged. "Just my nervous need for self-defense." Her eyes lit on the backpack he'd abandoned near the door. "Are you leaving?"

Was that disappointment in her voice…or wishful thinking in his interpretation? When Kate hadn't made it to dinner, he'd prolonged his leaving, not wanting to disturb her if she was resting. Now, as he gazed into her pleading eyes that looked downright electric in this dim light, he again felt the unintentional hold she seemed to have on him. Maybe he should have cleared out while he'd had the chance.

He glanced at his watch. "I'm catching the last ferry off the island tonight. I was just about to look for you so I could say goodbye." He tapped the knife handle. "Glad I didn't catch you by surprise, Norman Bates."

"Goodbye?" Her eyes shot to his. "But I was under the impression that you were staying the weekend."

"Yeah, I was under that impression too." He rubbed the back of his neck. "I just sort of changed my plans."

"Oh." Her face dropped, a jumble of thoughts parading across it. Was sadness at the news that he was leaving part of that?

He hesitated, not quite ready for what would no doubt be the final goodbye. Why couldn't he just say it? It wasn't like this was going to get any easier, and besides—he checked his watch again— he had a ferry to catch.

The sound of a door opening somewhere down that dark hallway turned their heads. The quiet tap of footsteps followed, then Mr. Cole appeared carrying an empty glass decanter. His look of surprise at seeing them quickly softened.

"Katie." His gaze on her seemed gentle and loving as he approached. "I thought I heard a noise a minute ago. Sounded like a scream. Was that you?" He stopped short of giving her a peck on the cheek, jerking back in alarm. "What's happened to you? You're a mess." His eyes darted quickly to Josh's backpack then to Josh. "Are you leaving us so soon, Joshua?"

"Yes, sir." Resisting the urge to point out that Mr. Cole had failed to wait for Kate's response, he gave his watch another glance. If he didn't catch the ferry in fifteen minutes, he'd be spending another night here whether he wanted to or not. Still, he didn't want to leave without sharing a private goodbye with Kate.

He put on a polite façade. "Unfortunately, my summer job has fallen through, and I need to get back to Seattle to start looking for work. If I don't get something, I can't start film school in the fall."

"Oh. I'm sorry to hear it. Well, a bright young man like you is bound to find employment. And remember the invitation remains open." Still holding the decanter in one hand, he placed the other on Kate's back. "One week from today. The wedding of the year."

Kate ran her hands over her hair. "Chase…" Her nonchalant tone seemed forced. "Where have you been all day?"

"Just as I told you." He crossed to the cabinet and set the decanter on top. "Sam and I had meetings all day in Seattle."

"Oh. So, that's where you've been this entire time?"

He nodded. "For the most part, yes." He removed a full decanter and two tumblers from the cabinet and eyed Kate as he poured a reddish liquid into one of the glasses. "What's the matter, dear? You look a little peaked."

"It's just that…" She looked at Josh like she might need him to back her up. "We *saw* you earlier today."

"Oh?" Mr. Cole's pleasant expression didn't waver as he filled the second glass. "Where?"

She let out a breath. "Driving off the ferry onto the island."

He gave her a light chuckle. "You must have better eyes than I do if you could make out my car from across the bay."

"No, I mean we were at the general store." She hesitated, glancing at Josh with a hint of remorse in her eyes, as if *she'd* been the one keeping inappropriate company. "It's just that, it was about four o'clock and I expected you to drive right to the house, and—"

"Katie." He capped the decanter. "You'll have to accept that I have business to take care of."

"You had business on Shaw Island?"

"Kate—"

"And who were you with?"

His face clouded, but Josh couldn't tell if it was from confusion or guilt. "What?"

"You had someone in the car with you."

"Of course I did." He chuckled dismissively.

"I told you I was with Sam."

"Yes, I know. But I saw—"

The click of footsteps from down the hall interrupted her, and they all turned to see a woman appear at the entry to the hallway. She was probably about Mr. Cole's age, with dark wavy hair and a plum colored skirt and blazer that flattered her shapely figure. A warm smile enhanced her chiseled, ethnic-looking features.

Josh recognized her immediately. The woman from the car.

Kate took a step back, smoothing her hair again.

"It's about time you two finally met." With just a slight shift in his expression, Mr. Cole handed one of the glasses to the woman as he countered around to Kate's side. He placed his palm on her shoulder. "Kate, this is Sam."

Kate's cheeks flushed. "Y...you're Sam?"

"Chase." Sam's mouth twisted. "Don't tell me you didn't warn her?"

Looking contrite, Mr. Cole took a sip from his own glass.

"Samantha Jordan." Reaching out to offer her hand, Sam gave Kate a conspiratorial look. "I swear, in all the years I've known Chase, he's never caught on that if he calls me 'Sam', people will naturally assume I'm male." She turned her raised-brow look on Mr. Cole. "For goodness sake, Chase, you gave poor Kate a start. She must have thought you were having some sort of tryst."

"I'm sorry, Katie." He gave her a quick sideways hug. "I tend to forget that Sam is a woman."

Looking aghast, Sam cuffed his arm.

"What I meant was," he made a show of preventing his drink from spilling, "that I respect you as a businessman…I mean *person*, and I forget that our being seen together might appear to be anything other than business related."

"You're not digging yourself out of this hole." Sam turned her attention to Josh and offered a confident hand. "And you must be one of Jessica's friends."

"Josh Collins." He took her hand, surprised by the firmness of her shake.

She turned back to Kate, her expression warm and friendly. "Sorry to be taking Chase away from you so much. We're at a critical point in the development of the new drug we're overseeing, and if Chase is going to take some time off next week, that necessitates extra hours this week. I hope you understand."

"Oh." Kate's shoulders stiffened. "Of course."

Sam's smile seemed genuine. "Chase, we should be getting back to work."

"Yes." Mr. Cole gave Kate an apologetic look, then snapped his fingers as if a thought had just occurred. "Oh, by the way. I have to fly out in the morning."

"Fly out?" Kate's eyes narrowed. "But the wedding is in a week. Where are you going?"

"Hm?" Clearly no longer fully present, Mr. Cole jerked into the realization that she'd just asked a question. "Oh. Vegas." He removed his hand from her back and waved it, as if casting aside the importance of her concern. "It can't be helped."

"But, you can't leave." Her cheeks darkened as her voice weakened. "I need you."

"If you need to go anywhere, just call the driver on the intercom." He nodded toward a white box on the wall. "He has an apartment above the garage and should be there whenever you need him."

"You mean," Kate said. "Someone else is on the grounds at all times?"

"He's a trusted employee, Katie."

"Fine." She started to wring her hands. "But I need you to protect me."

"Protect you?" He swirled his glass. "From what?"

"From…everything." A little girl quality had crept into her voice. "You know…like the press."

Josh tilted his head. Something struck him as odd about this exchange. How could she be naïve enough to believe that this man, whose previous wife had vanished, would be a reasonable candidate for the role of protector?

"Yes, of course." Eyes brightening, Mr. Cole

turned to Josh. "Joshua can have the job."

Josh snapped to attention. "Excuse me, sir?"

"Kate needs security and you need a job. You can start immediately." With a nod of finality, he turned and took a stride toward his office.

"But…" Kate tossed Josh a look of desperation as she attempted to limp after Mr. Cole. "You can't leave."

"Kate…" He faced her with the expression of a stern but loving father. "Don't ever interfere with my *business*." Taking his eyes off Kate, he exchanged a look with Sam before heading back down the hall.

Blowing out air through her teeth, Sam looked after him, then turned a conciliatory smile on Kate. "He's under a lot of stress. This new drug has run into some snags, and the press has started bothering him again."

A door shut somewhere down the hall, and Kate looked like she'd been kicked in the stomach. "I understand."

Eyes brimming with sympathy, Sam took a couple of steps toward her. "Besides, this will give us girls a little time together. Chase and I are business partners, but he's always been like a brother to me. I feel like I'm gaining a sister, and I'd like a chance to get to know you."

"Oh…okay." Kate seemed to be mentally reconciling this turn of events to whatever picture of her future here she had previously held. "I'd like that."

"Good." She reached out to give Kate's hands a squeeze, then scrutinized her disheveled appearance in a way that came across as more caring than critical. "Besides, I have a feeling that being the wife of a successful business man is going to be a big change for you. I'm here to guide you in any way you need. Think of me as a mentor." With a parting smile to them both, Sam turned to follow in Mr. Cole's wake.

With renewed hope that Kate might now reconsider her plans, Josh treaded lightly. "Are you okay?"

"Well…it's a relief to have another woman in my corner." She gave up a little smile. "Look, I understand if you don't want to accept Chase's job offer."

"I just don't think it would be a good idea." He looked at his watch. "But I'm staying one more night at any rate. I just missed the last ferry."

"Oh." She made a cute wincing face. "I'm really sorry."

"Not your fault." He wanted to smooth her hair, partly to help her, but mostly to see if it was as soft as it looked. Instead, he hooked his thumb in his pocket and tipped his head toward the door. "Come on. I'll walk you to the guesthouse."

She shrank back.

"Is something wrong?"

"No…it's just that…" She shrugged it off. "It's

nothing. The rain, that's all."

Josh peered out the front window. "It looks like the rain has let up."

She nodded, picking up the knife. "I guess I'd rather fall in the mud again than risk another run-in with Stuart."

"That's the spirit." He opened the door for her. "Besides, Stu's a jerk. Just ignore everything he says when he's had too much to drink."

"Which is…" She stepped out onto the porch and drew her arms to her torso for warmth. "…what percentage of the time?"

Following her out the door, Josh huffed an ironic laugh. "Unfortunately, I'd have to say he's batting a thousand in my experience." He helped her down the steps, watching as she gingerly braced herself on the railing. "But then I've only seen him when he's come on campus to party with Jessica and her friends."

"Isn't he a little old to be hanging out with the college crowd?"

"I guess we have to show him some grace." Josh shrugged his brows as they started down the path toward the guesthouse. "He was only five when he lost his mom."

"Five?" She let out a confused half chuckle. "But that just happened a year ago."

He glanced over at her, squinting in puzzlement. "You really *haven't* read about this family in the news, have you?"

"What do you mean?"

He paused, assessing her earnestness. "Stuart and Jessica didn't have the same mother. Stuart's mom was Mr. Cole's first wife."

She stopped so suddenly, he reflexively grabbed her by the arm to keep her upright.

She looked up at him, her face stricken. "His *first* wife?"

Josh hesitated. So she didn't know about what had happened to Emily Cole. Maybe that was why she thought this marriage was a good idea. She didn't know the whole story.

Thank You, God.

Good thing he hadn't left right after dinner, because it looked like he'd just been granted one more shot at preventing this woman from ruining her life.

Chapter 14

Kate had slid to an abrupt halt that would have sent her pummeling into the mud again if Josh hadn't caught her by the arm. *Mr. Cole's first wife.* The words seeped from Kate's ears to her stomach like poison. Chase had been married *twice* before. Why hadn't he told her?

Her entire body started to shake.

"Kate …" Josh firmed his grip on her arm. "You really didn't know?"

She shook her head, biting back tears as raindrops started to hit her face.

"I'm sorry." Josh encouraged her to continue down the path. "It really wasn't my place to tell you."

"It's all right." She treaded carefully down the incline, fighting that peculiar dazed feeling from the sudden shot of adrenaline. A sharp pain stabbed her knee and her fingers dug into Josh's arm in response.

Before she realized what was happening, he had scooped her up in his arms. Ignoring her feeble shriek of protest, he moved briskly toward the guesthouse.

"If you're not careful," he said with just the barest hint of admonishment, "you'll be in a cast by Saturday."

She gave in to the feeling of security she felt in his arms. Moments later, he set her down on the front step and reached out his hand. She stared blankly, then jarred back to harsh reality. Where was her key?

Horrified, she realized that in her haste she hadn't even thought about locking the door. "I think it's open." Her heart pounded at the implication. Thank goodness Josh was there with her.

He opened the door and helped her inside. She desperately needed him to stay until she could assure herself that there was no one in the house. How was she going to manage that without letting on the reason for her terror?

"You've had a rough day." He scanned the space, then lowered the dimmer switch that brought down the living room light to a more soothing level. "Do you want me to stick around for a while? I could make you some tea or something."

She blew out a sigh. It was as if he'd read her mind. "Thanks. I'd appreciate that." How many places in this house could a person hide? She had to somehow manage to check them all before Josh left. "I'm going to put on my sweats, then I want you to tell me everything you know about Chase's first wife."

He winced. "It's not really my place to—"

"Please. I mean…" She cast a wary glance around the living room then, taking what she hoped was a subtle side-step, did the same to the dining room and kitchen. "If you don't tell me, who's going to?"

Brow furrowing, he eyed her movements. "Are you sure you're okay? You seem really skittish."

"You're right." Unsure if she found his concern comforting or overbearing, she grabbed her elbows and went for a more relaxed stance. "I guess I was more shaken up today than I realized. And now with the storm, and the dark woods…" And the sound she'd heard earlier, but she hesitated to mention that.

"If it would make you feel better, I can double check all the windows and doors."

She smiled her agreement. Maybe he really *could* read her mind.

He met her smile with one of his own, reaching over to twist the lock on the front doorknob. She turned to go down the hall, glancing over her shoulder to make sure he wasn't following her with his eyes. She then did a quick investigation of the bathroom and the guest room before moving into the master bedroom. Her heart pounded as she cast her gaze around the room.

After making a thorough sweep of the master bath, she gingerly knelt down to check under the bed. Next, she surveyed the walk-in closet and, satisfied that all was as she'd left it, changed to gray velvet sweats and the same sweatshirt Josh had already seen her in.

When she limped back out to the living area, Josh was standing at the kitchen island pouring water from the kettle into a couple of mugs. He looked up when she walked in, then crossed to the living room. He set the mugs down on the coffee table and moved to help her to the sofa.

"Here." He scooted the ottoman in front of her and lifted her leg to help her rest it.

The feel of his hands on her calf sent a bolt of lightning straight to her heart. His touch was unassuming—not possessive or self-serving in any way. He was helping her, plain and simple.

As she settled in, he sat next to her on the sofa, then picked up both mugs and handed one to her. "I was worried about you when you didn't show up at the house earlier." He nodded toward the bag of fruit she'd left on the coffee table. "I hope that wasn't dinner."

Her head eased against the sofa back. "I just couldn't face Jessica and her friends." Breathing in the soothing scent of chamomile, she took a careful sip of tea. "So, tell me about the first Mrs. Cole."

He slowly tasted his own tea, as if deciding how to start. "Stuart's mom was named Emily. I guess she and Mr. Cole met in high school and got married right after."

Kicking off her ballet flats, she allowed this new information to seep in. "And they had Stuart."

"Right. He was an only child, and his mom died when he was five."

That detail sat like a rock in her stomach. "Poor Stuart." Her heart went out to him. Missing her own mother was painful, but at least she was pretty sure she was still alive. This story was almost more than she could take, but the need to know prevailed. "How did she die?"

He pulled in a breath. "Chase found her body in the pool at their house in Seattle."

Despair and disbelief gurgled from her throat. "He…he *found* her?" A dull pain formed in her temples as she tried to keep the image from storming the walls of her heart. "How horrible."

"Yeah. It was strange though, because she was a really good swimmer. She was a member of some kind of club that did things like swim across Lake Washington and race in the Puget Sound."

Her eyes narrowed as she clung to the solace of the hot mug. "Yet she drowned in her own pool? That just doesn't make sense."

"That's exactly what the public thought, given that the Coles didn't exactly have a peaceful, quiet home life."

That comment hit like a blow to her solar

plexus. "What do you mean?"

He sighed. "This is just what I read in the paper after Jess's mom went missing, but apparently Emily Cole had called the police to their house quite a few times over the years. Domestic disturbance calls."

"Domestic disturbance?" Her stomach buckled at the too-familiar phrase. "You mean she claimed he hit her?"

"I don't know exactly." His eyes pooled as if it pained him to have to say these awful things. "It's just what I read."

"But..." Kate's head swam with images from her early teen years. Her mother huddled in a corner crying. Her stepdad cursing at the top of his lungs as the police officers hauled him out of the house, only to release him a few hours later. The neighbors peeking out from behind closed curtains. "He wasn't ever arrested was he?"

"No. The papers quoted friends of Emily saying that the police would take him outside and Emily would hear them all laughing together, like it was a big joke. Then he'd go back in the house and that would be that." He took a sip of tea, probably to give her time to assimilate. "So when she died, it's no surprise that Mr. Cole was under suspicion."

"They always suspect the spouse." Her voice sounded muted, like she was speaking underwater. She folded forward, anguish getting a chokehold on her throat.

"Kate?" Taking the mug from her, Josh placed a supportive hand between her shoulder blades. "Are you okay?"

A chill traveled through her. What was she going to do? Chase was supposed to keep her safe, but how could she expect that from a man who had been suspected in the death of one wife and the disappearance of another? This was too much for her to even think about.

Lifting her chin, she blinked against the grit in her eyes. Her gaze flitted from the front door to the large living room windows, which had offered a magnificent and welcome view of the water in the daylight but now only served to add to her feelings of vulnerability. Why were there no window coverings in this room? A person could be standing just a few feet away from the glass, staring at her, and she would have no way of knowing.

"Hey." Josh leaned in to catch her gaze. "Is something wrong? You keep looking around like you think someone might be hiding in a dark corner."

She shut her eyes tight. It had become pretty clear that her thoughts were totally transparent around this guy. She opened her eyes and met his gaze. "It's just that earlier, I heard a noise outside." She nodded toward the kitchen window. "And when I looked out…I saw something."

159

"Something?" He frowned. "Like what?"

"An arm."

A corner of his mouth lifted. "*Just* an arm?"

He must think she was crazy. "If it was an arm, I'm pretty sure it was attached to a whole person." She blinked and looked away. What had she been thinking admitting this to him? It would only open up the door to more unanswerable questions. "But now that I think about it, I'm sure it was something else."

Looking more curious than fearful, he set down the mug and shifted forward to stand. "Would you feel better if I had a look around out there?"

"No!" Her fingers clutched his sleeve. "I mean…what if it's an animal?"

He gave her a slight smile. "You mean like a cat?"

"I was thinking something bigger."

"Sasquatch, maybe?" His tone teased. "It's okay. I was a boy scout." He started again to stand.

"No." Blood whooshed in her ears. If it was Joe, what would he do if he encountered Josh? Tightening her grip on his arm, she yanked him back down. "I shouldn't have said anything."

Some unidentifiable emotion flickered in his eyes as he looked at her hand on his arm.

Embarrassed by her sudden intensity, she released her hold. "I'm sure it was just the wind blowing a branch. I'm not used to being around so many trees."

He tipped her a narrow-eyed gaze. "They do seem to come to life when the wind whips them around, that's for sure."

The little titter she let out sounded false and forced. "I'm certain that's all it was."

She had to get a grip. She was on a gated property, and the storm had her nerves on edge. All she had to do was stay the course and everything would settle into place. She trusted Chase. She *did*.

Josh twisted to fully face her. "You know, considering your injury and all, maybe you'd feel better if you stayed in the big house tonight."

Warmth pulsed through her in sync with her throbbing knee. The idea of returning to the big house with Josh covered her like a blanket until she considered how it would appear to Chase in the morning. If she admitted to feeling fearful about staying in the guesthouse, he might start asking questions too. The last thing she wanted was to drive him away, either by revealing unsavory parts of her past or by causing him to suspect that she didn't entirely trust him. She couldn't lose him. He was her last hope.

"I'll be fine." Pulling herself to her feet, she remembered all the nights she'd spent in much worse conditions. Sleeping in doorways with one eye open. Locking herself in public restrooms. She was strong enough to handle a night alone in a secured house.

"Okay." Josh stood. "Just be careful of that knee."

"You bet." She started for the door. "I don't want to limp down the aisle."

"Hold on. You mean..."

Feeling his gaze at her back, she turned to face him.

He pinned her with a glare. "...you're still planning on going through with the wedding? After everything I told you—"

"Yes." She tossed him the best confident look she could muster. "I'm getting married on Saturday."

Placing his palms over his eyes, he let out a breath that was clearly meant to further support his stance on this. Lowering his hands, he raised his eyes to the beams of the ceiling, although she was pretty sure his focus traveled much higher.

After a pained moment, he met her eyes with his. "It's your life, I guess." His voice had softened in surrender. "And I changed my mind." He started for the front door.

Moving to keep pace, she shook her head, her tired mind failing to track with his thoughts. "About what?"

He unlocked the door, then turned to make eye contact. "I think I'll take that security job after all. Just in case."

Tears filled her throat, but she choked them

back, trying not to let her relief show on her face. "In case what?"

"In case Sasquatch comes back." Opening the door, he smiled. "You don't think I'm going to let you be the only one to see him, do you?"

Relief came out on a giddy chuckle. She tried to forget that what she feared was far worse than a close encounter with Bigfoot. "Thanks. That would be great."

Braced between the door and the jamb, she watched him step into the wooded area between her and the main house, which seemed slightly less ominous with him in it. He turned, raised a brow, and mimed a twisting motion with his hand. Grateful for his concern, she shut and locked the door, then leaned against it.

So Josh was staying. A sense of security that she hadn't felt in months filled her. She tipped her head back and closed her eyes, trying to shut away the image of his handsome face. He was a great guy, but he had made it clear that they shouldn't be friends once she became a married woman, and he was probably right. She couldn't deny that there was an attraction there, at least on her end, and it wouldn't be fair to Chase for her to spend time with him. Still, she was grateful to have him around for now. She might go crazy otherwise.

Recalling their conversation, she pushed herself away from the door. *Poor Emily.* Her death was sad, but there was no reason to think it had been anything but an accident. Surely Kate would know if Chase was the kind of man who had it in him to be physically abusive. Hadn't her years living under the same roof as her stepfather gifted her with that discernment?

So, she would proceed with her plans as if nothing had changed. And nothing really *had* changed. Everyone had a past, herself included. Chase must have assumed she knew about Emily, and if it wasn't a big deal to him anymore, that was a good indication of his innocence.

Casting aside her worries, she focused her thoughts on the big comfy bed that awaited her. If nothing else, she could at least look forward to a good night's sleep, knowing that she was safe. Things would no doubt look better to her in the morning.

She hobbled to the bedroom to get ready for bed. A few minutes later she emerged from the master bathroom, having decided her comfy sweats and sweatshirt were far more comforting than the flimsy silk nightgown she'd worn in San Francisco.

She crossed to the bed and reached to pull back the covers, but stopped cold. A slightly crumpled slip of paper sat atop one of her pillows. She frowned. That hadn't been there earlier…had it? It looked dirty, like it had been dropped in the mud. Hand shaking, she reached out and turned it over. The blood drained from her face as she read the hand-scribbled words on the other side.

You're Next.

Chapter 15

Josh sat at the window of his room with his computer in his lap and his Bible on the table next to him, staring out at the sunny, rain-washed morning. His concern for Kate had prevented peaceful slumber, so he'd taken advantage of the time to get on his laptop and do a little investigating.

His search for 'Chase Cole' had brought up article after article describing both Emily's death and Trina's disappearance. There was nothing new. Just a rehashing of everything Josh had previously read.

Running a hand through his hair, he allowed his gaze to drift out to the sparkling blue channel that cut between Shaw and Orcas. He couldn't blame Kate for wanting to live in such a pristine place, but at what cost? Something strange was going on here.

He blew out a long breath. Kate was afraid of something, but it wasn't Mr. Cole. On the contrary, she wanted Mr. Cole to protect her. So what exactly was she looking to him to protect her *from?*

Sure, the paparazzi were out to get her, but why did she find having her face appear in the paper so terrifying? What exactly was she hiding from—or more to the point, *who?*

He looked back down at the computer screen. If he wanted to convince Kate to change her mind, he needed answers beyond what even the internet could provide. He had to have some inside information.

Contemplating, he picked up his phone and checked the time. Just past seven thirty. Early, but if Eli had worked his regular weekend schedule, he'd be getting home just about now, making oatmeal and winding down after his graveyard shift.

Josh clicked on his best buddy's cell number, praying he'd be able to help him find what he needed.

Eli picked up after a couple of rings. "Hey, Josh. How are things in Camelot?"

"A far cry from happily ever after." He smiled at the ease he felt talking to his friend. "I need your help."

The clanking of a spoon against a saucepan confirmed Josh's familiarity with Eli's morning routine. Eli yawned. "What kind of help?"

Giving him a quick rundown of the situation, Josh did his best not to make his interest in Kate seem too personal.

"So," Eli swallowed a mouthful of oatmeal. "It

sounds like you might have more to gain here than just an interesting summer job."

Josh sighed. Leave it to Eli to read between the lines, even over the phone. "What are you getting at?"

"I mean 'security man' isn't really your style. That was always my gig."

"Okay, so maybe I do feel a personal obligation to this woman. She doesn't have anyone in her life to help her figure this thing out."

"Of course she does." Eli's smile came through in his voice. "She has you."

"Yeah." Coming from the guy who knew him better than anyone, those simple words confirmed Josh's suspicion that he wasn't entirely crazy in accepting this job. He was on a mission here. "So, do you think you can help me?"

"What exactly do you need me to do?"

"A couple of things. Is there any way you can run a background check on Kate?"

"I can't really do an official check, but I can put her name into the computer and see what comes up. Can you get me her social?"

Josh pinched the bridge of his nose. How was he going to manage that? "I can try."

"That would help. What else?"

"Well," he paused, carefully considering his words. "I've heard that Chase Cole might pay people off to make things go his way in his business."

"Yeah, I've heard that too. Nothing substantiated beyond the usual rumors about people who make a lot of money in things like pharmaceuticals."

"Right. But it got me thinking about the way the police have treated him." Josh paused, knowing he was treading on Eli's home turf. "Can you see what you can find out about the guys who investigated either of Mr. Cole's cases?"

"You mean like, find out if any of them were on the take?"

"I hate to even suggest it, but apparently the guy gets away with a lot."

Eli expelled a slow breath. "I can't promise anything, but I'll see what I can do."

"I owe you one."

Eli chuckled. "You owe me several."

As Josh clicked off the call, a movement outside snagged his attention. Kate walked tentatively up the trail from the guesthouse, looking over her shoulder as if she thought she was being followed. *Strange.* And why was she up so early? She must have had a hard time sleeping too.

Josh lingered at the window, watching her golden hair glistening in the morning sun. What wouldn't he give if they could just forget about all this nonsense with the Cole family and continue to get to know each other. He suddenly yearned to go vintage shopping, eat burgers and watch a marathon of old sci-fi movies with her.

Shaking off the thought, he covered his uncombed hair with his Mariners cap and headed out to greet his new boss.

By the time he got downstairs, she'd only made it as far as the porch steps. She looked up with wide eyes and gave him a pretty, if faltering, smile.

She looked beautiful in casual slacks and a short sleeve sweater, although the shadows under her eyes betrayed her lack of rest. He ached to see her getting comfortable in her own skin instead of putting on this act that didn't suit her at all, and clearly wasn't good for her health.

"Oh…good morning…" Her voice sounded clipped and out of breath. "I thought I should say goodbye to Chase before he leaves for Vegas."

"I think you're a little late." He shut the door and hurried to give her a hand up the steps. "I saw him leaving just before seven."

"Before seven?" The news seemed to confuse her. "I guess he wanted to catch the early ferry."

Without telling her? Josh frowned. Something just wasn't right here.

As she moved up the stairs, he noticed her face contort every time she put weight on her right leg.

"How's your knee?"

"Fine." Her shaky voice failed to support the affirmative answer.

He tipped her a disbelieving look.

Her shoulders drooped. "Okay, not so fine. I was really hoping it would feel better today, but I guess I twisted it worse than I thought."

"I think you should have it looked at before it gets serious." He led her to one of the cheerful white Adirondack chairs that adorned the porch.

"I don't want to make a big deal out of this, and you shouldn't either." She lowered herself into the chair. "Let's wait and see how I'm feeling later on, okay?"

"You're the boss." He shook his head at her stubbornness. "But at least let me get you some breakfast."

Holding up a hand, she rested her head against the chair back. "I still don't feel up to facing Jessica's crew."

"I don't blame you, but you're in luck. They partied till the wee hours last night, so I don't think we'll be seeing them for quite some time."

"Thank goodness." Though her words conveyed relief, a worried look clouded her features. "I don't have much appetite yet, though."

Her distracted gaze wandered around the yard and the woodsy area beyond. Could she really be that paranoid about paparazzi, or was something else bothering her?

He cast his gaze upward. *Six days, Lord. Six days to convince her not to go through with the wedding. Show me how to win her confidence.*

"Look, Kate." He waited till he caught her eye.

"If I'm going to be your security guard, we have to trust each other."

"Okay...." She cast him a wary glance, clearly unsure where he was going with this.

He calculated his words, not exactly sure himself. "I can tell something's bothering you. Something major that you're not telling me."

"No." Her mouth moved into the shape of a smile, but her eyes remained flat. "Just my knee." Her focus shifted again to the trees at the edge of the yard as the curve of her mouth drooped. "And the people out there who won't leave us alone."

"What people?" He noticed how tightly her hands clasped the arms of her chair.

"You know." Her glance darted away, as if she feared looking him in the eye. "The *public*."

Right. He nodded. "That's all?"

Smiling slightly, she couldn't manage to hold his gaze. "Uh huh."

He studied her for a moment. He liked the way her eyes caught the morning light and turned the soft color of bluebells as they scanned the yard. What was it going to take to earn her trust? "I want to keep you safe, but I can only do that if I know everything I'm up against."

Dropping the counterfeit smile, she looked at him, clearly considering his words. "Okay." She let out a resigned breath, then took something out of her front pocket. She paused for a moment before handing it to him.

He studied the loosely folded piece of paper that looked like she'd fished it out of a mud puddle. "What's this?"

"Read it."

He unfolded it and read. "'You're next'." He looked at her. "Where did you get this?"

"I found it on my bed."

"On your bed?" Alarm shot through him. "When?"

"Last night." She rubbed her upper arms. "I had left the front door unlocked, remember? I think someone got in while I was over here at the house."

A visible shudder ran down her body. Something was really frightening this girl.

"And you'd heard someone outside earlier." He studied the ominous scrawl. "You think someone wanted to post this outside the guesthouse, but went inside when they saw you leave?"

She nodded. "Maybe they tried to put it someplace near the door where they thought I'd see it, but the wind blew it down. That would explain why it's so dirty. Then they heard me leave and seized the opportunity."

"Wait a minute." He tried to gauge the seriousness of the situation. "You mean you knew someone had been in your house, but you spent the night there all alone? Why didn't you call me?"

"Because I don't have your number."

"Well, that's got to change. Did you call Mr. Cole?"

She lifted a shoulder. "I couldn't let him know about..." Clamping down on her thought, she looked away.

"About what?"

"You know." She took the paper from him and waved it for emphasis. "About *this*."

He shifted his chair so that their knees practically touched. "No, you were about to say something else. You couldn't let Mr. Cole know about *what?*"

Tears welling in her eyes, she seemed to run through and discard a number of possible answers.

"Please Kate." He placed a hand on the arm of her chair. "Just tell me the truth. What are you so afraid of?"

She drew in a slow, jittery breath. "Okay." She glanced at him. "I'll level with you."

He shifted in his seat, waiting for her to continue.

"You said that Emily had accused Chase of domestic abuse. I went through that with my stepfather, and I just can't do it again."

"Your stepfather?" Josh's throat tightened. "You mean, he hit you?"

She looked down, but she couldn't hide the tears that formed in her quickly reddening eyes. She nodded meekly. "He was an angry drunk.

Yelling and hitting were the order of the day in our house."

"I'm so sorry, Kate." The urge to give her a consoling embrace tugged at him, but he settled for rubbing her arm. "What about your mom? Couldn't she help you?"

"My mom is a pretty classic example of an abused wife. He raged at her too, but she was afraid to leave. I think she was scared of being broke, or of what he'd do if she left. So she went into denial and tried to make me believe things weren't as bad as I knew they were. It was crazy making."

"Oh, Kate." Some of the pieces fell into place. Of course she was drawn to a man who appeared to be the father she'd needed, but was in truth just a variation of the one she'd had. It was basic Psyche 101. He rubbed her arm again. "So, what did you do?"

She swiped at her eyes. "I got out. That's all that matters."

"And now you're worried that Mr. Cole might be the same as your stepdad. I get it."

"I don't know." She shook her head. "I just haven't seen it in Chase. He's always so sweet and gentle."

No surprise. Those guys were great at playing the part until they had some poor woman ensnared. Josh tried not to let his suspicions show. "You mean, in the weeks you've known him, you've never seen him get angry?"

"Never." She paused. "Well, there was this one time. We were in San Francisco and he took me out to a really nice restaurant. Everything was fine, and then the server brushed against Chase's arm and got Bordelaise sauce on the sleeve of his jacket."

"I've been a waiter, myself." Josh nodded. "It happens."

"Apparently not to Chase. He went ballistic."

"How so?"

"He didn't raise his voice, thank goodness, but I could see the anger in his eyes. He basically called the guy incompetent and told him he had gotten people fired for less than that. It was pretty awful."

"So, what did you do?"

"I…I just let it go. I mean, I figured the offence was worse than I realized because Chase is ordinarily so nice to everyone."

"Kate." Josh shook his head. "A person who is nice to you but brutal to the waiter is not a nice person. It's pretty much a given."

Her eyes creased and she bit down on her lip. "You don't think that…" She paused to blink away threatening tears. "That he could have killed anybody…do you?"

"It doesn't really matter what I think. What do *you* think?"

Inhaling deeply, she stared up at the wispy

clouds, as if the answer might be written there. When it clearly didn't appear, she leaned forward and wrapped her arms around herself. "I just don't know what to think."

"It's okay, Kate." He rested his lower arms on his knees to get closer to her. "Anyone would feel that way if they didn't have all the answers. The only way to get rid of those doubts is to find out the truth about what happened to Emily and Trina. But that's going to take some time."

"No." She shook her head, tears running down her cheeks. "I don't have time."

"Why not?"

"Because I…" She swallowed hard, as if the words she'd been about to say had burned her throat. She ran her hands over her face. "I can't postpone the wedding. And if I found out Chase was guilty, I don't know what I'd do."

"You'd move on. Don't be foolish, Kate. You can't marry him not knowing what happened."

She shot to her feet. "I don't want to know."

"Yes you do." Standing, he grabbed her arms and dipped down to catch her gaze. "I know you do. I know you want to look into the eyes of the person you're about to marry and know that you can one hundred percent trust him with your life. I know that, because that's what everybody wants."

She looked away, unable to argue. "But…" Her voice sounded weak. "How can I possibly find out for sure…?"

"I'm here to help you." An idea struck and took hold. It might not give them all the answers, but it would at least provide a starting point. Confident that she wasn't going to run, he let go of her arms. "What kind of clothes do you have?"

She stared at him like he'd sprouted a second head. "What?"

"I mean, do you have anything more casual?"

"I...brought a pair of jeans with me. They're old and worn-in, but they're my favorites so I couldn't get rid of them."

"Perfect." He gave her an assessing look. "You do know you look prettier without all that make-up, right?"

Her hands flew to her cheeks. "I didn't take the time yet this morning. I—"

"Then don't. I like you better this way."

An endearing blush crept across her face. "What are you getting at?"

"Do you trust me?"

Her forehead creased. "Is that a trick question?"

"I don't play tricks." Grinning, he took the cap off his own head and plunked it onto hers. "Trust me with this one thing. If I'm wrong, you can stay sequestered here for the rest of your life if that's what you want."

The blush quickly paled, and her eyes widened in fear. "I can't...I mean, I don't..."

He resisted the temptation to push back the

wayward strand of blonde hair that draped her smooth cheek.

This was a calculated risk, but he had a feeling it was one worth taking.

Chapter 16

Downtown Friday Harbor bustled as it had the day before—no surprise for a Sunday at the beginning of the tourist season. As Kate slipped cautiously out of Josh's car, she adjusted his cap on her head, pleased that no one seemed to be paying her any attention.

Stepping up onto the curb, she caught a glimpse of herself in a shop window. Except for the blondeness of the few strands of hair sticking out of the cap, she looked more like Kathy than Kate. The thought comforted her.

And it didn't hurt to know that Josh preferred her that way too.

"Remember…" Pocketing his keys, Josh joined her on the sidewalk. "I can do most of the talking if you want me to. You don't have anything to worry about."

"Famous last words." She forced a smile. Although a massive weight had lifted from her shoulders when she'd admitted her trepidations to Josh, she remained unconvinced that launching their own personal investigation into Chase's past was going to do any good.

Besides, unless she filled Josh in on the rest of her story, he would never understand the extent of her fear. If they uncovered information that confirmed Chase's involvement in either Emily's death or Trina's disappearance, Kate would be back at square one—terrified for her life with nowhere to hide. Maybe she would be better off remaining blissfully ignorant.

Except for one thing. All the bliss had drained out of this situation.

She pulled in a fortifying breath and kept pace with Josh. He was right. If she had to dive out of the frying pan, it was best to know the temperature of the fire.

As they neared the gallery, the pink flier in the window taunted her. Her courage faltered. "Are you sure this is a good idea?"

"You said Marion was Trina's closest friend. If anyone knows anything, it's probably her. And besides…" He held open the door. "It can't hurt to ask."

"Great." She crossed in front of him to enter the shop. "More famous last words."

Inside, only a few patrons milled about, much to Kate's relief. Marion stood behind the counter, studying a clipboard and paying no attention to anyone. Kate's knees buckled. Good thing Josh had such broad shoulders, because she might have to duck behind him if this woman decided to take a swing at her with that clipboard.

Dipping her head toward Marion, Kate spoke just above a whisper. "That's her."

Josh nodded, then headed to the counter a little more briskly than Kate would have preferred.

Marion glanced up, a friendly if insincere smile appearing where a scowl had looked so at home the day before. "What can I do for you?"

Kate let out a breath. So Marion didn't recognize her. Freezing up, she looked to Josh for support.

He put on that sweet smile that would soften even the meanest disposition, or so she hoped.

"My name is Josh Collins." He gestured toward Kate. "You met my friend Kate yesterday."

Marion's expression morphed like an apple drying in the sun. "Yes, I remember." She looked down her nose at Kate, as if simultaneously recognizing her and disapproving of her casual appearance.

Wishing now that she had at least put on some lip gloss, Kate tried for a nonthreatening smile.

Marion's hand went to her throat, where she fingered a large, probably locally-crafted necklace made of colorful gemstones. "I believe I said everything I had to say to her then." With an end-of-discussion finality, she lowered her head and scribbled something on the clipboard.

Josh's confidence didn't seem to waver. "We're hoping you can tell us something about

Trina Cole."

Peering over the top of her glasses, Marion's features sharpened. "This wouldn't be a good time. Everyone in town is upset." She fired a pointed glare at Kate. "Why can't people like *you* stop bringing trouble to our community? After what happened last night…" Shifting her gaze to what she could see of said 'community' just past the gallery window, she let her voice trail off cryptically.

"Wait a minute," Josh looked confused. "*What* happened last night?"

Marion gave him a distasteful look. "If you want to know, you can buy a newspaper." She glanced nervously at her other customers. "All I know is, it's not going to be good for business if things like this keep happening around here. I don't know why people think they can come to the San Juan Islands to escape their troubles. All they seem to do is bring their troubles with them."

"Oh," Josh persisted. "But I—"

"I'm going to have to ask you to leave."

"But if we could just—"

"Please." She scooped up the clipboard and stormed back to the room Kate assumed was her office, shutting the door with such force that the paintings on either side clattered against the walls.

Kate let out a breath. "What do you suppose she was she talking about?"

Looking uncharacteristically stymied, Josh

shook his head.

"A couple of sheriff's deputies were shot and killed last night." An airy female voice drew them both around.

Jocelyn, the clerk who had helped Kate with the sculpture, stood behind them, her eyes darting between them and the office door.

Kate exchanged a look of alarm with Josh. "*Killed?* That's awful…"

"Right here in Friday Harbor." Jocelyn spoke in a low tone, as if Marion might actually hear her consorting with the enemy through her closed door.

Josh looked concerned. "What on earth happened?"

The woman shook her head. "There was an incident at a home down on the waterfront. The police aren't saying much until they finish investigating. So far all we know is that two officers died at the scene and two others have been hospitalized."

Kate's hands went to her face. Was it possible that Joe could have somehow caused this?

Josh was apparently thinking more like an investigator than she was. "Did it have something to do with the bomb scare yesterday?"

"My guess is yes." Jocelyn flicked her gaze to the office door. "Nothing ever happens around here, then all of a sudden…" She opened up both hands like either a flower blooming or a bomb exploding.

Kate felt faint. Marion had implied that the shooting was somehow her fault. But if Joe had found her, he wouldn't waste time playing games or doling out warnings. He would come after her. Unless some poor police officers had tried to stop him. Could he have somehow had the wrong address on the wrong island? She shuddered at the thought.

"Was anybody else hurt?" she asked meekly. Like maybe a woman who could have been mistaken for her?

Jocelyn shook her head. "Not as far as I know."

"I'm really sorry to hear about the deputies…" Josh consulted her nametag. "…Jocelyn. But we were hoping Marion could help us understand what happened to Trina Cole. She was close to her, right?"

"Trina was her best friend." She gave Kate a consoling look. "But I'm sure Marion won't ever talk to you. She's pretty unhappy about this whole situation."

Josh nodded. "I'm sure it must be hard for her to see Chase moving on."

She waved a dismissive hand. "She has no use for him. None of us do."

"Oh?" Kate traded a cautious glance with Josh, not sure if she was ready to hear what might follow that statement.

Jocelyn's eyes brimmed with remorse. "I'm sorry. I didn't mean—"

"No." Kate gulped. "Go on. Please."

Jocelyn nodded. "It's just that everyone around here knows he's not exactly ethical in his business practices." She glanced around then leaned forward, as if to indicate they should huddle if they wanted to hear more. "There's talk that he greases palms to get his drugs pushed through the testing so they can get FDA approval and start earning profits faster."

Kate felt the bagel she'd eaten earlier at the Shaw Island General Store do a flip in her belly. "People say that?"

Jocelyn shrugged. "I guess you have to resort to that sort of thing in order to make money like he does. And we're grateful that he spends some of it on local art. That's how he met Trina, you know."

Kate grappled with this new bit of information. "By buying art?"

"Yes." Apparently noticing Kate's look of confusion, she clarified. "Trina worked here when she first moved to the islands. Back in...I think...about 1990. That's how she and Marion became friends."

"I see," Josh encouraged her to continue. "So Mr. Cole was a customer here?"

"That's right. Apparently, he liked Trina's work and he asked her to go out to see the house he was having built on Shaw."

An uncomfortable feeling gnawed at Kate. This acknowledgment that the man she was going to marry had experienced not just a life, but a *love* life before she was even born was unnerving to say the least. She glanced at Josh, certain that he was thinking the same thing.

If Jocelyn noticed her discomfort, she didn't let on. "Chase wanted her to advise him on which art pieces to buy. From what I hear, most of the art she placed is still in his home."

Kate thought about what she'd seen so far of the artwork in their house. The Native American and Pacific Northwest paintings and pottery. The intricately carved masks. The chandelier. Trina had chosen all of it.

Jocelyn's face crinkled. "It's so sad that Marion wouldn't sell you the seahorse. It just seems like it belongs in that house."

Kate twisted a glance at the window where the sculpture had stood the day before. Seeing that it had been replaced by a multi-colored vase, her heart sank. "Did she sell it to someone else?"

"She put it in her office." Jocelyn's brows formed a knot in her forehead as she looked back at the closed door once again. "I don't know why she's holding onto it. She knows its value, all things considered."

Maybe it was her ignorance about art, but Kate wasn't quite following Jocelyn's thinking. "I'd be happy to pay her what it's worth."

"Of course." Jocelyn smiled kindly. "But it *is* a little awkward to appraise, considering how we acquired it."

Josh's demeanor remained patient and conversational. "And how *did* you acquire it?"

"Oh, it was anonymously donated to the gallery. It just showed up one day with no return address and no information attached."

Josh furrowed his brow. "That seems strange."

"Very." Jocelyn turned a sympathetic eye on Kate. "I'll see if I can talk her into selling it to you. It just isn't healthy for her to be hanging onto it."

"Not healthy?" Kate asked.

"No. You know." She lowered her voice. "The reminder of Trina."

A chill passed through Kate. Why would that particular piece remind Marion of Trina?

Jocelyn straightened a display of brochures on the counter, as if fulfilling a need to look busy. "That's why Marion put it in the window. To draw the tourists into the gallery."

Kate flicked a questioning look at Josh, who tweaked an eyebrow in response.

Jocelyn seemed to take their reaction as cause to defend her last statement. "It might seem opportunistic, but business is business. If it hadn't been for Trina going missing when she did, Marion would have lost the gallery."

Kate frowned. What would Trina's disappearance have to do with Marion not losing her business?

The whoosh of a door opening stopped Kate's question before she could ask it.

"Jocelyn." Marion charged out of her office, still studying her notes on the clipboard. "Did you finish the press release for the group art show…?" She glanced up. Seeing Josh and Kate, she halted and her demeanor turned stony.

"I'll get right on that, Marion." Looking like she'd been caught with her hand in the cookie jar, Jocelyn scurried away.

Slowly narrowing the space between them, Marion hugged her clipboard. "What are the two of you still doing here?"

"We were talking to Jocelyn about the seahorse sculpture." Josh's tone remained confident. "My friend here is still interested in it. Would you mind showing it to us?"

Kate shot him a look. What was he up to?

Obviously wondering the same thing, Marion lowered her chin and countered him a look over the top of her glasses. "It's not for sale." She shifted her weight from one lace-up granny shoe to the other. "Now, please leave."

"Thank you." Josh put his hand on Kate's elbow. "But if you change your mind, let us know."

"I won't." Marion slapped the clipboard onto the counter. "See that you don't come back."

Standing outside a moment later, Josh let out a

long breath. "Well, that was strange."

"I'll say." Kate hadn't exactly expected a warm reception, but now she felt more confused than ever. "What do you suppose Jocelyn meant by Marion not losing the gallery because of Trina's disappearance?"

He shook his head. "The best I can figure is people heard that Trina used to work here, so that attracted the curious."

"Maybe. But I think there's more to it than that. And it has something to do with the artist who puts flecks of gold in her glass."

"Flecks of gold?" Josh's gaze narrowed. "Are you talking about the seahorse?"

"And Chase's chandelier."

"Wow, you're observant." His mouth lifted in an admiring smile. "You think they were made by the same person?"

"I don't know much about glass art, but they sure look like it." She tried to ignore the campfire his smile sparked in her chest. "And for some reason, the seahorse reminds Marion of Trina."

"Plus Trina picked out the chandelier. What do you suppose it all means?"

She shook her head. "Probably nothing. I bet we're wasting our time chasing down a rabbit trail." She turned to head back to the car. "Now I'm hungry and sleepy, and my leg hurts."

"Fine, Dr.Watson." Josh's mouth twisted as he made a show of matching her hobbly pace. "Let's scout out a drive-through while we plan our next move."

"Careful, Sherlock." She tossed him a playful look. "Someone might mistake us for friends."

The crooked smile she won with that remark made her blush. And she'd been warning *him* to be careful.

"Hey, it's not like I'm suggesting a date. Not quite." A twinkle glinted in his eye. "Well, *almost*."

She gave his arm a swat as he opened the car door for her. The thought of having a not-quite-but-almost date with Josh gave her a much-needed feeling of normalcy.

Settling into the car, she positioned her purse in her lap, and the reminder that the note still burned a hole in its outer pocket brought her back to reality. It was a warning that she was next in line as a victim, but of whom? The obvious answer was Chase, but did someone know about Karen? Were they telling Kate that she was 'next' to suffer the same fate as her?

The thought brought a shiver.

Josh slid into the driver's seat and flashed her a smile that stilled her nerves like a blanket of safety.

She pitched her purse to the floor. All her worries were, at least for the time being, held captive by that dimpled grin.

Chapter 17

Curled in a ball under a blanket on the passenger side floor of Josh's car, Kate let her thoughts wander. Sharing their take-out lunch of burgers and fries in the car on the ferry ride back from Friday Harbor had been more fun than she'd had in ages. In spite of her ongoing safety concerns, she had managed to relax and be herself. The only explanation was that she had come to completely trust this guy. She could be real with him without any fear of rejection or betrayal.

She chewed on her lower lip. Did that mean she could tell him the real reason she was afraid for her life? And more importantly, *should* she?

"We're through the gate."

Relieved to hear his muffled proclamation, Kate pulled the blanket off her head and groaned. She hoisted herself up onto the seat, then removed his ball cap from her head and shook out her hair. She rubbed her temples and tried once again to make sense of everything Jocelyn had told them.

None of it brought her any closer to knowing the truth, and the more she thought about it, the more her head hurt.

Josh eyed her. "Is the hat giving you a headache?"

"It's not that." She managed a light smile. "I appreciate your helping me keep a low profile. I'm just getting tired of feeling like one of Michael Jackson's kids every time I go out in public."

Josh chuckled. "If it makes you feel better, I didn't see any paparazzi outside the gate."

She huffed. "You mean I impersonated Shirley Temple in *Stowaway* for no reason?"

"We still can't be too careful, Shirley." His voice rumbled playfully, as if their biggest concern today was how to get the smell of greasy fries out of his car. "Sorry the only blanket I have to offer is covered in cat hair. It's the one Godzilla sleeps on when she goes for rides."

Kate laughed. "Godzilla?"

He returned a smile. "She's my tiny terror."

Josh found a parking spot around the side of the house next to the upscale fleet that belonged to Jessica's friends. He turned off the engine and gave Kate an assessing look. "Home, sweet home."

She folded her arms, in no hurry to move. "You really think I'm making a mistake, don't you? Marrying Chase, I mean."

He took in a long breath. "I just don't get it. You're engaged to a billionaire who's old enough to be your father. You should be taking your time to make sure he's everything he seems to be, but you're not willing to postpone the wedding. You don't seem like the gold digger type to me, so what's the rush?"

A gold digger? Kate pinched the bridge of her nose with her fingers. *Was* she marrying Chase just for his money? She had arrived here thinking she honestly loved him, but now she wasn't so sure.

"It's not like money itself is so important to me," she said. "I mean, not that I've ever really had any to speak of."

He chuckled lightly. "Yeah, I can relate."

"And it bothers me that people assume Chase earned his money by being dishonest."

"You think that's just an assumption?" Josh rested his hands on the steering wheel.

"What do you mean?"

"Well," he thought for a moment. "Money and morality are like two cars driving towards each other on a one lane road. Eventually one of them is going to wind up in the ditch."

She crinkled her nose. "You ever think of working for Hallmark?"

"My point is that the two usually don't go together. Personally, I'd rather eat Raman and keep my integrity."

Letting out a breath, she considered. An unsettled feeling had prevailed since her arrival, and nothing made sense anymore. She yearned for a happy life with a man she adored, but lately that yearning hadn't involved Chase. What was up with that?

She stole a quick look at Josh's strong profile and realized she had spent far more time with him since coming here than with Chase. No wonder she was so confused.

After a stretch of contemplative silence confirmed that the conversation had run its course, they both got out. Kate leaned against the car, giving her stiff knee a stretch. Now that she'd been fed, she longed for a nap, but where? The guesthouse no longer felt safe, and the main house was overrun with living examples of spoiled entitlement. What was she going to do?

As Josh crossed around the front of the car, the sight of his muscular form under his 'Seattle International Film Festival' t-shirt almost provided the boost she needed without the shuteye.

A sudden urge to confide in him collided with her previous misgivings. Maybe she *should* talk to him about Joe and her theory about the real meaning behind the note. Tell him about the money and Karen and…everything. She slipped her hand into the pocket of her purse and fingered the folded paper.

"Are you okay?"

She looked up, only then realizing that he had reached her side of the car. She leaned her hip against the car door. "Josh." She took the note out of her purse and held it up to him. "I think there might be something more to this note than I told you."

Brow furrowing, he reached over to take it, but his fingers grazed hers and they stood there, hands touching and neither of them letting go of the paper. Their eyes locked and all the air seemed to vacate the vicinity.

"What..." he cleared his throat. "What is it?" His voice sounded husky, passionate, concerned.

As she looked into his eyes, part of her had to admit that she didn't really want the life she had come here to live. She yearned for a life of passion, of being really and truly known and understood by the one person she could know and understand in return. She longed for love. If she had that kind of love, wouldn't she feel protected?

Suddenly, her need to feel safe consumed her like a hurricane. Images from the past flicked across her mind—of her stepdad lashing out at her, and of the look in Joe's eyes as he angrily slashed with his scalpel. If she expected Josh to keep her safe, she had to tell him everything. It was the only way he could know what to do.

She caught enough breath to speak. "I have to...tell you—"

"There you are!" A cheerful feminine voice yanked Kate from the brink of total vulnerability. She twisted a look behind her.

"I saw the car come up the drive and I hoped it was you." Sam approached them, clearly having just rounded the corner of the house.

Abruptly shifting gears, Kate somehow managed to smile through the fog of her own scattered wits. She sensed Josh's frustration, left hanging as he was on her crazy near-admission.

She shook herself. Why had she almost disclosed everything to him? It was *Chase* she needed, and the safety he could provide.

Reaching them, Sam showed no awareness of the bubble of emotional confidentiality she'd just burst. "I hope I'm not interrupting." A gentle wind ruffled her breezy white blouse and cream rayon pants as she raised a hand to block the sun from her eyes. She looked casual yet completely pulled together in the way that Kate could never quite manage. Sam was clearly a very classy lady.

"No," Kate heard herself answer. "You're not interrupting."

"Good." Sam's warm smile accentuated her exotic features, the ethnicity of which Kate couldn't quite decipher. "I was hoping you'd have time for our tête-à -tête this afternoon."

Sam's desire to get acquainted somehow reassured Kate that that her own life must not be as wildly out of control as she thought. A smile pressed on her lips. "I'd love to. But..." She looked at Josh, not for permission but to assure that he wouldn't feel left out. "What do you think?"

He held up a palm. "I was actually going to suggest that I should head back to Seattle."

Kate's tired nerves jolted. *Seattle?*

"Josh." Sam folded her arms. "Don't tell me you're leaving for good?"

"No. I'll be back. I just need to go pack a few more things if I'm going to be working as Kate's security for the summer." He locked eyes with Kate. "Or however long she needs me."

Kate felt a shift in the ground underneath her that if she'd still been in California, would have registered on the Richter scale.

"Will you be okay if I go?" Josh lowered his voice a notch. "I could be back by tonight."

"Oh…" Her knees felt weak, not just because of the injury. "Sure."

"We can talk more about this later." He moved to hand her something and she realized that when Sam had startled her, she'd released her hold on the note.

She took it, wishing it and the message it carried would just disappear.

His narrow-eyed gaze assessed her. "I don't think you should stay in the guesthouse anymore. Not even for an afternoon nap."

"Is something wrong with the guesthouse?" Sam creased her brow in what read as motherly concern.

A déjà vu-like comfort overtook Kate. There was something about Sam that, in spite of the awkward circumstances of their introduction the previous evening, told Kate she could trust her. She reminded her of her mother.

The paper crinkled between her fingers. There was no reason why she shouldn't show it to Sam. She held it out for her to take. "I found this on my pillow last night."

Sam took it, her face contorting. "This is strange. Any idea where it came from?"

Josh spoke up. "Probably just someone's idea of a joke, but we don't want to take any chances."

Sam nodded. "I understand." She folded the note and handed it back to Kate, resolution firming her gaze. "I think you should stay with me until Chase returns from Vegas. That will only be a couple of days, but Josh is right. You really shouldn't be alone."

"Oh…well…" Kate looked from Sam to Josh and back again. "I'd love to…but, where do you live?"

Sam fanned her arm out toward the bay. "On the yacht."

Kate looked out to where the *Magnificent Obsession* sat some distance from their dock. "You mean…*Chase's* yacht?"

"Yes. I have a condo in Seattle, but I stay on the yacht when I need to be near Chase for business." She frowned. "Don't tell me he didn't tell you that either."

"No." Kate flapped a hand in an awkward effort to downplay Chase's selective communication.

"It is going to be *your* yacht too, after all." The

congratulatory tone in Sam's voice implied actual accomplishment on Kate's part. "Besides, it'll be fun, and whoever wrote that note won't be able to taunt you out there."

"What do you think?" Kate looked to Josh for confirmation. "You could stay out there too, in your capacity as security guard."

"No thanks." He held up a hand. "But if you're set, I think I'll stay tonight in my apartment and head back here tomorrow. Besides," he leaned in slightly and lowered his voice. "It wouldn't be proper for me to be out there alone with two single women."

"Such a gentleman." Sam elbowed Kate's arm. "Most men would jump at that chance to stay on a yacht with a couple of babes like us." She dipped her head at Josh. "I find your conviction refreshing."

Kate smiled. She did too.

Sam clapped her hands together. "Well, now that that's been decided, why don't you get your things together and meet me at the dock."

"Okay." She eyed the span of water between the dock and the boat. "But how do we get out to the yacht?"

"Oh, it's easy. We just take the dinghy. I'll show you how to start the motor so you'll be able to come and go whenever you please."

Eyes narrowing, Josh scanned the steep grade past the guesthouse and down to the water. "I'm not sure it's such a good idea for you to take that trail, Kate." He looked at Sam. "She twisted her knee pretty badly and she needs to take it easy."

The concern on Sam's face made Kate think she might produce a first aid kit and fix her up on the spot. Instead, she settled a consoling hand on Kate's shoulder as she instructed Josh.

"Don't worry, you can drive down to the dock." She pointed. "The little road is just past the guesthouse. You'll see my Volvo when you get to the parking area." She let out a breath as if she'd just remembered something. "I want to go check on Stuart. He and Chase had an argument last night and I'm a bit concerned."

An argument? Not knowing how to respond, Kate bit her lip and nodded as Sam headed for the house.

A second wind rushed over Kate at the prospect of seeing the yacht. Thank goodness she hadn't told Josh the whole story about Joe, opening her emotional closet and dumping out her alarming collection of skeletons. She needed to keep up her boundaries with this guy if she wanted to set her heart back on the right course.

"Come on." She started for the guesthouse. "I need to repack my suitcase."

"Hold up." Josh stopped her with a hand to her shoulder. "You're not getting off the hook that easily."

The intensity of his concerned brown eyes

reeled her back in. *Hook? What hook?*

Chapter 18

Looking at Kate, Josh contemplated which was a prettier shade of blue, her eyes, or the bay behind her. For a second, he actually forgot why he had reached out to stop her.

Right. The note.

He drew his hand from her shoulder. "So, what were you going to tell me?"

Her eyes slitted. "About what?"

He smiled. She was adorable when she got lost in thought. "About the note. You said there might be something more to it?"

"Oh." She looked away, not like she'd forgotten, but more like she'd hoped *he* had. "It was nothing. I just…" She glanced over her shoulder, then looked him confidently in the eye. "…wanted to say that I shouldn't sleep in the guesthouse anymore, but you beat me to it."

He gave her a skeptical look. So they were playing that game again. "Uh huh." He tipped a nod toward the guesthouse. "Let's go get your things then." Hopefully, she'd eventually own up to what she was *really* going to tell him.

A few minutes later, he loaded her hastily-packed suitcase into his trunk, then got into the car with her. Her gaze rested out on the yacht, which gleamed a bright white on the sparkling bay.

He started the car. "So, you think you'll feel safe staying out on the boat?"

"Totally." A slight quiver in her voice clashed with her confident tone. "No one's going to bother me on the water."

Backing out of the parking space, he cast her a sideways glance. "You haven't seen *Dead Calm*, have you?"

"We'll be fine." Amusement danced in her answer. "I'll be with Sam, and something tells me she can hold her own."

"True." If Sam hadn't offered to keep an eye on Kate, he wouldn't have decided to stay away for the night. It was great to have someone else around here with whom Kate seemed to feel at ease.

"Besides," she tucked her purse onto the floor by her feet, "it will give me a chance to ask her about Emily and Trina."

"Now you're thinking like an investigator, Dr. Watson."

"Why thank you, Mr. Holmes." She smiled, seeming to relax a little. "You should at least check out the yacht before you leave."

"No thanks." He carefully took the turn from

the main driveway onto a narrower one that led down to the dock. "The yacht itself might be okay, but I'd rather jump out of a plane than get into a dinghy."

"You don't like boats?"

"Oh, I like boats just fine. It's the water underneath them that bothers me."

Surprise came out on a cute little sputter. "You're afraid of water? Why?"

"Because I almost drowned once." The words sounded like someone else's answer to that question, since this was something he never talked about. Not that he minded. It was just that no one ever asked.

"Seriously?" Her eyes widened. "What happened?"

He shrugged. "I was just a kid—seven years old. I was swimming in a lake we always went to with a bunch of my older cousins. The adults were talking, not paying enough attention. I wanted to show off and I swam out further than I should have and I somehow went under." A lump caught in his throat. It had been a long time since he'd allowed himself to relive the emotion of that day, or think about the impact it'd had on his life.

Pulling up next to a silver Volvo, he continued. "I came to the surface just long enough to see that no one had noticed. They were all looking the other way, and when I tried to cry out, my mouth filled with water."

Kate shivered. He appreciated her clearly feeling the intensity of the story without him having to give many details.

"Whoa. Then what happened?"

"I don't even really know." Shutting off the engine, he let his head rest on the back of the seat. He looked out at the glittery sheet of blue, scarcely registering its deadly potential. "I felt like I heard a voice tell me to be still. I stopped thrashing, and all of a sudden I felt myself being lifted up to the surface. There was a big branch sticking way out over the water and I grabbed it. I pulled myself up and when I looked down to see who had lifted me, there was no one there."

She blinked. "That's spooky."

"Maybe. But I learned something that day. We can't always count on other people, but I know God had my back that day, even though I was just a kid and I didn't know anything yet about believing in Him. He always has my back." He shot her an angled look. "He always has yours too."

Emotion creased her pretty forehead. "But you're still afraid of water."

Sadness lifted the corners of his mouth. "Let's just say my faith is strong but imperfect. I still wrestle with the fear."

"That's some story." Kate let out a breath. "Thanks for sharing it with me."

Giving her a half-smile, his eyes met hers. He

wanted with everything in him to take her away from all this, but he couldn't. He could no more control her decision to follow Jesus than her choice to marry Mr. Cole.

The peripheral sight of Sam trudging down the trail toward the dock broke the hold Kate had on him.

"Come on." She opened her car door. "I'm dying to get on that yacht."

She limped carefully toward the dock, waving to Sam while Josh went around to the trunk to retrieve her suitcase. Glancing over at the bobbing boats and the frothy waves pounding against the rocks, he braced himself. There was pretty much no way he was going to get out of being a gentleman and helping her board the dinghy. Stepping out onto that narrow strip of wood planks was going to take every ounce of nerve he possessed.

Sam spoke enthusiastically to Kate as Josh approached with the suitcase. "You are going to forget all your troubles out on the water, I promise."

Josh smiled at Sam's reassurance. She seemed like a hip version of his mother, and he found that comforting.

Kate's smile dropped as she looked down at herself and let out a sigh. "Oh, man. I left my purse in your car." Looking at Josh, she scrunched her face in apology. "Would you mind?"

"No problem." Leaving the suitcase, he walked back over to the car, pleased by the sound of the happy female chatter that met his back.

At the car, he easily located Kate's purse where she'd left it on the floor. As his hand touched the soft leather, the top of the bag fell open, revealing a matching wallet on the inside. He froze, remembering his conversation with Eli. This would be so easy, but did he dare?

Before he could talk himself out of it, he pulled out her wallet and opened it. There in one of the plastic sleeves was the item he'd hoped to see—her social security card.

He quickly committed the number to memory and placed the wallet back in her purse, sending up a quick prayer for forgiveness.

Kate's trusting smile as he returned only compounded his sense of guilt. He handed her the purse.

"Oh," Sam reached into the pocket of her billowy pants. "Before I forget, I grabbed a remote for the main gate so you'll be able to get back in."

"Thanks." He took it, appreciating her thoughtful gesture. It was a major indication of trust, especially considering the circumstances. Fingering the remote, he turned his gaze on Kate. "If I make that 10:20 ferry in the morning, that will put me back here at around 11:15. Call me if you need anything."

"I will. But don't worry about me." She gave

him her pretty smile that he could have sworn made the ground underneath him shift.

He would probably worry. And he would definitely miss that smile.

Chapter 19

Sam had dropped anchor at the opening of Blind Bay, a little further out than it had been before, and Kate had a sense of freedom she hadn't experienced in a long time. Being out on the yacht felt like a vacation.

Limping only slightly, she exited the dining room and admired the view that spanned three sides of the main salon. To her left, the lights had started to pop on in Chase's house and in those of their Shaw Island neighbors. To the right, the town of Orcas lit the tip of Orcas Island. A glass door at the end of the room revealed a gorgeous pink-and-amber-streaked sunset over the boat's luxurious hot tub deck.

Catching her own reflection in one of the expansive windows, Kate smoothed the Ann Taylor spandex tuxedo trousers and striped boat neck top Chase had picked out for her in a swanky San Francisco shop. It wasn't the vintage style she loved, but it was comfy and she liked the way she looked in it.

She eased into the room, happy that her knee

210

seemed to be stinging a little less. Sam had given her an elastic bandage, an ice pack, and a good talking-to about self-care, which Kate had accepted with humility and gratitude. Motherly concern had been missing in her life for a long time, and she found herself soaking it up.

Weaving her fingers together, she studied the array of nautically-themed Pacific Northwest artifacts displayed in the room. Old maps and compasses adorned the walls, along with a whale whittled out of something that looked like bone. Most intriguing was a long piece of carved wood which rested on two wrought iron hooks above the sofa. It had a sharp spear on one end that had been chiseled from rock. Kate leaned in to get a better look.

"Ugh. I just hate that thing." Sam entered from the dining room carrying a tray which held a French press coffee pot, two cups, and some kind of dessert. "I wish Chase would sell it so I wouldn't have to look at it anymore."

"What is it?" Kate resisted the urge to touch the splintery wood.

Sam set the tray down on the coffee table. "It's an old Makah Indian whaling harpoon. Chase sees it as a historical artifact, but all I can think of when I look at it is the poor whales."

Trying not to dwell on that image, Kate perched on the curved beige sofa and ran her fingers over the soft suede. "I just can't get over how amazing Chase's boat is."

"It's going to be *your* boat soon too." Smoothing the fabric of her pants, Sam sat next to Kate. "I hope you don't mind my staying on it once in a while. It's so helpful to be in close proximity to Chase when we're getting ready to close a business deal."

"Oh, I don't mind." Kate shook her head. Talking to Sam at dinner had made Kate realize how much she'd missed being around other women. She could see Sam becoming not only a mentor, but a friend.

Sam smiled. "I've thought of buying a little place on the island, but I have to admit to dragging my feet. I mean, who can resist the occasional yacht retreat, right?" She pushed down on the top of the coffee pot. "But I realize things will be different, now that Chase is taking the plunge again. The last thing I want to do is to interfere with your lives."

Suddenly overcome with a need for a female confidante, Kate wanted to encourage Sam's presence. "If we're using the yacht, you could always stay in the guesthouse."

"Oh, don't you just love that place?" She filled Kate's cup with the dark brown liquid. "But Chase likes to keep it available for entertaining business associates. I really do need to invest in a place of my own. Our business has been so crazy lately. It seems like I'm out here half the time."

Kate bent slightly, inhaling the intoxicating aroma of the coffee. "I had no idea it took so much work to get a new drug on the market."

"More than you'd ever believe. Some of the hoops we have to jump through…" She paused as she offered Kate a small pitcher of cream. "You've probably heard talk about Chase and his business practices."

Recalling Jocelyn's comment, Kate answered with an innocent shake of her head as she accepted the pitcher.

"The truth is that when you get into big business where a lot of money changes hands, sometimes you have to make decisions that might seem unethical to some people. That's just business." Sam shrugged as she poured a second cup of coffee. "But Chase is a good man."

Uncertain as to why Sam had felt the need to explain that, Kate picked up a small spoon and gave her coffee a fervent stir.

"I swear," Sam went on, "between the reporters and the police, it's hard to say who's better at putting a negative spin on a perfectly innocent situation."

Kate stopped, mid-stir. "You don't trust the police?"

"Not after what we've been through." Spooning raw sugar into her cup, Sam nodded toward a plate of elegantly decorated bite-size cakes. "I hope you enjoy these. I'm trying out a new French pastry chef and I've been told her profiteroles are to die for."

Eyes widening, Kate took one of the gooey pastries and bit into it. She savored its melt-in-your-mouth sweetness, but noticed that Sam hadn't taken one. Probably how she kept her figure so trim.

As Kate washed the other half of the pastry down with the best coffee she'd ever tasted, a realization struck. She swallowed. "So you and Chase work out here sometimes. This must be where you were yesterday after I saw you get off the ferry."

Nodding from behind her tilted cup, Sam made an affirmative sound. "That's exactly right." She set the cup back on its saucer. "Chase knew if we went to the house, we wouldn't be nearly as productive, and he was right. With all the pre-wedding excitement swirling around, who can focus on work?"

Kate twisted her mouth. "I don't think anybody else is all that excited about the wedding. Jessica and her friends are just happy to be done with school."

Compassion filled Sam's eyes as she set down her coffee and patted Kate's hand. "Don't worry about Jessica and Stuart. They'll both come around and welcome you into the fold eventually." She gave Kate's hand a squeeze before releasing it. "They've been through a lot, and they don't always behave as respectfully as they should."

Kate pursed her lips. Now *that* was an understatement.

Sam eased back into the cushions. "Poor Stuart has always needed extra care, especially since Trina left. I try to be available for him as much as possible."

"You two are close?" Kate hoped she'd masked her unfavorable impression of *poor* Stuart. If the guy had a positive side, so far he'd done a terrific job of keeping it hidden.

A kind smile crossed Sam's lips. "I've literally known him his whole life. Whenever he's upset about something, he comes to me. Even when Trina was here, he and I had a special bond. He needs someone to turn to for motherly advice."

"You know…" Setting down her coffee, Kate welcomed the easy segue. "Stuart said something strange to me. He said I remind him of his mother. Do you know why he'd say that?"

"Blonde hair. Blue eyes." Sam waved a hand as if the resemblance were more amusing than concerning. "Chase always goes for the same type. You know how men are."

Type? Kate pulled in a breath to steady her unease at the reminder that the man she was engaged to had 'gone for' other women before her.

Not to mention the disturbing suggestion that if she had picked her second hair dye option—Katy Perry Midnight Black—Chase would have struck up a conversation with some other woman that first night at the club. Was he really only attracted to her because of a quality that wasn't even real?

"Chase and I have been friends since high school." Sam topped off their cups, seemingly unaware of Kate's discomfort. "We were both a couple of social outcasts back then, and we kind of leaned on each other."

Kate absentmindedly sipped her coffee, trying to picture what they must have looked like back then. Both their attractiveness and success made it hard to believe either of them had ever been on the unpopular track.

Sam continued. "Before Chase met Emily, he'd spent two years obsessing over a cheerleader named Rebecca who had the same gorgeous blonde hair and blue eyes. He finally got the courage to ask her out, and she humiliated him."

"That's awful. What did she do?"

"First she laughed at him, then she told all her cheerleader and football player friends about it. They made fun of him for months."

"How horrible."

"It was. I'm sure that girl had her regrets when Chase made his first million."

Kate twisted a strand of blonde hair around her finger. "I'm sure."

"Anyway, he started dating Emily not long after, and I teased him that he was only doing it to prove something to Rebecca."

"Was that true?"

"Maybe at first. But eventually he fell head over heels and I figured if I didn't make friends with Emily too, I'd never see him. Of course, they were a couple, so I made sure I wasn't around all the time. But the three of us had similar interests, so it worked out."

"Oh, you were a swimmer?"

"Oh no. Chase and I were more into boating. But we'd go to Emily's swim meets to be supportive."

The notion that swimming and boating were 'similar' intrigued Kate, but only until a more pressing thought caught her in its grip. "So, you were there when Emily died." She flinched at the sound of that. "I mean, not there when it happened, but you *knew* her then."

Sam shifted, as if the statement had hit a raw nerve. "I was the first person Chase called when he found her."

A horrible picture swirled in Kate's head, hitting her gut with a nauseating wallop. Her brain somehow overlaid the image of Emily's floating form with the memory of Karen she'd tried so hard to block out. Try as she might, she couldn't stop the red of Emily's swimsuit from bleeding out from her torso, forming a circular pattern in the water. The gentle waving motion of her body became the last remnants of a violent struggle to hold onto life even as it was stolen away.

Drawing in a breath, Kate tried desperately to snap herself out of the unwelcome reverie. She couldn't go there. Not now. "How awful," she eked out. "For both of you."

Sam nodded. "He was a mess, as you can imagine. I had to call 9-1-1 for him when I got to the house."

"And Stuart?" Forcing her focus from her own embellished memory back to Sam's story, she swallowed a lump of agony. "Where was he?"

"Upstairs asleep, thank goodness. I was the one who had to break the news to him that his mother had drowned."

"Oh. How horrible." The story at least gave some explanation as to why he was such a mess as an adult.

"And as if that wasn't bad enough, people accused Chase of having something to do with it." Sam's eyes hardened. "People have no idea what happened. And of course the police just want to find someone to blame. Sometimes I think they'd rather convict the wrong man just to be able to say they solved a case."

Weariness weighed on Kate, tempting her to call it a night. But too many questions remained unanswered. "So...how *did* it happen?"

Sam pushed a hank of dark hair behind her ear. "The truth is that poor Emily had two unfortunate habits—drinking alone, and swimming alone. That night the combination proved deadly." She leaned back even further into the cushions and crossed one long leg over the other. "Poor Emily had a blood alcohol level of point one six, and had suffered a blow to the skull. The coroner concluded that she must have dived in and hit her head, knocking herself unconscious. Since no one was there to help her, she drowned." Sam blinked away tears. It had been more than twenty years, but the emotion still thickened her voice.

Kate cleared her throat and spoke gently. "So, Chase wasn't home at the time?"

"He was being interviewed at a major radio station. There was even a live audience present." Sam reached over and gave Kate's hand a squeeze. "You can rest assured, Kate. Emily's death was an accident."

Kate let out a breath. If anybody knew Chase, it would be the friend he'd had since high school. This was definitely the reassurance she'd been looking for. That just left her with the question of what happened to Trina.

She urged Sam to continue. "So then Chase moved to the islands."

"Yes, and it was a good move." Pulling in a deep breath, Sam leaned over and grabbed her purse from the other end of the sofa. "This was where he met Trina." She took out her wallet and opened it to a small photo in a plastic sleeve. Her eyes lingered on it for a moment before she handed it to Kate.

Kate studied the photo of a thirty-something Chase next to a very young blonde. "Trina was…younger than Chase?"

"By about ten years." Sam crinkled her brow as if considering the significance of that for the first time. "Now that you point it out, Chase's brides have always been about the same age. Funny, isn't it? The groom ages but the brides stay the same."

Failing to find that truly *funny*, Kate handed back the photo. "I heard that Chase hired her to decorate his house."

"That's right." Sam closed her wallet and put it away. "He loved her work. She mostly made things like vases and colorful ornaments."

Kate felt a twinge of annoyance. When would she stop feeling like a candidate for Outsider of the Year? "So, Trina was a glass artist?"

"Oh…you…didn't know?" Sam gave another *oh-Chase* shake of her head. "She shared studio space behind her friend Marion's gallery with a metal-working co-op. She used to sweep up their metal shavings to put in her glass. That became her signature technique."

Kate felt a chill run through her. "You mean…Trina made the chandelier in Chase's dining room?"

Sam nodded. "She made it as a wedding gift for him."

Kate's heart pinched. What a fool she'd been to think she could compete with that.

"In fact, that was the first time she used her technique. It was so unusual, she actually had it patented."

Patented? As in, no one else could make glass that way? Kate thought of the seahorse, fashioned from bits of glass containing metal flecks. Something wasn't adding up. "Did she ever make other things out of her glass, like mosaic sculptures?"

Sam shook her head. "No. I know she wouldn't have done a mosaic. She loved the pure form of the blown glass."

How strange. It was as if the artist who made the seahorse had shattered Trina Cole's artwork to create her own. But why donate it anonymously?

A thought began to take form. "Did Trina sell her work through Marion's gallery?"

Sam nodded. "Exclusively. Her work was quite popular with both locals and tourists." She lifted her gaze toward Chase's house, as if the conversation had stirred up memories. "Unfortunately, it took the scandal to give her work the widespread popularity it deserved."

A sick feeling started to form in Kate's stomach that made her regret eating that pastry earlier. "What do you mean?"

Shaking her head, Sam reeled in her focus. "It's just the way things work in the art world. The story of Trina's disappearance was such big news, and that made people want to own her work. Of course when the demand goes up, the prices skyrocket."

Her words struck Kate. Jocelyn had said that if it hadn't been for Trina, Marion would have lost her gallery. Was that what she had meant?

She set that thought aside as another one edged its way in. "Jocelyn at the art gallery told us that Trina's friends didn't like Chase. Do you have any idea why?"

Sam rolled her eyes. "Trina's friends don't understand Chase. They see a man who's successful and knows how to take control, and they assume he's somehow abusing his wife. Chase would never hurt anyone."

Kate blinked back a surprising rush of emotion that followed on the heels of Sam's statement. "I...that's...good to know."

"You can put your mind at ease." Sam laid a hand on Kate's knee and looked her in the eye. "I know there are people who think you're headed for trouble, but they don't know Chase the way I do. He's a good man." She gave Kate's knee a firm pat. "You're lucky to have him."

Kate felt considerably better, but one question remained unanswered. "So, what do you think happened to Trina?"

Sadness rimmed Sam's eyes. "The truth is that Trina was fed up with her life."

"Fed up?"

"That's right." She clicked off a list on her fingers. "With Chase working so much. With Stuart and his drinking. With Jessica acting like a spoiled brat. She wanted to make a clean break from all of it."

"So, you're saying she just left?"

Sam shrugged. "Trina never wanted to behave like the wife of a successful businessman. She wanted to live like an artist—on the edge. She got involved with a summer resident. A guy who lived on his boat. One day the guy and his boat were gone and so was Trina."

"But…why disappear when she could have asked for a divorce?"

"This is where things get complicated. Chase and I couldn't explain this part to the police without stirring up questions we wouldn't know how to answer." Sam lowered her voice, as if someone might overhear if she spoke in a normal tone. "Can I trust you?"

Acid burned in Kate's throat as she nodded.

"Good," Sam affirmed. "You see, Chase is very gifted when it comes to getting our projects moved to the top of certain people's priority lists."

Shifting in her seat, Kate fought back that acid. "You mean, he pays people off?"

"It might look that way to some people." Sam lifted a palm. "Anyway, Trina never understood our business. She felt that some of the things Chase had done were going to land us in prison, her included. I think she got scared. And that would explain her wanting to just disappear and start fresh."

"So, the story Chase told the police is true? She really did leave him for another man?"

"It's one hundred percent true. To Chase, it's humiliating and heartbreaking. The poor guy has been through so much." She shook her head. "But of course there are people who just don't want to drop the investigation. Poor Chase."

"Yes. Poor Chase."

"Kate." That caring, motherly look that had filled Sam's eyes narrowed into something more pointed. "Chase is my dearest friend, and I need to know something."

Kate's heart rate increased at the directness of her gaze. "What?"

Sam tipped her head just a little. "Exactly why are you marrying him?"

"Because I…" Kate swallowed hard against a lump in her throat. "…I love him, of course."

"But it's more than just that, isn't it? Level with me, Kate." Sam's eyes zeroed in with laser beam intensity. "You're not just taking advantage of Chase for his money, are you?"

Kate felt the breath whoosh from her lungs. Taking advantage of Chase…. *Was she?*

 *Chapter* 20

Josh unlocked the door to his apartment, happy to be home. He'd called Eli from the ferry to give him Kate's social security number, then had spent the next two and a half hours attempting to appease his guilt for the sneaky way he'd acquired it.

A pressure against his ankles drew his eyes down to a big ball of gray dappled fur. "Hey, Godzilla." He reached down to pet his beloved cat. "Did you miss me, girl?"

"I'll say she did." Eli, entered from the hallway, his hair askew. "I'm glad you made it back before I took off for the night shift." He headed for the kitchen. "Coffee. Then we can talk."

Eli disappeared into the small kitchen, and Josh heard the familiar clanking of the coffee pot against the side of the sink, then water running. He headed to the dining room, where Eli had set up his laptop next to a stack of papers on the table. It felt a little like any ordinary Sunday during the school year, when Josh would have been sitting there at the table studying, after having spent a good part of the day at his church a few blocks away.

"You know," Eli called out from the kitchen, "talking to the guys at work about this Chase Cole situation has made me really glad I'm not in homicide."

"Yeah." Josh flicked on the computer. "I hear it's a real killer."

Eli sputtered out a fake laugh. "Funny, Josh. You really should consider writing sitcoms instead of documentaries."

Crossing around to the far end of the table, Josh took a look out the window down at the University Way, or 'The Ave', as the locals called it. He'd been very aware that the press could take an interest in him and wanted to be sure he hadn't been followed. He could handle it if his name got dragged into the rumor mill, but for Kate's sake, he wanted to be careful.

Satisfied that there was nothing unusual—just the typical students carrying backpacks or Starbucks cups—he leaned on the window frame and thought about his neighborhood. While the countercultural lifestyle of the area held little appeal to him, and the transient teens and young adults known as 'Ave Rats' could make him uneasy, he'd enjoyed the proximity to campus. Sharing this apartment with Eli had been a good experience, but he wouldn't mind relocating when the time came.

He glanced at the papers on the table. "So did you find out anything about Chase Cole?"

Eli appeared in the doorway with a carton of milk in his hand. "I managed to track down a retired officer who worked on the Emily Cole case back in 1990."

"No kidding?" Josh moved closer to the table. "And he was willing to talk to you?"

"Hey, for a cup of Starbucks it's amazing what you can get out of people. He was real open about it, but I'm not sure I found out anything you haven't already read in the paper." He crossed to the table and pulled what looked like a police report from his stack of papers. "Emily Cole drowned all right. Right there in the pool behind the house in Magnolia she owned with Chase Cole."

Leaning over, Josh studied the report. "Did the guy say anything about the domestic disturbance calls?"

"He said he never went on any of those calls, but he remembered hearing a couple of officers talking about it. They said Emily was the one with the temper and that she'd get mad at her husband and accuse him of being abusive with her."

"Do you buy that?"

Shrugging, Eli turned his head at the sound of the coffee gurgling into the pot. "There's really no proof that Chase ever hit her."

"So, there was nothing to suggest he might

have done something to cause her death?"

"Nothing." Eli moved back to the kitchen, raising his voice to be heard. "And Chase Cole had a solid alibi. He left the house that night to do a live radio interview, so people saw and heard him."

"That seems solid, all right." Josh felt his hope melting away. Not that he wanted Mr. Cole to turn out to be guilty. He just wanted something definitive so he could walk away knowing Kate would be happy and safe.

He played his last card. "What about Trina?"

"Everything I find points to no evidence of foul play." Eli spoke past the sound of coffee meeting ceramic. "And again, Chase had an alibi. He was out of town on the last day people saw Trina Cole. And with no body…" He poked his head through the doorway. "…it's pretty hard to prove a murder." He disappeared back into the kitchen. "Everyone's holding their breath waiting for the second Mrs. Cole to surface."

Josh shuddered at the choice of wording. "You think that's likely to happen?"

"The more time passes, the less likely it gets. I don't know. I wish I could have dug up something more solid to give you."

Eli entered with a couple of mismatched thrift store mugs that Josh had picked up strictly because they reminded him of some his grandma had owned since the 1970s. He set one down on the table for Josh, taking a sip from the other as he took a seat. "I found out some things about your friend Kate that you might want to sit down for."

Sufficiently alarmed, Josh lowered himself into one of their old wooden chairs. "What?"

Eli consulted a piece of paper torn from a yellow legal pad. "Well, the social you gave me belongs to Katherine Jennings, and she seems to have gone by Kathy up until recently."

Josh shrugged his brows. That on its own wasn't too strange, but he knew there was probably a reason. Still, it felt weird to think of Kate as a 'Kathy'.

Eli went on. "So this girl, Kathy Jennings, was reported missing back in 2008."

"Missing? As in, she ran away?" Not surprising, considering what she'd told him of her family life.

"Apparently. She was seventeen, and never reported as found." Eli handed him a copy of the report, which had a picture of a teenage girl clipped to it.

With her wavy, shoulder length brown hair, she resembled a young Elizabeth Taylor. Her blue and green flowery dress looked like something out of a 1950s Technicolor movie. Josh couldn't help but stare for a moment. She was mesmerizing.

"That's Kate all right." He took a long swig of coffee and a moment to process. "She told me her stepdad was abusive. Do you think he's the one she's afraid of?"

"Maybe, but he's not the only one."

"Meaning?"

"Meaning, Kathy Jennings is wanted for questioning in a homicide case in San Diego."

"What?" Josh nearly dropped his coffee. "You mean she's a suspect?"

Shaking his head, Eli handed him another police report. "It says 'possible accessory to criminally negligent homicide'."

"Whoa." Josh shook his head, not able to even get a grasp on the right questions to ask. This would explain so much about her odd behavior. "What on earth happened?"

"I talked to the detective on the case down there. He's a real charmer. One of those guys who thinks intimidation is the key to getting people to cooperate. Apparently, Kathy...*Kate* had a job in a clinic that's under investigation for perpetrating a scam called 'psychic surgery'."

"What's that?"

"You remember that movie *Man on the Moon?* You know, where Jim Carrey plays Andy Kaufman?"

"Oh, right. I remember that scene. Kaufman had cancer and he went to a clinic in the Philippines or somewhere to have that New Age 'cure'."

"Right. It's a really popular hoax. According to this detective..." He slid a finger down his handwritten notes. "Detective *Johnson*, it's hard to build a case because people are either convinced it actually works, or embarrassed when they realize they've been taken."

Josh shook his head. Fake surgery. Healing with the mind. It was a shame more people didn't put their faith in the Almighty as the real healer.

Eli continued. "Johnson needed some inside help, and he said he picked the office manager, Kathy, because he knew she probably wasn't aware that it was a scam. Also because she seemed easily intimidated."

Josh's back went up at the thought of that guy targeting Kate.

By the look on Eli's face, he fully agreed. "Anyway, Johnson told Kathy that he was going to arrest her unless she helped him gather evidence to prove her boss—a guy named Joe Malone—was swindling people."

"So, what happened? Someone died?"

"A gentleman named Carl Hingston. He had lung cancer and went to the clinic against the advice of his family. Apparently, he was convinced that the 'surgery' worked and refused to seek conventional treatment. He died, and a few days later this guy Joe went on the lam."

"And let me guess. Kathy went missing too." Josh ran a hand through his hair. Was this what she'd wanted to tell him about the note? That it might have been written by someone who knew about this situation? And what had made her change her mind?

Eli read from the yellow paper. "Johnson tracked her to a place called the Club After Five. It's some kind of gentleman's club in San Francisco. Apparently, he talked to someone who tipped her off that he was on her trail, because she disappeared from there too."

"So, that's the so-called 'tough bind' she was in when she met Mr. Cole." Josh frowned. "But that's been weeks, and she's been in the news. Why hasn't this detective come up here to get her?"

"He says he really doesn't care about getting her. It's Joe Malone he wants. He thinks he fled to Mexico, but extradition from that country can be tough."

"So she's going nuts trying to keep her face out of the newspaper because she's afraid this detective will see it and find her. Meanwhile, he already knows where she is and doesn't really care." Josh ran his hands across his eyes. "And she's marrying Chase Cole because she thinks he has the financial resources to keep her hidden." He shook his head. "What would happen if she just turned herself in?"

"She'd tell them everything she knew about Joe Malone's shady operation and that would be it. Johnson admitted he wouldn't pursue prosecuting her as an accessory."

Josh let out a long breath and picked up the picture of innocent teenage Kate. He had to explain all this to her, and pray that she wouldn't be too angry at him for prying into her personal life.

He had about a hundred more questions flying around in his head, but before he could flag one down, his cell phone rang. Seeing a number that didn't look familiar, he sent Eli a do-you-mind look, and clicked 'accept'.

"Josh Collins? This is Mark Hughes from Homegrown Productions."

All Josh's nerves were instantly on alert. Homegrown was one of the hottest documentary production companies in the country. Was this call for real?

He tried not to let his voice shake. "What can I do for you?

"I'm looking to hire an assistant director for a doc we're filming this summer. It's about an artist who does all his paintings on the walls of caves. Then he photographs them and sells the prints. You heard of the guy?"

Josh's head was still spinning. *Had he?* "Uh…no, I don't think so…"

"He's one of those crazy people who live on the fringes. Perfect subject for a doc. Anyway, I got your name from one of your profs at the U who thought you'd be a great addition to our team. We're in production for six weeks and post-prod for another six after that. I'd need you up in Vancouver in a couple of days. Are you interested?"

Was he interested? Was he *dreaming?* This was the kind of call he hoped he'd get after logging a few more years of school, but who was he to question the judgment of one of his profs?

He started to say an enthusiastic but composed "yes", as if he got this kind of offer all the time, then stopped himself.

Kate. He couldn't take this job because it would mean abandoning her. What was he supposed to do?

He rubbed his temple, and Eli sent him a questioning look.

Josh cleared his throat. "I'm really interested, but can I take a little time to see if I can rearrange my schedule?"

"I know it's short notice." The man sounded understanding, but businesslike. "Go ahead and think it over, but I'd like an answer by the end of the day tomorrow."

Tomorrow. *Monday.* That shortened his timeframe for proving to Kate that she shouldn't walk down the aisle on Saturday.

Mark went on. "Why don't you take the details and get back to me as soon as you know."

Josh reached for the yellow paper that held Eli's notes and flipped it over. He wrote quickly as Mark elaborated. After ending the call, he gave Eli the news.

"Great." Eli looked pleased. "So, you're taking it, right?"

Was he? Josh tapped his phone on the table and looked at the photo of young Kate. No way could he just bail on her.

This would require not only serious thought, but serious prayer. One way or the other, he had to return to Shaw Island for the things he'd left there, but it would be good to talk to her about it now.

Not to mention that he wouldn't mind saying goodnight to her.

He scrolled for her number and prayed for the right words.

Chapter 21

Kate paused, allowing Sam's unanswered question to hover in the air between them. She wasn't marrying Chase just for his money. The fact that he was a hard worker with a soft heart only added to her reasons for loving him.

As she opened her mouth to speak, the muffled sound of her eerie sci-fi ringtone stopped her, and she glanced around for her purse.

"It's here." Extending her arm, Sam retrieved the bag from the end of the sofa.

"Thanks." Kate fished for her phone, reminding herself that if everything went as planned, she'd have to change that ring to something more befitting the wife of a successful businessman. Something by Bach or Beethoven, maybe.

Expecting to see Chase's name on the screen, she frowned. The call she'd just missed had been from Josh.

"Was that Chase?" Sam swirled what was left of her coffee, apparently deciding whether to finish it.

"No." Kate slipped the phone back into her purse, which she then tossed onto the floor, making a mental note to check for a message later on. "Just Josh."

"Oh," Sam nodded. "So, you were about to answer my question."

"Right." Kate stretched out her leg. As much as she wanted to defend her own motives, she *had* needed certain resources to ensure her safety, and Chase had offered them to her. While she really didn't owe anybody any explanations, Sam had been kind enough to give her the reassurance she'd needed. The least she could do was to give her some reassurance in return.

But how much did she dare tell her?

"I do love Chase." She looked at Sam. "But there *is* more to it." She pulled in a breath. "I think I'm in danger because of something stupid I did."

"Danger?" Sam leveled a look of concern. "What kind of danger?"

Still collecting her thoughts, Kate peered out the door at the cozy outside deck. The sky had darkened to a vivid cobalt and the thought of fresh air appealed. "Do you mind if we sit outside for a bit?"

Sam stood. "That's a good idea."

As they stepped through the glass door, the cool air felt refreshing against Kate's cheeks. Sam flipped a switch, and pools of soft golden light washed the deck, which was almost as big as the salon inside. A hot tub, with a bar rimming one edge of it, stood at the center, and various kinds of seating surrounded it. On the far end, two sets of batwing gates opened to stairs leading down to the lower level swim platform. Kate recalled coming up that way earlier after Sam had tied the dinghy to the back of the boat.

Sam flicked another switch, illuminating the orange glow of a couple of heat lamps which flanked a long white sofa. As Kate sat, Sam looked over the railing at the swim platform. "I thought I heard someone."

"Someone?"

She shook her head. "It's no one." She eased down onto the sofa. "I'm just half-expecting Stuart to come paddling out on his kayak."

"He's still upset?"

"He just has some things to work through."

"Oh." Settling into the soft cushions, Kate let her gaze drift over to the hot tub, with its neatly folded white towels and a champagne bottle in a shiny silver bucket gracing its edge. This really was the life.

She took a deep breath and began. "I came from a pretty bad family situation and I left home before I graduated high school. I wound up in San Diego with no money and no job skills. I answered an ad to be a customer service rep for a clinic, and it was kind of a lifesaver. See, a bunch of us were in the same boat, down and out or runaways. The

guy who ran the company—his name was Joe...."
A shiver ran up her spine when she said his name.
"He had a condo and let anybody who needed a
place to live move in. It wasn't exactly 'home', but
it was a place to sleep. Sounds pretty dismal,
right?"

Sympathy brimmed in Sam's eyes. "Go on."

"So the job turned out to be a sales job. Some
of the people who had been there longer tracked
down names and contact information for people
who were critically ill. Then they'd send us out to
talk to them about the clinic. We'd make fifty
bucks for every person we convinced to come in to
experience a healing."

"A 'healing'?" Crinkles formed on Sam's
brow. "What kind of healing?"

"I didn't really know at first. Just that Joe had
all kinds of people saying they'd been cured of
various things. Like it was some kind of miracle."

"Uh huh." Sam sounded skeptical. "Go on."

"So after a while, I realized that Joe was
making a bundle of money, but I didn't really
question it because it was keeping me off the
street."

Sam raised a disapproving eyebrow. "It
sounds like a tenuous situation."

"It was. But I had a small group of friends I
could count on. Shari and Ben, and Iowa. We
called her that because she hardly ever talked and
no one knew her name. All we could get out of her

was where she was from, so that's what we called her." Kate smiled at the memory. "But my favorite was a boy named Dakota. That really was his name, not where he was from." A lump formed in her throat. "He was just a kid—only fifteen when he first got there."

"Fifteen? You mean this man employed children?"

"He kind of looked the other way, I suppose. Anyway, Dakota's seventeen now, but he still seems so young. He has Downs Syndrome, and he really needs looking out for. I kind of took him under my wing."

Sam pulled her legs under herself, clearly getting involved in the story. "Did he do the same job as you?"

"Yes, and he was great at it. He'll talk to anyone, and he's a hard worker. Plus, Joe had him telling people a story about how he couldn't walk or even speak until Joe healed him."

"Was that true?"

"No, but people believed him. He's so sweet, I don't think it registered to him as a lie." Kate pulled her good leg up, mirroring Sam's position as best she could. "Anyway, after I had been there for a while, Joe offered me a promotion to office assistant. I was thrilled not to have to solicit patients anymore, and it was kind of exciting. I was let in on all the inner workings of the clinic, and I finally got to witness actual healings."

"So, what happened in these 'healings'?"

"Well, they took place in the room Joe called the 'Operating Theatre'. It looked just like an operating room, but he had a place along one wall where a small audience could observe. It was my job to help guide the audience members in and tell them what to expect. I also made sure they knew the rules."

"Rules?"

"Like to stay in their seats and to not cross the line on the floor. Joe didn't want anybody to get too close to him while he was working on the patient."

Sam shuddered. "That sounds ominous."

Kate expelled a jittery breath, hating the memory of this part. "It was weird, but people who are sick or have sick loved ones want so badly to believe in miracles, that maybe it didn't seem so strange to them. The patient would be all prepped on a table with a sheet covering them. Then Joe would come in wearing surgeon's scrubs, complete with mask and the whole bit. He'd pull back the sheet to uncover whatever area of the person's body was most impacted by their illness." She clasped her hands to keep them from shaking.

"Then he'd take a small knife, like a surgeon's scalpel, I guess, and he'd cut into them. You knew he was really cutting because blood would…" She had to pause to subdue the memory and its accompanying emotion. "Blood would spurt out.

Then he'd reach into the person's body and pull out the thing that was making them sick. It always looked like a tumor or something. Then he'd rub his hand over the incision and say some kind of chant and the incision would heal. It was weird, like I said, but he really convinced people that he had some kind of healing power."

Disgust rolled across Sam's face. "And you believed it?"

"I really wanted to. It was all a little weird and cult-like, but it was a job and I liked my friends. Plus all the patients seemed to think they were either cured or at least better after their healing, so there was every reason to believe it was real."

An image of Mr. Hingston clung to her as fresh as the day he'd visited the clinic. Kate brushed back a tear. Karen had tried to talk him out of it, right up until he'd gone in for pre-op. She was the only family he had and since she hadn't wanted to watch, there had been no audience for that surgery.

Mr. Hingston was such a sweet man, and he'd been so certain that the healing was going to cure his cancer.

It hadn't.

A wave of sadness washed over her. "Then it got a little scary towards the end."

Sam rubbed her upper arms. "What happened?"

"Well…. One day I walked across the parking

lot to get a sandwich at the mini-mart. A man walked up and started threatening me."

"Threatening? What did he say?"

"He asked if I worked for Joe Malone and I said yes. Then he said he was a detective and that if I didn't do everything he told me to do, he'd arrest me."

Sam frowned. "On what grounds?"

"Well, he told me that Joe was perpetrating a scam and that I would be charged as an accomplice if I didn't help to gather evidence against him."

"What kind of evidence?"

"He said that what Joe did wasn't real surgery, but that it's a sleight of hand, and he wanted me to get close enough to take a video. I was so scared of this detective, and of going to jail. I mean, he really had me terrified."

"I can understand that."

"That afternoon, I cut a little hole in the pocket of my lab coat so you couldn't tell I had the camera in it. I was so scared when Joe started the healing. It was dark in the room except for the bright lights shining right on Joe and the patient. I eased closer and closer to that line. I hoped he wouldn't notice, but he kept glancing over at me."

"Kate, that must have been so frightening."

"It was. Finally, I was standing right on the line but I still couldn't get a good view of his hands. So I took a big step, and he kind of jerked his arm up and looked at me. A thing that looked like a kidney fell out of his sleeve and splatted on the floor, and the audience gasped. It was really awful. Joe did his best to try to save the performance, but it wasn't very convincing. To make matters worse, I knew I hadn't gotten anything on video."

"So what happened?"

"Well, after the surgery, Joe wanted me to go into his office and talk to him in private. I reminded him I had to get to the bank before it closed because I always took the day's money in to deposit. Joe only let people pay in cash so there was always a lot of it. I took the money pouch out of the safe and shoved it in my backpack like I always did. Joe said we'd talk as soon as I came back, and he went into his office."

She stopped and took a deep breath. She couldn't admit that Karen Hingston had picked that moment to storm into the clinic, furious that her father had died that morning.

What happened after that was the *real* reason Kate had run. Would the story still make sense if she skipped ahead?

"Kate?" Sam touched her arm.

Jerking back from the memory, Kate realized she'd been staring off into space. "So I grabbed my backpack and ran. I didn't know what else to do."

"You couldn't call the police?"

"Maybe I should have, but I was afraid

because of what Detective Johnson had said. I thought if I went to the police, they'd arrest me. So I ditched my lab coat and kept moving till I made it to the Greyhound station. I looked to see when the next bus was leaving, and it happened to be going to San Francisco."

"You ran away a second time?"

"Yes. The good thing was that I always kept my most important possessions with me in my backpack." She took in a deep breath, confident that she should include the next part. "It wasn't until I was holed up in a seedy motel room in San Fran that I remembered I also had the money pouch. I took it by accident."

Sam raised an eyebrow.

"Please don't tell Chase," Kate quickly added. "I haven't told him that part yet."

With a slow blink of understanding, Sam nodded. "And you couldn't return it because you were afraid of Joe?"

"Right. And of Detective Johnson finding me."

"So, how much was in the pouch?"

Kate gulped. "Almost a quarter of a million."

"A quarter million *dollars?*" Sam's eyes shot open. "That was his take for one day?"

"Yeah. It was a good day."

"So what did you do?"

"The only thing I could think to do. I dyed my hair blonde, changed my name from Kathy to Kate, and got a job in a place called The Club After

Five".

"Is that a restaurant?"

She took in a breath. "Sort of. It's more of a Gentleman's Club. Anyway, I got asked to move into an apartment that five of the girls who worked there shared. It wasn't great, but it was in a safer neighborhood than that motel and it was good to have people to walk home from work with."

"So the club is where you met Chase?"

She nodded. "He came in one night with a group of guys for a business meeting. He was so nice, and *different* than the other customers. He seemed kind of protective of me in a way."

"It sounds just like Chase to want to protect a pretty young woman."

"Especially one with blonde hair and blue eyes?" Kate looked down, still feeling conflicted about that point. "He came in a couple more times, by himself. He just sat at the bar and had a drink, and struck up a conversation when he saw me.

"Then one night I went in to work and there was Detective Johnson sitting at the bar. I panicked. I ducked back into the room we used for our breaks and one of my roommates confronted me. She said he'd been asking around about me, and told me that if I was in trouble with the law I'd have to move out. I knew I couldn't stay at my job either if Johnson was onto me. Chase happened to walk by and he heard me crying hysterically. He asked if there was anything he could do to help me. I just sort of blurted out my story." She looked away. "Except the part about the money." *And Karen.*

She sniffed and went on. "He told me he wanted to help me, and he took me to a nice hotel and put me up in my own suite. All by myself with no strings attached. Over the next few weeks, we just got to know each other. And he meant what he said. No strings attached."

"That does sound just like Chase. He has such a big heart."

"I honestly don't know what I would have done if he hadn't shown up in my life. He was a real angel. That's why I have a hard time believing he could have harmed anyone."

"Trust your instinct, Kate. I've known Chase most of my life. He's had a couple of rough breaks, but the man you met in San Francisco is the real Chase."

Kate smiled.

"And I'm relieved to know you're not marrying him for his money."

Kate thought back on everything she had just told her. Had she made that clear?

Sam met her questioning gaze. "I know that, because you have enough money to keep yourself safe."

"Oh, but…" Kate cut herself off. She had never even considered using the stolen money, but if knowing she had it assured Sam of her intentions with Chase, then maybe that was okay.

Sam let out a sigh. "And now, it's getting late." She stood, stretching her arms over her head. "I'm guessing you could use some good rest."

Kate couldn't help a yawn. "You're right about that."

A few minutes later, Sam began checking all the doors as Kate braced herself for her careful trek down the stairs to the lower level.

"Oh, Kate." Sam stopped abruptly as if jarred by recollection. "I meant to tell you this earlier." She crossed to the wall near the top of the stairs where Kate stood, and put her hand on a white box, similar to the ones in the house. "I don't want you going up and down the stairs any more than necessary. If you need anything, just call me on the intercom. There's one right next to your bed."

"Thanks, Nurse Sam."

Sam's eyes twinkled. Clearly, she enjoyed the opportunity to dote on people.

After making the slow journey to the lower level, Kate hobbled down a short hallway and entered the master suite. This room occupied the tip of the boat and made Kate feel like royalty. She quickly changed and slipped into the humongous bed, which was situated in the middle of the room. She reached over and turned off the light, sinking into the fluffy pillow and gazing at the windows making up the V-shaped end of the room.

As she looked out at the lights of the Shaw Island ferry landing in the distance, a sense of security warmed her as much as the downy duvet. Joe couldn't get to her out there.

She allowed her eyes to close and a feeling of peace to claim her. She would dream of Chase and the life they would share together. Yachting. Maybe even traveling once the media frenzy died down. Life would be good, and filled with love and passion.

Passion….

As she started to drift off to sleep, an image soothed her mind. Embraced by warm, strong arms, a sense of love and security which she had never known before surrounded her. In the soft haze between sleep and wakefulness, she felt her head tip back to look into the eyes of the man she adored.

Josh.

Her eyes popped open. *Josh?*

She sat up, her heart hammering in her throat. Her mind had wickedly shone a light on the secret her heart had kept hidden for the past three days. An ache…no a *yearning* for Josh.

What had triggered the release of this longing that her logical mind had known was best kept concealed? His phone call. That was it.

She let out a groan. Getting so caught up in her conversation with Sam, she'd completely forgotten to check for a message. She was way too comfy now to trudge all the way back upstairs, and in spite of Sam's instruction, she would feel like a total brat asking her to bring her purse down to her. It was no big deal. Even if Josh had left a message, it could wait until morning.

Closing her eyes again, she listened to the soft sloshing of the waves outside and the occasional cawing of some kind of a bird. She'd gotten what she needed—reassurance, from a reliable source, of Chase's innocence. Everything would be okay.

With her course laid out before her, she finally felt truly safe.

Cautiously, she closed her eyes again, praying that a certain handsome future filmmaker wouldn't invade her dreams.

Chapter 22

Relaxing into one of the cushy chairs on the deck of the main house, Kate suffered a sudden pang of consciousness. All night and through breakfast, she'd done such a great job of pushing Josh to the back of her mind that she'd forgotten to check for a phone message. With a resigned sigh, she grabbed her purse from the floor next to her and began diligently digging through it.

Sam glanced at her from behind the morning newspaper. "Did you lose something?"

Kate frowned into the depths of her purse. "I know I put my phone back in here last night."

Compassion filled Sam's dark brown eyes. "Maybe it fell out and slid between the sofa cushions. We can check once we're back out on the yacht."

Kate gave one last look before giving up. How she managed to own minimal possessions yet still collect so much useless junk in her purse was one of God's great mysteries.

A quick glance at her watch told her that it was nearly eleven fifteen. Even if she'd missed a message from Josh, it didn't really matter now. He'd be here soon anyway.

Setting her bag on the cushioned ottoman which supported her leg, she massaged her knee and let her gaze wander. The vibrant blue sky promised a brighter day, just as the details Sam had shared the night before had assured her of a secure future.

"It's warm this morning." Sam placed the newspaper down on the table between them, then slipped off her beige linen jacket and tossed it onto the chaise behind her. "But the paper predicts a storm later on. We should enjoy the sunshine while we can."

Noticing for the first time that a dramatic patch of gray loomed in the distance, Kate decided to drop the weather-paralleling-her-life analogy. This was just the climate of her new home. Unpredictable and constantly changing. There was no reason to think her happy ending would follow the same pattern.

Angling her wrist to check her watch for the umpteenth time, she caught herself. What was she doing? If her happy ending was secured, why did she keep wondering when Josh would show up?

She sighed. It wasn't any big mystery, really. He was an attractive, single guy who happened to share some of her interests. But her life was what it was, and she couldn't change that. She might not get to have the passion she longed for, but that was part of the price she'd pay for her safety. Things were working out perfectly with Chase, and Josh had just been a temporary distraction.

Unfortunately, there was nothing she could do about his being there. He needed a job, and it had already been promised to him. Controlling her thoughts, and acting like a boss, not a friend, would be the only way to hold her emotions in check.

Tipping back her head, she studied the wispy clouds directly above. Thank goodness she hadn't told Josh about Joe. How did she know he wouldn't have told his best friend, the cop, and blown her cover completely?

The rustling of newspaper brought her out of her thoughts, and she glanced at the section Sam had just set on the table.

"Oh my gosh." Snapping it up, she read the headline. "'*Shania Hane Faked Death to Elude Stalker*'."

"Isn't that something?" Sam looked up. "She was living in Friday Harbor under an assumed name."

"Josh and I met her the other day." A tingle danced down Kate's spine at the thought of telling him. "He swore it was her and I told him he was crazy." She chuckled. "I guess I owe him another chocolate shake."

Sam made a tsking sound. "That poor woman was being stalked to the point of having to kill her real identity and go into hiding."

"Yes." Kate bit her lip. "Kind of like me."

A soothing look of motherly concern slipped over Sam's features. "Don't you worry." Her words sounded soft and reassuring. "You won't have to hide forever."

Kate gave her a light smile. Something about her certainty made Kate think she should believe her.

The French doors behind them clicked and Kate twisted around, hoping not to see Jessica or Stuart. The sight of Josh stepping out of the house in jeans, a t-shirt, and a cobalt blue cotton jacket sent all hope of controlling her thoughts sailing out into the bay. The best she could hope was for her emotions to not show on her face.

"Josh." Twisting back around, she grabbed the newspaper and waved it in her hand as he crossed in front of her. She tried to suppress the heat that rose to her cheeks. "You're not going to believe this."

Ignoring the paper, he tipped a courteous if subdued greeting at Sam before returning his attention to Kate. "Why haven't you been answering your phone?"

Both his tone and his demeanor held an edge Kate hadn't experienced from him before. Her heart sank. Had something changed?

Lowering the paper, she sputtered, "I...I lost it."

"Well, that explains it." Though softened, his voice left her with the distinct feeling that her carelessness had let him down.

His concerned gaze settled on her. "How are you feeling?"

"Sam wrapped my leg." She gave a light smile that didn't feel as reassuring as she hoped it looked.

"Kate is a very cooperative patient." Sam rose to her feet. "And now that you're here to look out for her, I'm afraid I have to head to the mainland."

Kate gripped the newspaper, as something just short of panic crept in. She had assumed they'd have the day together to work on wedding plans. The idea of spending time alone with Josh now that…she gulped…now that her feelings had intensified, made her stomach hurt.

She looked at Sam. "I hope I haven't been keeping you from your work."

"It's not a big deal." Sam pushed to her feet and smoothed a hand over her linen pants. "Something's come up and I need to go meet someone."

Kate tried not to let her distress show. "Are you taking the yacht?"

"Oh, no. I have a friend on the other side of the island who sometimes loans me his powerboat. It's easier than the yacht, and I hate being a slave to the ferry schedule." Sam bent down to give Kate's hand a reassuring squeeze. "I'll be back later today and we can return to the yacht together."

Kate watched as Sam headed into the house. Cautioning a look at Josh, she chewed on her lip, anxious to regain the rapport they'd had up until now but needing to let him know she had set her boundaries.

He stood there next to the deck rail, neither leaning nor sitting, as if he might be planning on leaving too. She looked down at the newspaper she still held in her hands, then tossed it onto the table. Even if he wasn't interested in discussing the article, surely he'd want to hear what she'd learned about Chase. She attempted to sound earnest. "So, Sam told me everything about Emily and Trina. She's known Chase since high school. Can you believe that?"

"Uh huh." He seemed hesitant to hold her gaze, which was totally unlike him.

Kate went on. "She was actually there with him after he found Emily, and she was one of the last people to talk to Trina before she vanished. It looks like Chase's story about her leaving him for another man is true."

He pulled in a breath, but let it out in a heavy, wordless sigh.

Why was he acting so distant? Was he really this upset about her not answering her phone? Or was there something else?

She buried her apprehension behind a

plastered-on smile. "So, we don't have to do any more investigating. We can focus on getting ready for the wedding."

He worked his jaw, like he wanted to say something but couldn't decide how to start. Her heart quivered. She missed the banter they'd had just the day before.

Act like a boss, Kate. Not a friend.

"So, we might as well get started." She swung her leg off the ottoman and pulled herself to her feet. "I need to decide where we're going to stand for the ceremony, and where the guests are going to sit. Just think…" She took a cautious step, her knee responding with a dull ache. "In a few days, you'll be calling me Mrs. Cole." Forcing a smile, she turned for the door.

"If that's what you want." His voice sounded firm and solid, like he wasn't moving to follow. "Or maybe you'd rather I call you *Kathy.*"

She froze, the word stabbing her like a cold blade. Slowly, she turned, gaping at him in confused disbelief. "How did you…?"

Stepping toward her, he pulled some folded papers from his inside jacket pocket and held them out.

She took the papers with trembling hands. The heading of the top page screamed at her. *Missing Persons Report.*

A shockwave skittered through her. Her mother had reported her missing. Of course she had.

A copy of an old photo of her was clipped to the corner of the page. It was all she could do not to fold into a heap on the deck as she pictured her mom, frantic, responding to a policeman's request for a recent photo of her by extracting this one from its frame on the living room wall. Had her stepdad been with her, offering comfort? Or had he made her go through this alone?

She flipped to the second page—a yellow paper filled with handwritten notes. Her eyes swept over the murky mass of words. *Kathy Jennings…Emily Cole…Detective Johnson…Carl Hingston.* Then out of the blur of pencil markings, a phrase took shape. *Possible accessory to criminally negligent homicide.*

Her knees buckled and Josh reached out to clasp her arms.

She tried to pull away from him, but her strength failed. "How…where…?"

His eyes, which had seemed so distant just a moment before, now brimmed with compassion. "Eli tracked this down for me."

Her breath caught. He'd had her investigated? Betrayal surged in her chest till she could scarcely breathe. "Why?"

"Because I asked him to."

Fury mixed with fear, forming a potent brew that threatened to erupt like a volcano. Wrenching free from his grasp, she took an unsteady step back. "You…you had him check up on me?"

"I'm sorry, Kate." Remorse filled his voice. "But I just had a feeling there was something serious going on that I should know about. Why didn't you tell me about any of this?"

"Because it's none of your business." The papers crumpled between her shaking fingers. "Didn't that ever occur to you?"

He shook his head. "No. That didn't occur to me because I happen to care about you. I want to protect you, and not just because Mr. Cole hired me to."

He cared about her. She looked into his eyes, not sure if she wanted to see a deeper meaning in them. Her outrage faltered. "But…you had no right…"

"I understand why you're running." With an extended hand, he took another step toward her. "And why you're trying to hide inside a loveless marriage."

Loveless? The word gave her anger a reboot. Josh couldn't tell her how she felt. He had no idea.

His suppliant gaze connected with hers. "But you need to know that the detective isn't interested in arresting you. You don't need to hide anymore."

Her head started to spin, and she grappled for a chair to catch her weight. Getting arrested for her involvement with the clinic was really the least of her worries now. Did Josh know the rest of the story? Did anyone?

She scanned the yellow page again, looking for any mention of Karen or of the stolen money. Seeing nothing, she flipped it over. There she saw more notes, but in different handwriting. Something about a documentary and some numbers behind a dollar sign.

She looked up at Josh. "You got offered a job on a movie?"

His eyes narrowed in confusion, then widened in realization. He let out a long breath and took the papers back from her. "I got a phone call while I was home."

"Really?" She pressed her lower arms to her belly. "When does the job start?"

"Well, they would need me to be in Vancouver tomorrow."

Tomorrow? Pain squeezed her chest, where the happiness she felt for him made a confusing contrast to the sorrow she felt for herself. "So…you're leaving?"

He let out a breath. "That's why I was trying to call you. "I haven't given them an answer yet. I wanted to talk to you first."

Anguish filled her throat. He had wanted to talk to her. Like what she thought mattered in his decision. Like *she* mattered.

She couldn't let herself think that way. "But you're taking it, right? I mean…it's what you want."

"Kate." He knelt next to her. "I made a

commitment to you."

As she met his gaze, her body weakened in an exodus of spent adrenaline and rage. With everything in her, she wanted to just go with him. To get into his dented-up Toyota and drive away from all her fears and concerns. Into a life filled with passion and the kind of love that was formed by a thousand colored dots of different emotions that only made sense when you stood back to see the picture they formed.

She looked away, afraid of what she might say if she looked into those eyes again. If love could build a strong fortress around her she'd be safe, but it couldn't. No matter how badly she wanted it, love would never be enough.

Pulling herself painfully to her feet, she crossed to the railing and focused on the creeping patch of grey in the sky. At least with her back to him and that small distance between them, she could fake a strength she didn't feel.

"I think you should take the job." She blinked back a tear. "It's a great opportunity, and I can't stand in your way."

The sound of his steps behind her carried over the soft sloshing of the waves below them.

"Kate…I need to know you'll be okay."

His hand touched her shoulder, and she turned. Unable to help herself, she looked up at his molten eyes drilling into hers.

She slowly shook her head. "You can't keep

me safe." It came out in a choked whisper.

"You're right. I can't." He removed his hand, but she could still feel its warmth. "No one can guarantee your safety, Kate. Not Mr. Cole. Not me."

The tears started to come in spite of her best efforts to restrain them. "Then what am I supposed to do?"

Dipping down to recapture her gaze, he spoke softly. "You have to have faith. Just know that God is in control."

Wrapping her arms around herself, she turned again and wiped her eyes. "You don't know what I need, Josh."

"You're right. But I wish I did." Resting his hands on the railing, he eased up next to her. "Kate...*Kathy*...I..."

Turning to meet his gaze, she felt her heart skitter in her chest. She leaned in closer to him, longing to allow everything she had worked for all these weeks to slip from her grasp so she could follow her heart's lead.

Don't be a fool, Kate.

Stumbling back a step, she held up a hand. "I know what I want." She pulled in a breath for strength. "I want to be Mrs. Chase Cole." Overcome with a need to get away from him, she started for the stairs that led down to the water.

"Wait." Alarm cut through his voice. "Where are you going?"

Good question. Her first step down reminded her that putting stress on her knee was not a good plan. "I'm going to the yacht to wait for Sam."

He moved to follow. "At least let me drive you."

She held up a hand. "It's not your job to take care of me, Josh." Emotion mixed with pain, doing little to convey a sense of self-assurance. "I think you should go."

He wavered, then let out a long sigh. "Fine." The word was low. Resigned. "If you're sure that's what you want. I'll just go inside and get the rest of my things." He took a step, then stopped and met her gaze. "I won't bother you again…Mrs. Cole."

As he headed back to the house, Kate stood motionless—torn between the need to flee and the desire to go after him.

The door clicked shut behind him, and a tear rolled down her cheek. She quickly swiped it away, then grabbed hold of the railing with both hands and made her way down the stairs. By the time her feet touched the soft ground at its base, the periphery of her vision had blurred, and her throat had tightened. The throbbing of her heartbeat echoed in her ears.

Focusing on what she could see of the dock through the trees, she started down the trail, the thin soles of her ballet flats providing only minimal traction on the dewy stones. This was a stupid move, tackling this trail. But she'd needed to get away from Josh.

All she could think of as she edged into the thicket of trees that enveloped the trail as it wound past the guesthouse, was her desire to get back to the yacht. And what then? She didn't even have a key to get inside.

Another wave of uncertainty tightened her throat. It would be okay. Josh would leave, and she could start to feel like a normal bride with nothing worse than a case of pre-wedding jitters. Then when Sam returned, she would help put things into perspective.

She passed the front of the guesthouse, then followed the trail as it wound down below the beams that supported the decks she had so looked forward to spending time on. Keeping her head down, she focused on the pine-needled path and tried not to think about which stabbing pain hurt worse—the one in her knee, or the one in her heart. Both seemed to be gaining intensity with each step. How could she have let herself get so caught up in caring for a man who wasn't hers?

The truth was, she felt drawn to Josh in a way she would never be to Chase. But even if she could stay with Josh, what kind of life could she offer him? Her past would forever haunt them. And unless she decided to spend the stolen money, which would create a whole new set of problems, she needed Chase's resources. That was just the way it was.

As she passed the stairway that led up to the backdoor of the guesthouse, she paused and looked around. She hadn't realized that from this section of the trail, there was no view of either the main house behind her or the water in front of her. Aside from that staircase and the mostly obscured guesthouse above the trail, there was nothing but a shroud of trees on either side.

A chill passed through her, and she attempted to hasten her steps, even though the steep downhill grade of the path made that very difficult.

Behind her, something crackled. Before she could turn, a hand took a firm hold of her shoulder and jolted her to a stop.

Chapter 23

Raking his hand through his hair, Josh climbed the stairs to the second floor. Why hadn't he talked to Kate calmly, the way he had planned? Whatever chance he'd had with her had crashed and burned in a blazing trail of the trust he had failed to instill in her.

Confusion blurred his thoughts. To stay or to go. He'd prayed for guidance in making this decision, and her words had seemed like the answer. But if he'd been able to talk to her about it last night, would her response have been different?

Entering the room that had been his over the weekend, he contemplated. The question of Mr. Cole's innocence wasn't really the issue anymore. Josh had to face it. The real issue was that he couldn't stand the thought of someone else marrying his Kate.

His Kate? He jarred at the thought. When had she become *his* Kate?

He tossed the few items he'd left out into his backpack. He should be totally stoked right now. Working on this movie could set him on the career path he'd dreamed of for years. But taking it meant walking away from Kate, the woman he could have sworn, if he didn't know better, was the woman he was meant to be with.

Get a grip, man. No matter how badly he wanted things to be different, Kate wasn't his. If he stayed, things would only get more complicated.

He closed the zipper on his backpack and tossed it onto the bed, then grabbed his phone from his jacket. He took the papers from his other pocket, wishing again that he had handled the situation differently. He scanned his scrawled notes for Mark Hughes' phone number. This was for the best. But why was he still so torn?

Mark picked up after a couple of rings, and Josh told him his decision. It definitely gave him a boost to hear Mark's enthusiasm over the news that they'd be working together. As Mark filled him in on how to get to the hotel and the first location, Josh glanced out the window toward the pristine bay. There was no sign yet of the ferry, but it would be coming soon. He might as well board the next one and just make a clean break.

He allowed a look at the woodsy area below. From what he could see through the trees, there was no sign of Kate either. Small wonder. On that leg, it would take her a while to get down the trail. Why hadn't he insisted on driving her?

Grabbing his backpack, he confirmed with Mark that he'd see him in Vancouver that night, then ended the call. Stepping out of the room, he prayed that his fervor would match his new boss's by the time he crossed the border.

"Well, hey." The sound of a female voice drew his attention to the end of the hallway, where Kim rolled a sleek silver suitcase out of her room. She started toward him. "Looks like we're planning to catch the same ferry."

Hoping to conceal his indifference to that prospect, Josh shouldered his backpack and reached out to take Kim's bag for her. "I thought you'd be staying for the wedding." Small talk felt hollow, but at least it might help to take his mind off Kate.

She shrugged as they started for the stairs. "I would, but duty calls. I'm heading to Bowen Island for a marine biology summer internship. If all goes well, it'll lead to a job in the fall."

Pausing at the top of the stairs, Josh tamped down the extended handle of Kim's suitcase and angled her a look. "You're going to be a marine biologist?"

"That's the plan." Sliding a wisp of hair behind her ear, Kim tipped a playful half-smile and started her descent. "I know you probably thought I was just another party girl. That's the clever façade I managed to maintain at school to keep my social life from drying up. What guy wants to date a science nerd, right?"

He smiled, going along with her self-deprecating barb.

When he didn't say anything, she reined in the flirtation. "Are you headed back to Seattle?"

"Vancouver, actually. I got a job on a film that's being shot up there."

"Seriously? We're going to be neighbors. Bowen Island is just north of Vancouver." Kim smiled, giving him a flash of nearly-perfect teeth. "You'd love that place. It's where they shot *Clan of the Cave Bear*." Her smile turned coy. "Maybe we can get together some weekend."

"Yeah, sounds good." The idea wasn't exactly unappealing, and it might be nice to have an old friend to explore with. Not that he'd get a lot of free time, but still.

Reaching the bottom step, he popped up the suitcase handle. The wheels hummed across the smooth wood of the floor as they made their way to the front door. They stepped out into what had quickly turned from warm sunshine to a shadowy chill.

"Looks like we're heading out just in time." Kim shivered. "A storm's brewing."

Josh scanned the overcast sky as they headed down the porch steps. He'd always made the most of this atmospheric Seattle gloom by pretending he lived in a black and white film. Right now, the sudden gray only served to enhance his mood.

As they walked around to the side of the house, his eyes wandered again to what he could see of the trail leading down to the dock.

"We'd better hurry if we want to catch this next ferry." Kim reached out her hand and clicked her key fob, opening the trunk of her sports car.

Shifting his focus, Josh hoisted her suitcase in. She gave another click to shut.

"I guess I'll see you on the boat." She crossed to her door and opened it. "It's a long ride. Maybe I'll challenge you to a game of chess." She winked and got into her car.

As she pulled out of the driveway, Josh tossed his backpack on the passenger seat of his Toyota, and pulled in a slow breath. He'd forgotten Kim was as much of a chess nerd as he was. A game might be just the thing to refocus and clear this whole insane situation from his mind.

Casting one more long look at the trail, he considered strolling down just to make sure Kate wasn't sitting on the ground rubbing her knee. He checked his watch and shook off the thought. Kim was right. If he didn't hustle, he'd miss this ferry, and the last thing he needed was to find himself with time to kill on Shaw Island.

Besides, Kate was an adult, and she had made her own plan. Clearly, there was no place for him in it.

The wind blew a sudden gust through the trees, sending a chill through him like a whispered warning. He needed to move on.

He got into his car and started the engine. As

he pulled around the horseshoe curve of the driveway, he exhaled long and low. This was all for the best.

He eased the car past the guesthouse and toward the gate, away from any ridiculous hope he might have harbored of a life with Kate.

Chapter 24

Kate jerked forward, freeing herself from her assailant's grasp. Her leg twisted and she stumbled downhill, landing in an excruciating heap on her hands and knees. Heart pounding, she contorted to get a look over her shoulder.

Stuart towered over her.

Her frantic mind registered his wild hair and shirttails sticking out from the waist of his khaki pants, which looked as though he had slept in them.

His arm flailed in the direction of the guesthouse. "Aren't you staying there?"

The strangeness of the question baffled her only slightly less than the strangeness of this whole situation. Keeping her eyes on him, she tried to push herself upright, but the slope of the path combined with the pain shooting from her knee made the effort impossible. "No...not anymore."

"Aw..." His head lolled back and he pounded the heel of his hand against his forehead. "Stupid,

stupid…"

Leaning on her right hand, she managed to lever herself to a sitting position, facing him. She held up her other hand in defense in case he came at her again. "Please, just leave me alone."

Rubbing his eyes, he stumbled backwards, and for a second Kate thought he was going to fall over. She grappled for something to use to pull herself to her feet, but all she could reach was a moss-covered tree root.

"I get it now." He shook his head. "It figures."

Fear welled in Kate's throat. Why hadn't she accepted Josh's offer to drive her? If she had, she'd be on the yacht right now instead of sitting on the ground in a tangled heap, facing an overwrought alcoholic who might or might not be dangerous.

He looked at her, his eyes glazed as if it required all his effort to focus in on her. "How am I supposed to live without money?"

An odd question, considering that his dad was a billionaire. She pulled her left foot under her in an attempt to get solid footing. "I…don't know. I—"

"Dad says I have to leave after the wedding. Get a job or get out." He narrowed his reddened eyes into a fiery glare. "It's because of you."

The blood drained from Kate's face. This was all starting to make sense. "You think he's asking you to leave because of me?"

"What I think is that if you were gone,

everything would go back to the way it was." His hard glare didn't waver. "I have a good thing going, and there's no reason for it to end."

Kate's mind reeled. If he came at her, she'd have no way to defend herself. She was in the thick of the woods, with little chance of being heard if she screamed, and less chance of being seen.

She looked past Stuart up the shadowy trail. If only Josh would come to check on her, but why should he? She had told him to leave. Now, she had no choice but to try to reason with Stuart.

"Listen." She attempted to make her voice soothing, the way she used to speak to Dakota when he was upset. "Maybe I can help you."

"Help me?" The fire in his eyes cooled slightly into an amalgam of anger and suspicion. "How?"

"You know…" Stretching to reach a tree root, she managed to push herself onto her good leg. "To get a job. Or go back to school—"

"*Or…*" He held up a finger, as if an idea was brewing. "You could get me a place of my own. In Seattle. With a view of the water."

Her heart pounded. Did he think Chase had given her access to his bank account? "You mean…you want me to buy you a house?"

"What I *want*…" he clenched his hands at his sides. "…is for you to make up for what you've ruined."

"Okay…" She tried to smile as if his demand were actually rational. "I'll do whatever I can."

He stared down at her, a mixture of unreadable emotions crossing his features. He jutted out his jaw. "You think I'm some kind of loser."

Her hand shot up like a shield. "No…. I just think you've had a rough life in some ways—"

"In some *ways?*" His glower reignited. "I practically saw my mother die. That's not something a person just gets over."

She gaped up at him, confused. "What do you mean, you *saw* her?"

His gnashed his teeth and looked away, moisture dimming the intensity in his eyes. "You wouldn't believe me."

"Stuart." Kate managed to push herself off the ground to an unsteady standing position. "This is really important." She hopped a couple of steps, then braced her weight against a tree. "What exactly do you remember from that night?"

As he stared off into the distance, some of the hard lines of his face softened. "I woke up because my parents were fighting. I heard it all."

"All…*what?*"

"You know. Yelling. Doors slamming. I heard my mom go downstairs and I knew she was going to the pool. She swam all the time, especially when she was mad at my dad." His voice drifted off.

"So, she went down to swim." She had to keep him focused. "What do you remember after that?"

"After a while, I got up and went to the room

across the hall. I looked out the window down at the pool, and that's when I saw her."

"And what was she doing?"

"Lying face down next to the pool." He swallowed hard. "Not moving."

Next to the pool? Kate's heart drummed in her ears. "Where was your dad?"

"I don't know. Gone."

"So, what did you do?"

"I got back in my bed and hid under the covers until Sam woke me up to tell me my mom had drowned."

"Oh…" The absence of emotion in his voice alarmed her. "Did you tell Sam what you had seen?"

"No." He shook his head. "But later, I told my dad."

"And…? What did he say?"

"He said I was wrong. But I know what I saw."

Kate's head swam. If this was true, there was more to Emily's death than just a simple drowning. But Stuart had been a little boy. How reliable was his memory, especially considering the years of alcohol abuse that had followed?

She considered her words, not wanting to trigger his anger. "So you never said anything to anyone else?"

Shoulders drooping, he stared off into the distance. "I told Trina."

"Trina?" Her breath caught. "When?"

"Last year, when I was in rehab. She believed me." His voice lowered to a near-whisper. "That's why she disappeared."

Kate stiffened, taking care not to let her distress reflect in her expression. "Why would she disappear because she believed you?"

"Because she confronted my dad about it."

"Oh?" Kate swallowed past the tightening ball of fear in her throat. "And what happened?"

"They had a fight. Then my dad said he was going out of town, and he left. The next night, Trina disappeared."

"So, you think her disappearance had something to do with her confronting your dad?"

Stuart lifted a shoulder in what seemed to take more effort than the resulting shrug. "All I know is, everyone thought my dad was out of town the last night Trina was here. But he wasn't."

"Oh…and how do you know?"

"Because I saw him. He was here." He looked around ominously. "Hiding in these woods."

An involuntary shiver that had nothing to do with the chill in the air passed through Kate. "Why would he do that?"

"I don't know." His gaze pierced her with an alarming directness. "Why don't you ask *him?*"

The wind kicked up, stirring the trees around them to life. Then a different, familiar sound emerged through the rustling of the branches. The sound of a car starting up. *Josh.*

She pushed away from the tree she'd been leaning on. "I...I have to go." She stepped, but her knee buckled in a detonation of pain.

Stuart shifted to his left, blocking her way. "They're going to find her."

"What?" Eyes watering, she looked past him up the path. Josh was so close. If only she could cry out. The distinctive rattle of his engine grew louder, and she caught a flash of teal blue moving past the opening at the head of the trail. She was too late. He couldn't help her.

"They're going to find her."

Stuart's ominous words joggled her focus back to him. "What? Who?"

"Trina. Then what's going to happen to me?"

Not knowing how—or even *if*—to respond, Kate took a step down the trail.

Stuart blinked, as if his lids were weighted, then regarded her through narrowing eyes. "Where are you going?"

Reaching out again to the tree for support, she took a couple of careful paces backward. "To the yacht to wait for Sam."

"Right..." He nodded in glassy-eyed recollection. "She's coming back..." His eyes shot open and he looked at her with a newfound alertness. "So...you're going out there. Yeah. That's good."

With a sudden deftness that caught Kate off

guard, he made a couple of clumsy strides up the trail. He faltered, regained his balance, then continued up the hill, laughing like some sort of deranged mad scientist.

She frowned. Had critical connecting points in his brain been shorted out by his excessive alcohol intake, or was it just his personal policy to be cryptic in his behavior?

Grateful to have him gone, she turned and took a step toward the dock, bracing herself for the pain she knew would follow. She stumbled, but kept going. There was no way she was going to stick around with Stuart acting so unpredictable and crazy. She had to get out to the yacht.

A few minutes later, she reached the dock and carefully slid into the dinghy. It wobbled unsteadily under her weight as she worked her way to the seat next to the motor.

She stared at it. If she couldn't get the motor to start, at least the dinghy had oars. She could row if she had to, but who knew how long that would take.

Remembering that Sam had said it was easier to pull the cord from a standing position, she carefully pushed herself back up, keeping all her weight on her one good leg. She pulled the cord, but the engine sputtered and she fell sideways, nearly clocking her head on the edge of the dock.

Great. She was lucky she hadn't taken a plunge.

As she clutched the edge of the boat in an attempt to push herself back onto the seat, something in the water under the dock hooked her attention. Cautiously, she leaned as far over as she dared, then gasped.

From deep down under the surface, the hollow sockets of a skull stared back at her.

Chapter 25

Kate slumped down in a chair on the deck of the main house, shivering and clutching a cup of tea which had long since gone cold. Tears choked her, and she'd hardly gotten a good breath since making her gruesome discovery several hours before.

Trina. It had to be Trina.

Her stomach roiled at the grisly recollection of seeing a dead person. It was too horrifying to bear. Just like last time.

Last time. Poor Karen.

She blinked against the memory. She'd have to wash her mind clean of it, along with today's discovery, if she ever wanted to live a normal life again.

"Why aren't they doing anything?" Jessica leaned against the railing, shifting from foot to foot in an effort to get a better view of the dock below. "All they're doing is standing there talking."

"I...I don't know." Bleary-eyed, Kate glanced down through the trees at the sheriff and several deputies on the dock. There had been a bustle of activity when the sheriff's boat had first arrived, and they had questioned everyone on the property before hemming in the area with crime tape.

Now everything seemed so quiet. The dark clouds had chased the sun nearly to the horizon, and a cold breeze had kicked up from the water. A rainstorm hovered just above, adding to the heaviness in the air.

Shuddering against the wind, Kate raised her eyes to where the *Magnificent Obsession* sat out in the bay. She wanted more than ever to just be out there relishing the safety of the boat and hearing Sam's assurance that everything was going to be okay.

Kate tapped a nervous finger against her cup. Where *was* Sam? If only Kate had her phone, she could call her and make sure she knew what was going on. And she could call Chase and ask him to explain the things Stuart had told her.

She sighed. If she was honest with herself, the first person she'd call if she found her phone would be Josh. A hollow feeling inside her grew. Josh was gone. Off to live his life. A life in which there was no place for her.

The news of her discovery probably hadn't reached him, since he'd been traveling on the ferry then in his car with the broken radio. When he heard, would he call her? She looked out at the yacht again. She *had* to find that phone.

She looked around, unnerved by the silence.

"Where is everybody?"

"Gone." Jessica sniffed. "After the sheriff talked to all my friends, he told them they were free to go, so they bailed. Who can blame them, right?" She wrapped her arms around herself and stared out at the dock. "I mean, who wants to be around my freak show of a family?"

Cognizant of the ease with which she could respond the wrong way, Kate settled for a sympathetic nod. She watched as Jessica pulled her sweater closer around herself and chewed on her thumbnail, wondering if she dared say anything to her about her 'freak show' of a brother. She opted to tread lightly. "Where's Stuart?"

Jessica rolled her eyes. "He's probably drowning his sorrows…" Her voice trailed off as she tossed Kate a guilty look. "Sorry. Bad choice of words. I'm sure this news sent him over the edge." She blinked at her second poor word choice. "He and my mom had a rough time with each other, but the last couple of years she was here she really tried to help him. He appreciated that."

"Help him with his drinking, you mean?"

She nodded, taking a couple of steps closer to Kate and leaning on a glass-topped table. "She actually got him into rehab. He was clean and sober, and Mom was really proud of him."

"Clean and sober?" Kate thought about what he'd told her about the last day Trina was seen alive. "So the day she disappeared, he was lucid?"

"Oh yeah. Then her disappearance sent him into a total tailspin. I think it reminded him of his own mom. You know…he's never gotten over that."

Kate nodded. Small wonder, especially with no resolution to his own memories of the incident.

She calculated her words. "How was your mom getting along with Chase…your dad, before she disappeared?"

The look on Jessica's face told Kate more than she would have liked. "I told the police my parents never fought, but that wasn't exactly true. He can get pretty angry."

Kate's stomach lurched. Could she really have been so wrong about Chase?

Jessica sat on the chair next to Kate, her eyes filling. "I know what everyone says about my dad, but I just couldn't believe it. I kept hoping Mom would come home." She wiped her eyes with the sleeve of her sweater. "I was awful to her. I thought she must have left because of me. I've spent the last year hoping she'd come home so I could tell her I was sorry for the way I acted. For all the things I said."

Jessica's sentiment hit Kate with a painful familiarity. She longed to tell her own mother the same thing.

Jessica blew out a breath. "But now, I have to admit that what everyone says happened might really be true. I have to face that she's not coming back."

A scuffling sound pulled their attention to the stairs leading up from the shoreline.

"Excuse me, ladies." The sheriff reached the top step, stopping a courteous distance from them. Dark splotches marred his taupe, button-front shirt in a pattern that suggested he'd gotten as close a look at the body as he could without actually diving in to join it.

Kate kept her head down. The man had questioned her earlier, but she'd still been in shock. It hadn't really occurred to her then that the local law enforcement might study the national fugitive lists. Sure, she'd changed her appearance, but she lived in terror of being found out for what she had done.

"I'm sorry to tell you, but we won't have any answers for you tonight." He spoke in a compassionate, fatherly tone. "I called for a CSI unit, and they'll be here tomorrow." He cautioned a step closer. "It's going to be getting dark soon, and they'll want to bring the body up in full daylight."

"Of course." Kate lifted her eyes to meet his. To her relief, his expression didn't give any hint of suspicion of her. "But, is it safe to just leave it…you know…overnight?"

His smile reassured. "Deputy Sheriff Joel has volunteered to stay to keep watch over the dock area."

Kate shuddered. Keep watch over a submerged corpse? That was one job she wouldn't be caught dead doing.

A sob slipped from Jessica's throat.

Shifting from foot to foot, the sheriff winced. "Is there anything we can do for you, Miss Cole?"

Jessica turned to face the water, shaking her head and wiping her eyes. "I just can't believe she was…right…there." Her words came out between gasps, as if the full weight of the situation had just hit her. "Under the dock. This whole time."

The sheriff drew in a long breath. "Not likely this whole time. My guess is that the tide dragged her in."

Kate looked up, alarm choking her. "The tide?"

"We did a thorough search of the waterfront when Mrs. Cole went missing last year. They would have seen her if she'd been close to shore. It seems most likely that she started out somewhere in the bay or even beyond and washed in. That's the thing about the water. It has its secrets, but you wait long enough and the tide with tell the truth." He grunted, clearly not seeing a need to elaborate further.

Kate exchanged an uneasy glance with Jessica. The whole idea that Trina had been out there in the water for an entire year horrified her. Looking out at the bay, she clutched her elbows, wishing she'd thought to grab a sweater off the yacht that morning.

She perked up at the sound of a powerboat slapping against the water as it rounded the tip of Shaw across the bay. Sam had said she was taking a powerboat. Maybe this was her.

It reduced speed before curving into the bay and heading toward the yacht. If this was Sam, she might have slowed at the sight of the yellow crime tape swathing the dock.

"I hate to ask." The sheriff ran a hand through his thinning hair. "But do either of you ladies know the whereabouts of Chase Cole?"

Jessica paled at the implication of the question. She just shook her head and turned away.

Feeling ridiculous for not being in better touch with the man she was supposed to marry in a few days, Kate offered up what she knew. "He's in Las Vegas. I would have tried to call him, but I lost my phone and…" Realizing how pathetic she sounded, she let her sentence go unfinished.

The sheriff's chin dipped a fraction, as if this were an uncomfortable topic for him as well. "It's important that we speak as soon as possible. If you hear from him, I'd appreciate you passing on the message."

Kate nodded again, losing sight of the powerboat as it pulled around to the other side of the yacht. It must be Sam, but what was she doing?

She glanced over at another officer making his way up the stairs, a look of urgency creasing his young face. As he reached the deck, he tipped a greeting to Kate, then let his gaze rest on Jessica.

"What is it, Joel?" The sheriff's voice rasped with weariness.

The younger man—apparently Deputy Sheriff Joel—cleared his throat. "I finished securing the perimeter. It looks like someone might have tried to get over the fence down a ways from the front gate."

A fresh wave of terror spiked in Kate's veins. *Get over the fence?* Her entire plan had rested on the theory that no one could get to her here. Had she been wrong to believe that?

Chapter 26

The sheriff pinched the bridge of his nose. "Do we need to send someone to do some repair work on that fence?"

"No." Deputy Joel shook his head. "I just noticed that a tree on the other side had a branch hanging down low, kinda resting on the spikes at the top. I thought it looked like someone might've tried to use it to climb over."

Startled, Kate considered the implications.

"I'll have a look tomorrow." The sheriff ran a hand over his chin. "I've about had it with those reporters. They'll do anything to get a lead on this story."

Deputy Joel straightened with an almost-military air of efficiency. "I told Mindy to let any media people who get wind of this know that you'll give an official statement when you get back to the station."

"Good." The sheriff grunted. "The last thing we need is to have them poking around here right now."

"I don't think we have much to worry about."

Deputy Joel went on. "That situation over in Friday Harbor has taken the focus away from the Cole family. Every reporter in the area is trying to get an exclusive with Shania Hane. No one even seems to know about what's happening here."

Thank goodness. Kate made a silent vow to thank Shania Hane in person if she ever had the opportunity. It was horrible what she'd gone through, but at least the timing had been fortuitous.

With a promise to return to the house as soon as possible in the morning, the sheriff retreated down the stairs.

Jessica rubbed her temples. "I can't stay here." She wiped her hand across her eyes and looked at Deputy Joel. "Tad, is it okay if I go stay with a friend in Seattle?"

Tad? Kate couldn't help but notice a slight upturn in the young man's demeanor at Jessica's use of his first name.

He cleared his throat. "I don't see why not."

Redness crept up his neck, a sure sign that it had been more than professional obligation that had motivated Deputy Sheriff Tad Joel to volunteer for the unsavory position of night watchman over a dead body.

"If…you…" He stammered a little. "…want to leave me your contact information, I can let you know if anything new comes up."

Smooth, Tad. Kate put her hand to her mouth

to conceal a smile.

"That's sweet." Jessica actually sounded sincere. "But I'm worried about you. You're not just going to sit out on the dock all night are you? I mean," she glanced up at the dark clouds overhead that were quickly turning an ominous black with the setting of the sun. "The sky's about to open up."

"It's nice of you to worry, Miss Cole." He shrugged. "But we keep a squad car behind the general store for when we need to get around the island. I can park it down by the dock and stay nice and dry."

"Oh." She nodded. "Well, I could take you to get it. When I go to the ferry, I mean."

"Great." He brightened at the suggestion. "My boss would appreciate not having to swing the boat over to the main dock to drop me off."

Kafe rolled in her lips as Jessica and the starry-eyed deputy retreated into the house.

As she turned back to see if the speedboat had left the yacht, something on the shore below hooked the corner of her eye. It was Stuart. She watched as he picked up the tip of a kayak and dragged it into the water.

She frowned. Between the discovery of Trina and the brewing storm, it seemed like a strange time to go for a boat ride, but maybe that was how he blew off steam.

Watching him step into the small vessel, she

felt like a ping pong ball that had just been batted back to the doubts-about-Chase side of the table. Stuart wasn't the only one who would be adrift if Chase were arrested for Trina's murder.

A cold gust blew a wisp of hair across Kate's face. As she turned her head to flick it away, something caught her attention on the chaise behind her. Sam's jacket. Shivering again, she reached for it. It was almost as if Sam had left it for her, knowing she'd need it. She slipped her arms into it, instantly feeling not only warm, but protected.

The reminder of her need to be mothered was almost too much for her to bear. Sinking into a chair, she put her face in her hands and allowed the tears to come. Thoughts raced through her mind too quickly to dwell on any one. Her mom…Dakota…Josh. So many people she cared about but had pushed away. Why did she do that?

For several minutes, she allowed her crying jag to run its course. When she finally lowered her hands from her face, her bleary eyes caught the movement of a ferry, glowing a soft pink against the royal blue water as it made its way toward Shaw Island.

The quiet thought that Jessica would make it onto this boat quickly led to an unsettling realization. If Jessica and Tad had gone, that meant Kate would be left alone in the house with Stuart. The thought propelled her to her feet.

She scanned the water, but there was no sign of the kayak. It was getting dark, so it was only a matter of time before he returned.

Glancing down at the dock, she noted that the sheriff's boat was gone. A cold awareness that she was alone and unprotected cloaked her. She had to get out of there.

Just as she started for the stairs, the muted sound of familiar sci-fi music jolted her to a halt. *Her phone.* But where was the sound coming from?

She quirked an ear and quickly honed in on…*herself?*

Then it hit her. The sound was coming from the pocket of Sam's jacket.

Perplexed, she plucked the phone from the pocket, giving the screen a fleeting glance. *Chase.* Adrenaline shot through her, numbing the connection between her brain and her voice as she clicked 'accept'.

"Hello? Katie?" Chase's voice sounded tinny and distant.

"Ch…Chase." Her voice came out in a squeak. "Did you hear what happened? That I…found her?"

"Yes. Yes, I know." His tone seemed clipped, dismissive. "Are you all right?"

All right? How could she be? "I…I'm fine." Her mind whirled. Should she say something about what Stuart had told her? That he had seen Emily's body, not in the pool but next to it? And that he had seen Chase here the night of Trina's disappearance?

No. Trina had confronted Chase about Emily, and if Stuart's theory was correct, she had died because of it. She couldn't say anything to Chase about that. It was too risky.

"Good." His voice sounded stern. Businesslike. "Where's Sam?"

"Uh…" Kate shifted on her feet. If the powerboat was still on the far side of the yacht, she couldn't see it, and she didn't know if that had been the one Sam had borrowed anyway. She stammered into the phone. "I…I don't know. She went to meet someone."

He muttered something incoherent.

She pressed the phone closer to her ear. "What? Chase, I can't under—"

"Katie, listen." He came off sounding like a drill sergeant. "Go to the guesthouse and stay there."

The guesthouse? But she'd only feel safe on the yacht. Then it registered that Chase didn't know about the note, or the noises outside her window. "But, I can't. I—"

"Don't open the door to anyone."

His disregard for her objections grated on her. How could she talk to him if he wouldn't listen? "Chase, the sheriff needs to speak to you."

"You've spoken with the sheriff?" Anxiety threaded through his tone.

"Of course." She frowned. "You need to call him right away. Tell him again that you don't know what happened to Trina."

There was no answer, just ambient noise on the line that made her wonder where he could be.

"Chase…" This ambiguity was killing her. Josh was right. She had to know the truth, and now that she was a safe distance away from Chase, this might be her only chance to ask.

Rallying all her courage, she carefully considered how much she should say. "You *don't* know what happened…right?"

He made an uneasy sound in his throat. "Katie…this situation is so much more complicated than…" He cut himself off.

She huffed out impatience. Out of fear, she had kept quiet about Karen, and Joe had gone free. If she had been courageous enough to speak up, would he have been arrested? She couldn't make the same mistake twice.

She blurted out the words. "Because…I talked to Stuart."

"Stuart?" The slightest quiver in his voice suggested that he knew what was coming.

"Yes. He told me that he saw you here at the house the night Trina disappeared. Why were you here, Chase?"

There was no answer. Just an indistinct announcement of some kind blaring in the background. Where was he? An airport?

She felt her fear falling away. "He also told me he remembers the night Emily died. That he saw her lying next to the pool. Do you know anything about that?"

A long moment stretched out in which she heard nothing from Chase but the sound of his breathing. When he spoke again, his voice was low and fierce. "Tell me you didn't repeat any of that to anyone."

The question jolted her. "No...I—"

"You didn't tell the sheriff, did you?"

Had she? Thinking straight suddenly seemed impossible. "Chase, I just need to know—"

"Or to Joshua?"

"What? No." Confusion overtook her. "Josh is gone."

"Gone?" Something clanked in the background followed by the far-off sound of someone shouting. "What do you mean, he's gone?"

"I mean I didn't think I needed him anymore and I let him go."

"You let him..." A loud jangling noise overlapped Chase's next words, making it impossible for her to decipher them.

It didn't matter, because all she could think was that he wasn't answering her questions. That could mean only one thing. He was guilty of one or both of his wives' murders. And now he knew that Kate knew.

Her blood felt like ice water in her veins.

"Listen to me, Kate. Stay in the guesthouse. Don't let anyone in, do you understand?"

Mind racing, she picked her purse up off the deck and secured it over her head and one shoulder, calculating how long it would take her to hobble down to the dock. Then all she'd have to do was get the dinghy out to the yacht. Sam would be back soon and Kate would tell her everything she'd found out. Together, they would make a plan. It was all going to be okay.

Across the bay, the ferry pulled into the terminal. Its horn sounded, followed by a faint echo.

Kate's stomach jumped. That hadn't been her imagination. She'd heard the horn, then a slightly delayed repeat of the same sound *over the phone.*

Chase wasn't in Vegas. He was on the ferry.

Chapter 27

Panic seared through Kate like wild fire. Trina had turned up dead because she had confronted Chase about Emily's death. How could Kate have been so foolish as to have done the same thing?

The threat of Joe finding her suddenly felt distant and unreal. Chase was equally dangerous, and he'd be there in a matter of minutes.

Gripping the railing, she started down the stairs. All she had to do was get to the dock, and pray that she could start that motor.

Moving as quickly as her leg would allow, she made it down the stairs and onto the trail. Groaning from pain and effort, she stumbled past the guesthouse to the place where Stuart had accosted her earlier. Her eyes darted around as she made sure she was alone this time. Steeling herself against the pain, she looked at the path ahead. *Almost there.*

Thank goodness she had left her suitcase on the yacht so she could run and not look back. Her habit of keeping all her most important possessions in one place had always served her well. Automatically, she ticked off her mental inventory. Her sweatshirt. Her favorite jeans. The money pouch. Her photos.

She lurched to a halt. *Her photos.*

It all came back to her. Sitting at the kitchen island in the guesthouse talking to Josh. She had stashed her photos between the cookbooks, intending to move them later, but she hadn't.

She reeled around and stared at the guesthouse looming above her. There was no time to vacillate. Those photos were all she had left of her childhood. Of her mother. She had to get them.

Somehow, she managed to pull herself up the stairs while fumbling for the house key in her purse. Praying that she'd make it before Chase arrived and found her there, she scrambled to unlock the back door. As it creaked open, the shadowy kitchen eased into view and an eerie sense that something was wrong crept over her. She reached for the wall next to the door and flicked a light switch, then froze.

All the cabinets and drawers had been flung open, their contents scattered across the floor. In the living room, the cushions had been pulled from the sofas. A lamp lay on its side in the middle of the room.

Panic propelled her back to the doorway, but she stopped. Her photos were just a few feet away. She couldn't go without them.

She listened. If whoever did this was still in

299

the house, had she made enough noise to alert him to her presence? Gingerly, she limped to the center of the room, hearing nothing but the wind outside and her pulse thrumming through her veins.

Bracing herself against the edge of the kitchen island, she quickly made her way around to the other side and knelt in front of the bookshelf. Just as she began to paw through the volumes, something behind her clicked. *A key in the front door.* She popped up just as it opened and the shape of a man materialized in the doorway. Her breath caught.

Chase.

She drew back. His normally impeccable appearance had transformed into something careless and desperate. His wild eyes seemed tinged with fear, an emotion she'd never seen him show.

As he stepped into the room, he registered the condition of the house. "Katie…. What happened here?"

She used the counter to steady herself as she scuttled to its other side. "I…I…don't…" She looked around, gauging the distance to the back door. But even if she made it outside, how could she hope to get down to the dock without him catching up to her?

"We need to go," he commanded in a tone that left no leeway for discussion. "Quickly, before someone comes."

Look around, she thought. *Someone already has.*

"Come on." Marching toward her, he reached out a hand. "They'll be here soon."

Shaking her head, she attempted to draw back. "Who?"

"Reporters…the police." He rounded the counter with an uncharacteristic swiftness and grabbed her arm. "I expected them to be at the gate, but now it's only a matter of time."

As he yanked at her, she cried out in pain. "Chase, my knee!"

Hesitating, he shot her a confused glare. "What about it?"

"I think I sprained it."

With a disgusted grunt, he hoisted her into his arms and started for the front door.

"Chase, stop!" Trying hard to ignore the amplified pain caused by his hand digging into her leg, she held fast to his shoulders to keep from falling.

He charged through the door he'd left open. Kate shivered, both from the bracing wind and her growing fear.

Grunting with the exertion, he slowed slightly in response to the incline of the trail. "We need to get off the island before the place is overrun."

"But, where are we going?"

"Never mind." He struggled to catch his breath. "We'll talk in the car."

"But, I—"

"You have to trust me." Reaching the driveway, he set her on her feet next to his car. "Get in."

"I don't understand." She stepped back as he flung open the passenger door. "Why can't you just talk to the police?"

Grabbing both of her arms with so much force it made her yelp, he glared at her. "You don't understand what they've got on me, Kate. We have to move!" He shoved her into the car.

The slamming of the door was followed by a soft *click*. She scrambled for the handle but it wouldn't budge. Her fingers found the switch for the lock, but the door still held. He had her locked in. Like a child who needed to be restrained.

As he crossed around the front of the car, panic held her in its grip. She had to get away, but how?

He got into the car and started the engine.

"Chase, please tell me where we're—"

"There's so much you don't understand." His hands shook on the wheel as he started down the driveway.

She stared at him. He was right. She didn't understand.

Darkness overtook them as he drove out of the open area and onto the part of the driveway that was lined by tall, swaying trees.

"Chase, we can't leave. There aren't any more ferries tonight."

"I keep a seaplane on the other side of the island. Once we're away from here, I'll call the pilot."

"Won't he know? About the body being found? And that you shouldn't leave the island?"

"For the right price, he'll fly us to the moon if I ask him to."

Her heart raced. That would explain how he had managed to be on the island the night Trina disappeared without anyone knowing. He could buy people's silence.

"You have to understand, Kate. They want to put me in prison."

Her stomach reeled. "Oh…?"

"And now that Trina has been found…" He chewed on his lip, clearly not used to things being out of his control.

Suddenly, his eyes widened and the car jolted to a stop. Hurtling toward the dashboard, Kate caught a glimpse of something moving in the driveway ahead. A sheriff's car. It was Tad!

The squad car swerved at an angle and stopped squarely in front of them. Chase pounded his hand against his steering wheel and barked out an expletive, the intensity of which made Kate cower.

Tad got out of his car and shone a flashlight as he approached. "Chase Cole?" His voice sounded small, as if he wasn't sure he was up to this. "The sheriff needs to talk to you, sir."

Chase worked his jaw as his eyes skirted around the car in front of him. Kate drew in a jagged breath. What was he thinking of doing?

Tad stopped a few feet from Chase's window and waited. Looking ill at ease, He shone the light at Chase, who sat rigid, gripping the wheel and refusing to budge. "I'll have to bring you in for questioning, Mr. Cole." He took a couple of steps back. "Wait right there. I'm going to radio our office."

Chase shifted gears and his car started to move in reverse.

"What are you doing?" Kate shrieked, grasping at the dash and the console between them for support.

Without answering, Chase shifted again and started to peel forward.

Whipping around, Tad reached for his holster. Raising his gun, he dove into Chase's path. "Whoa, stop right there!" He yelled, his voice and hands clearly shaking.

As Chase attempted to run his car through the narrow space between the squad car and the trees, Tad hurtled his body in front of him. There was a sickening *thunk*, and Tad flew in the air, landing in a heap in front of Chase's car.

Kate screamed as Chase hit the brake and she flew forward again.

As she pushed herself back from the dash, all was silent except for Chase's wheezing breath. He stared ahead with fear-filled eyes, but there was no movement outside the car.

"What have I done?" Suddenly, he opened his door and leapt from the car.

Kate leaned forward, watching as he knelt down next to Tad's prone body.

Emotion rendered her frozen, but only for a moment. Then the sheer will to survive kicked her into action. Without thinking, she slid over into the driver's seat and shifted the car into reverse. Chase looked up, confusion flashing across his face.

Sitting forward so she could reach the pedals, Kate turned her head, backing the car until she reached the narrow road down to the dock.

Scooting forward in the seat that was adjusted for Chase's longer legs, she gasped for breath. What was she doing?

She couldn't second guess herself now. Not when this might be her only chance.

Raindrops pinged against the windshield and she fumbled unsuccessfully to find the switch for the wipers. Giving up the search, she aimed blindly down the drive, relieved to make out a row of dim lights that delineated the edge of the dock.

Reaching level ground, she slammed to a halt and removed the keys from the ignition. A vague thought that Chase must have a key to the yacht on this ring made taking it seem like a good idea.

Yellow tape fluttered in the wind like a flag as she dragged herself out onto the dock.

She tried not to look at the area where she knew the body rested, or to think about poor Tad, who was supposed to be there watching over it. She stumbled to the dinghy, praying that the engine would start this time.

She sat down on the cold, wet dock and slid her body carefully into the unsteady craft. She pulled the start cord. Nothing. She did it a second time. To her relief, the engine came to life. Quickly, she pushed in the choke, looking toward the shore. All she saw was Chase's car, but no sign of him.

It took everything she had to focus on remembering the steps Sam had taught her, but she managed to pull the boat away from the dock and aim it toward the softly lit form of the yacht. A light rain hit her face and danced down her neck and the small boat rolled on the wavy water.

She fought tears along with nausea. How had her life gone so wildly out of control?

A long minute later, she pulled up next to the yacht, then killed the motor and reached for the metal bar at the edge of the swim platform. She tied the rope at the tip of the dingy to it. Soaked and shivering, she fought the movement of both vessels on the undulating water, and pulled herself onto the wet platform.

Depleted of strength and afraid to stand on the slippery, unstable surface, Kate crawled to the closer of the two stairways that led to the hot tub deck. She grasped at the handrail and managed to pull herself to a standing position on the bottom step, then started up, grateful at least that the rain had subsided.

Hearing an odd sound, she glanced down to her left. Something was in the water, scraping against the side of the boat.

A kayak.

She froze. It hadn't even occurred to her that Stuart might have come out to the yacht. Her mind raced. Why hadn't she remembered what Sam had said about him coming out here whenever he needed to talk to her?

Before she could move, a scuffling sound from up on the deck jolted her down to a crouch on the stairs. Expecting to see Stuart, she leaned back and peered through the batwing gate at the top of the stairs.

Her blood ran cold. It wasn't Stuart.

It was Joe.

Chapter 28

Terror and disbelief engulfed Kate as she bent down and prayed that Joe hadn't seen her. Her mind whirled. What was he doing on the yacht?

Instinct told her to make a dash for the safety of the dinghy but before she could move, a sound from the deck below caught her attention.

Peering through the space between the stairs and the metal half-wall which concealed her, she saw Stuart stumbling out of the door to the lower bedroom level and onto the swim platform. The boat rolled, and he banged against the wall below the stairway opposite her, dropping something and letting out an expletive.

She looked down as he bent to pick up whatever it was he had dropped. She gasped in recognition. *Her money pouch!*

Joe must have heard him too, because in an instant he stood at the deck railing, just a few feet away from Kate's head. She could barely see him through the space between the half-wall and the railing.

"What are you doing?" He shouted down at

Stuart. "I thought you left."

He thought he had *left?* Did they know each other? Heart pounding, Kate crouched lower, praying that neither of them would see her. The boat rolled on a wave, sending a surge of queasiness through her stomach.

Clutching the pouch to his chest and struggling to maintain his footing, Stuart looked over his shoulder and up at Joe. "I...I had to get something."

The money. He'd come back to get the money, and he didn't want Joe to know.

But how had Stuart found it? Had he come here looking for Sam and decided to go through Kate's suitcase? The thought amplified her queasiness.

And if Joe had tracked her here, why hadn't he found the money first? Surely he wouldn't have wasted any time, but he must have started his search elsewhere.

She cringed. The thought of either of them going through her things made her stomach roil. Holding her breath, she prayed that Joe would go back inside and that Stuart would get into the kayak. Then she could safely bolt for the dinghy.

Joe glowered down at Stuart, his gray eyes flaring, as he apparently assessed the situation. Then, lifting his gaze, he scanned the distant shoreline. Watching for her? That prospect made her shiver.

Suddenly, his face darkened. "Wait a minute."

She followed his gaze. The dinghy! It was a dead giveaway of her presence.

Her eyes flicked up at Joe, who frowned as if trying to remember if it had been there before.

"What's that?" Joe pointed with his chin as he started for the other stairway.

Kate exhaled, grateful that he hadn't chosen the stairs on which she hid. She had to act quickly. At the pace he was moving, he'd be able to see her hiding place in a matter of seconds.

Crouching low, she scampered soundlessly to the top of the stairs, then under the batwing gate to where Joe had been standing just a few seconds before. She peered down from under the railing. He now stood right next to where the dinghy was tied. That had been close, but what was she going to do now?

"This boat wasn't here before, was it?" Joe's voice sounded over the noise of the wind and the water. "Isn't this what Kathy was supposed to use to get out here?"

Kathy. The sound of him saying her name made her want to retch.

Looking around, she thought fast. If she moved quickly, she could crawl to the other side of the hot tub. That would conceal her while she made a dash for the door to the salon. Once inside, she could lock herself into a bathroom and call for help.

Ignoring the searing pain in her knee, she prepared to make her move. Joe was angry and had caught on that she was on the boat. She had to hurry or she'd be sunk.

Just as she was about to move, the boat pitched and her purse slipped from her shoulder. As she reached to retrieve it, she saw Stuart stumble again, raising both arms to keep his balance and inadvertently revealing the pouch in his hand.

"Hey." Joe started toward him. "That's mine!"

Stuart tried to dive for the kayak, but Joe flew at him, grabbing for the money.

"It's not yours. It's Kate's." Stuart wrapped his arms around the pouch and hunched over as Joe tried to get at it.

Looking furious, Joe reached into his shirt pocket. He fingered something, then raised his arm over his head. "Give it to me or I'll kill you!"

Recognizing the object in Joe's hand, Kate went numb. A scalpel.

No! Stuart might be a creep, but she couldn't let Joe kill him over something that was her fault. If only her legs would move, she could call for help. But how long would it take them to arrive?

There was no time. She had to do something now.

She grabbed hold of the railing, then pulled herself to her feet. "No!"

Both men turned to stare up at her.

"Just give him the money, Stuart." She shouted to be heard over the whipping wind. "It's not worth it."

Stuart clung to the cash. "But you said you'd help me."

She frowned. Was that why he had thought she could buy him a house? He knew about the money even then?

"I'm not kidding, Stuart." She regarded the scalpel, which Joe had lowered but not retracted. There was no time for discussion. "He says he'll kill you and he means it." When Stuart still looked unconvinced, she added, "He's done it before."

Joe's face hardened, a fire of realization igniting in his eyes.

The air left her lungs. What had she just done? If he hadn't realized before that she knew about Karen, clearly he did now.

Taking a step backward, she waved Stuart toward the kayak. "Hurry, Stuart. Forget about the money. Just go."

In one swift motion, Joe reeled around, grabbed the pouch out of Stuart's hands and plunged the scalpel into him.

Stuart made a choking sound then fell back in a heap. Joe pulled the scalpel free and started for the stairs.

Kate gasped. She moved as quickly as she could toward the door to the salon, but Joe grabbed her arms and shoved her forward. Her upper body slammed against the covered hot tub, knocking the wind out of her. She pushed herself around to face him.

"You saw, didn't you?" He stood just inches from her, the money pouch in one hand and the blade in the other.

Fear tightened her throat. "S…saw?"

"You know what I'm talking about, Kathy. You know about that Hingston woman, don't you?"

"I…I…I don't…" She wanted to lie, but denial seemed futile.

"You *saw*." He fingered the scalpel. "How else would you know?" He waved the weapon in her direction. "Who did you tell?"

"Nobody." She stared at the red smear on the blade and fought lightheadedness. "I mean, I haven't told anybody." She cringed. So much for denial.

"Don't play games with me, Kathy." He spit out the words.

"I'm not, I swear."

He regarded her for a long moment, then backed off slightly. "I *had* to kill her, you know." He tucked the pouch into the front of his shirt. "It was the only way to shut her up."

She nodded, as if his reasoning made perfect sense. Maybe if she got his mind off Karen, she could make him think they were allies. "I…I took the money by mistake, and I'm sorry. But everything's fine now. You can go back to running the clinic, just like before."

He pierced her with a glare. "There *is* no clinic. It's closed."

Closed? She didn't care about the clinic, but it had been a safe haven for her friends. If the clinic was gone, where was Dakota? "What happened to everyone?"

"How should I know?" His voice rumbled low and menacing. "That Hingston woman was going to turn me in. Send me to jail for scamming her poor sick father." He clucked a maniacal laugh. "Stupid woman. No one will connect her to me, and even if they do, I'll be back in Mexico."

Slowly, Kate nodded. There had to be a way out of this. She'd been through too much to give up now.

His focus on her sharpened. "But I'm not dumb enough to take any chances." He raised his arm, and the blade glinted against the dark sky.

Kate flailed. Her hand clasped the neck of the champagne bottle on the bar next to her. She raised it high, then swung it at his arm. The scalpel flew from his hand and skipped across the deck.

As Joe let out a roar of pain, Kate attempted to run. At the top of the stairs. he grabbed her from behind, cursing.

She thrashed against him, but she was no match for his strength. He struck her hard across the side of the head, sending her tumbling sideways, her upper body hurtling over the railing at the edge of the deck. Before she could push herself upright, Joe took hold of her legs and heaved her over. She caught a dizzying glimpse of the inky black water as she careened toward it, then felt herself being consumed by its freezing depths.

She thrashed and fought to get back to the surface, but it was no use. Her damaged right leg had been rendered motionless, becoming more anchor than oar.

She was going to die, and there was nothing anybody could do to prevent it.

Depleted, she stopped fighting. As she drifted toward unconsciousness, something Josh had once said pressed to the forefront of her mind. *God always has my back.*

He was right. She had been turning to people to keep her safe, and they hadn't saved her. She should have been turning to God all along. That was what he had been trying to tell her without pushing it on her.

A sensation of sinking into silent darkness seemed strangely comforting. She had fought hard in this life and done the best she could, but she couldn't fight any more. At any moment, she'd give in and surrender her final breath.

Then something brushed her arm, jerking her back to wakefulness. A hand grabbed her and she started moving upward.

All of a sudden, her head popped through the surface and her lungs filled, not with water as she'd expected, but with life-affirming air.

"Kate!"

Her name sounded both distant and contained in her own head. She gave in to the sensation of being dragged out of the water and onto a solid surface.

"Kate! Kate!"

The voice seemed familiar. She forced her lids to open, blinking past both ocean water and raindrops as she coughed and wheezed. She tried to focus on the face of her rescuer, just inches from hers, framed by the black night sky.

She smiled. "Josh…"

"Thank God." Josh's voice seemed to come from a dream.

Sputtering out something that combined a laugh with a cough, she reached up to touch his cheek, assuring herself that he was indeed real.

The rocking motion of the surface on which she lay brought her back to the reality of the situation. She was once again on the yacht. On the swim platform.

"We have to get you out of here." As Josh sat back, a dark, hazy form appeared behind him. A raised arm. A familiar glint.

She tried to scream as Joe lowered his arm, clearly aiming for her chest.

"No!" Josh shouted, launching himself at Joe.

Terror swelled through Kate like a wave as both men crashed onto the platform. She struggled to pull herself to a sitting position, and when she looked up again, Joe knelt less than three feet from her. His eyes glowed with heated determination. Slowly, he drew his arm over his head, and Kate put her hands to her face, bracing herself for the impact of the blade.

Suddenly, there was a loud *thwump*. She looked up to see Joe tumble off the end of the platform. In front of her, Stuart wavered on unsteady legs, wielding an oar in his hands. A gasp of disbelief quivered from Kate's throat as Stuart collapsed like a marionette to a sitting position.

Relief quickly turned to horror as she registered the motionless shape on the floor next to him.

"Josh!"

Letting out a weak sob, she clambered to him on her hands and knees. He lay on his side with his arms outstretched. The sight terrified her.

As she rolled him onto his back, his hand fell away from his chest. Kate saw that it was covered with something dark that dripped away with the rain.

Blood.

Chapter 29

Tears mixed with the raindrops streaming down Kate's face as she bent over Josh, relieved to feel his warm breath against her cheek. She looked up as the distant wail of a siren offered a ray of hope.

His eyes fluttered open.

"Hold on, Josh" Her voice came out barely above a whisper. "Help is coming."

He tried to raise his head. "I'll…be okay." His words were thready, and not very convincing.

"Of course you will." Kate glanced over at Stuart, who was waving an oar to get the attention of the approaching sheriff's boat, then returned her focus to Josh. "You shouldn't have come back."

"I had to." He flinched, barely managing to meet her gaze. "You needed me."

Kate swallowed a sob. In spite of everything she'd been telling herself for the past several days, she could no longer deny the obvious. She loved Josh. He was the one for her, not Chase. And now he might die because of her.

She tried to give him a reassuring smile, but a

growing circle of blood on his shirt gave little comfort. She had to keep him alert until help arrived. "But…you're afraid of water. How did you manage to dive in?"

"I…pretended I was the…hero in that movie. You know the one…" His words came out between shallow breaths. "*The Ugly Swamp Thing That…Ate the World*. I had to rescue you from the…bad guy in a…cheap costume."

"With a zipper down the back." Blinking back tears, Kate grabbed his hand. "Did you ever notice that?"

"Yeah…" He smiled. "Sure sign of a…" His grip on her hand tightened. "…low…budget."

Blue lights flashed across the platform as the sirens ceased. Kate looked up to see the sheriff's boat pull in next to the yacht along with what looked like an ambulance boat. Stuart dropped the oar and fell back onto the stairway.

In an instant, the buzz of a police radio and a flurry of activity filled the yacht. A female deputy helped Kate to her feet while a couple of medics went to work on Josh. Kate glanced over at Stuart, who was sprawled on the stairs, also being tended to. The thought that either of them might die because of her was more than she could bear.

That thought brought a fresh reminder of the danger they'd faced and the reason for it. She looked out at the water, to the place where Joe had fallen in. "The…the man who did this…. He's out there."

"Don't worry." The deputy put a calming hand on her shoulder and tipped her head toward the sheriff's boat, where an officer escorted a handcuffed and soaking wet Joe into the cabin. "One of our deputies apprehended him making a lame attempt to paddle away in a kayak." She stopped just short of an eye roll. "Landlubber."

Kate nearly collapsed against the woman's shoulder. Joe had been arrested. Her nightmare was finally ending.

"Miss Jennings." The sheriff appeared, looking even more overwrought than he had earlier in the evening. "You've had quite a day."

She gulped, then reeled in her courage. It was time to come clean.

"That man who attacked us…his name is Joe Malone. He's responsible for a murder in San Diego. And a scam that led to at least one death, probably more."

The sheriff gaped at her for a moment. "Well now. I think you and I need to have a long talk."

A wave hit the yacht and everyone took a sidestep to compensate. The movement gave Kate a painful reminder of her injury. She bent slightly, unable to keep herself from wincing.

The sheriff reached out to offer her some support. "Looks like your statement can wait till tomorrow. Right now, we need to get you to the ER along with these boys."

With an assurance that he would see her at the hospital in Friday Harbor, the sheriff helped her to a seat in the ambulance boat, then left to deal with Joe. Someone wrapped a blanket around her shoulders as she watched Josh being hooked up to an IV.

The boat started moving, but to Kate's surprise, it headed toward Chase's dock. All her nerves clenched. Why hadn't she remembered to tell the sheriff that Chase was on the island?

"Excuse me." She spoke to a female medic who was preparing to administer a shot to Stuart. "Why are we going back toward Shaw?"

The woman answered without looking up from the syringe she tapped. "We have an officer down."

Tad. With everything that had happened, Kate had forgotten about him. "He was hit by a car. But how did you know…?"

The medic held up the needle and studied it. "We received a 9-1-1 call from a nun."

A nun? Had she heard right?

The three male medics flew into action, grabbing a stretcher and a couple of bright red bags. Kate looked at Josh, grateful that the female medic was apparently staying on the boat while the others went to get Tad.

With her nerves on edge, Kate watched the men make their way toward shore, their heavy-duty lights shining through the driving rain. Squinting, she recognized the outline of Chase's car, and of a second car next to it. She drew in a breath. It was the squad car.

That seemed strange. Had Chase brought Tad down to the dock and called for help? Where did the nun fit in? And more importantly, where was Chase now?

As the men opened the doors of the squad car and dove into rescue mode, Kate scanned the area. There was something behind the trees at the end of the drive. She leaned closer to the window, making out the shape of a third car. Sam's Volvo!

She pushed to her feet. What if Chase got to Sam?

She had to do something. "Excuse me." She moved toward the medic, who was busy scribbling on a clipboard. "Could you let the sheriff know that Chase Cole might be on Shaw Island?"

"Chase Cole?" The woman frowned, barely looking up. "Why didn't you say something sooner?"

Kate sputtered. "Well, I...I..."

"You can tell him yourself at the hospital." The woman turned away, adjusting something on a machine next to Josh.

Feeling dismissed, Kate stepped back. She couldn't just stand here doing nothing when Sam might be in danger.

Pulling the blanket over her head to protect herself from the rain, Kate carefully made her way out of the boat and onto the dock. With eyes watering from the by-now familiar pain, she inched toward the parking area, hoping to be able to see if Sam was inside her car.

As she neared the squad car, the sound of the medics shouting out to each other alarmed her. She peered around them, hoping to catch a reassuring glance at Tad. When she couldn't see him, she hobbled around the front of the car.

Just as she was about to look in through the other open door, a hand grabbed her shoulder. Startled, she whipped around.

"Sam!"

Sam gave her a quick hug, then held her at arm's length. "You're soaked. Come get into my car."

Kate allowed Sam to help her across the small parking area, then through a stand of trees and into the passenger side of her car.

Once inside, Kate let the tears flow. "Oh, Sam. So much happened after you left."

"I know." Sam rubbed her arm. "I'm so sorry I wasn't here. I came as soon as I got the call from the sheriff's office."

"Joe was on the yacht. He wanted to kill me." The words tumbled out of her mouth, practically overlapping each other. "He pushed me over the edge, but Josh rescued me."

Sam's face creased with concern. "Do you know how Joe found you?"

Kate shook her head. "Not really. And I don't know how he knew to find me on the yacht."

"It doesn't matter." Sam took both Kate's hands in hers. "You're safe now. But we need to get you some dry clothes. We can go to the house and get something of Jessica's." Releasing Kate's hands, she reached for the gearshift.

"No!" Kate practically spit out the word. "We can't go to the house. Chase might be there."

"Chase?"

"Yes. He came for me. He tried to get me to go with him, but then he accidentally hit a deputy with his car, and I managed to get away."

Sam's eyes widened. "But…why—"

"Chase is guilty, Sam. He killed Trina. Maybe Emily too."

"What?" All emotion washed from Sam's face. "How do you know?"

Kate quickly relayed everything that Stuart had told her, and what had happened since. She finished just as the medics carried the stretcher onto the boat. "Oh, we need to go." She reached for the door handle.

"No. Wait." Sam started the car. "You're coming with me."

Kate frowned. "But, I need to get back on the boat. Josh is—"

"You're soaked." She backed the car up enough to allow her to pull it out of the space between the trees. "You need a shower and dry clothes. Then we can go to Friday Harbor together."

Kate's heart sank. "But, if we can't go to the house, where—"

"Just let me figure it out." Making a U-turn in the parking area, Sam grabbed her phone. She punched in a number, then turned on her headlights and started up the drive, struggling to see past the rain hitting the windshield.

Kate's thoughts whirred as she twisted around in her seat to see the boat pull away from the dock. It would have made more sense for them to have gotten on it, but it was too late now.

Sam held the phone to her ear and spoke. "Pick up. *Pick up.*" The words shot out like bullets.

Kate gripped her armrest, anxious for Sam to hang up so she could focus on driving.

"I'm coming over to borrow the boat again." She continued to speak into the phone as she curved onto the main drive.

Kate tried to relax. At least now they were on level ground, but it was still impossible to see more than a few feet in front of them. She tried to keep the nervousness out of her voice. "So…we're taking your friend's boat to Friday Harbor?"

Sam seemed not to hear her question. "I know you're not supposed to fly in the dark, Dennis, and only a fool would risk it on a night like this."

Fly? Kate cast her a puzzled glance. What was she talking about?

Sam continued her message. "And I know Chase is there. Don't tell him I'm coming."

"Chase?" Kate's stomach clenched. "You mean your friend with the boat is also Chase's pilot?"

Wordlessly, Sam clicked off the phone and tossed it into the cup holder in the console.

Kate started to panic. "Sam, if you know where Chase is, shouldn't we call the sheriff and tell him?"

"Shut up." Sam focused on the dark road ahead through the rain-pummeled windshield. "You ask too many questions."

Kate stared. "I don't…I mean, I didn't—"

"You ruined everything." Sam's voice hardened along with her features.

A fresh surge of adrenaline renewed Kate's alertness. "What do you mean?"

"You little fool." Sam shook her head. "I've waited for years for Chase to realize I'm the one he belongs with."

"You…" Kate's body went numb. "…you're in love with Chase?"

Sam didn't have to answer. The melancholy filling her eyes did it for her.

Kate shuddered. Why hadn't she seen it before?

"You were supposed to leave with Joe." Sam

struck a fist against the steering wheel. "That was our deal."

Their *deal?* Kate's blood flash-froze in her veins. "You were the one who told Joe where to find me? But…how—"

"You left your purse on the floor. I took your phone to check your contacts. Of course, I wanted that detective to come up here and arrest you, but he was really just trying to scare you to get you to help him collect evidence against Joe. So I found Joe's number instead. He agreed to get you out of my way as long as he got his money."

Kate's teeth clattered in fear. "So that was who you had to go meet today? Joe?"

"I had him flown in. Then I took him to the yacht."

Kate closed her eyes, fighting a wave of nausea as she remembered the small boat that had been near the yacht earlier. "But…if you had told me you loved Chase, I would have understood. We could have worked something out."

Sam leaned forward, squinting, as the car crept ahead. "That was the mistake I made the other times."

Kate slowly turned her head to look at Sam. "*What* other times?"

"The women who got in my way." Her words dripped like melting icicles.

"Emily and Trina?" Kate swallowed against mounting fear. "You killed them? Both of them?"

"I didn't intend to." Sam lifted one shoulder. "Emily tried to fight me when I told her I was in love with Chase. But she was drunk. It wasn't my fault she slipped."

"She...she slipped?"

Sam nodded. "Hit her head. I left her there, but then I realized how easy it would be to get her out of my way. When I went back, she was still unconscious. I dragged her to the pool and pushed her in. She tried to fight, but I held her down till she stopped moving."

Kate let out a small sob. The thought of poor Emily and how confused she must have been made her even queasier.

Sam sniffed. "Then I went home and waited for Chase to call me. I must be a good actress, because he never suspected I already knew she was dead." A sickening smile played on her lips. "Then he protected me without even realizing it."

"Protected you?"

"The policeman wrote in his first report that it looked like a homicide staged to look like an accident."

Something struck Kate as strange. "His *first* report?"

Sam nodded. "Even though he had nothing to do with it, Chase knew that would make him look guilty. So he paid the man to change the report. Drowning. No one ever figured out the truth."

"And...Trina?"

"Trina." Sam shook her head. "Stuart told her just what he told you about the night that Emily died. She came to me, frantic, thinking Chase had done it. So, we took a little cruise out on the yacht. A ladies' night. We sailed out past the bay, and…" Her look turned fierce. "She never deserved Chase. All she wanted was financial support so she could be free to do her *art*. Then she took up with that transient. She was planning to leave soon anyway."

"But…couldn't you have just let her go? You didn't have to—"

"I didn't *mean* to. We were fighting, and she was acting crazy. It was stormy. A wave came and jostled the boat, and she went over the side. She just…never surfaced."

"So…that wasn't your fault."

Sam snapped her a fiery gaze. "Of course it wasn't. Trina was my friend. But once it was done, I realized that she was out of my way. I gave Chase time to mourn. Then just as he was starting to see I was the one he needed, you had to come along and ruin everything."

"But if I had known—"

"I have to get rid of you. And this time it won't be by accident!"

The car slowed, and Kate looked up. They were approaching the gate. She had to get out before they left the property.

"You're just using him for his money."

Reaching for the gate remote on her visor, Sam stopped the car. "The same as Trina."

In one swift move, Kate grabbed Sam's phone and jumped from the car.

Her feet hit the muddy road, and she fumbled with the phone as she tried to run. She felt for the '9' on the dark pad and it lit up. All she had to do was hit 1-1, but the rain beating against her face all but blinded her.

Hearing Sam coming from behind, Kate twisted a look over her shoulder. Sam lunged at her, wrapping her hands around her throat. Struggling for air, Kate tried to loosen Sam's grasp with one hand, while desperately prodding the phone pad with the thumb of the other.

As lightheadedness threatened, Kate thought she saw a figure step in front of the headlights behind Sam. A guttural sound reverberated in her head. As she felt herself start to succumb to the lack of oxygen, a vague thought registered.... *Sasquatch?*

In an instant, Sam's hold on her was relinquished and Kate fell backwards, hitting the swampy road with a thud. Fighting back from the fog of near-unconsciousness, she identified the black-sweat-jacket-clad figure wrestling Sam to the ground.

Scarcely able to speak, she rasped out recognition.

"Dakota?"

Chapter 30

Kate sat at a table on the deck of the main house watching as the divers prepared to go into the water by the dock. The thought of what they were going to bring up was only slightly less horrifying on this bright sunny morning than it had been when she'd discovered it the day before.

Resolving to focus on the bright side, she thanked God again that Josh's stab wound hadn't turned out to be life threatening. He might even get to leave the hospital today if everything went well.

Pushing the black hood off Dakota's head, she watched him dig into a huge bowl of oatmeal. "It's getting warm, Dakota. Are you sure you don't want to take off that sweat jacket?"

Chewing, he shook his head. "The truck driver said I…I…I could keep it."

"I know." Kate smiled at his endearing way of repeating words while his brain caught up to his tongue. Downs Syndrome had denied him precise enunciation, but not the ability to put thoughts into words. "It was smart of you to figure out where I was."

"Iowa saw you on the T...TV." He shoveled in another bite as if he thought he might not get a chance to eat again soon. "The man called you 'K...Kate', but I knew he got it...got it wrong. He said you were marrying a man on...*Sha'island*."

Kate smiled at his focused pronunciation of the two words, as if they were one. "And did you know where that was?"

"No, but B...Ben told me." He smiled proudly. "Washington."

"So you started to walk? Didn't you know how far Washington is from California?"

"No." He shrugged. "But I was happy when that tr...truck driver...stopped for me."

She gave Dakota a reassuring smile. "He must have been an awfully nice man to drive you all the way to Seattle from San Diego."

"Then he helped me get on the bus and told me how to...to...get to the..." He paused, as if trying to remember the correct word. "The *ferry*."

"And then how did you get onto the property?"

"Easy." Dakota shrugged. "I saw a big tr...tree and I climbed it. I swung right over the fence."

"Well, I'm glad you came to find me, but I don't want you to hitchhike ever again, you understand?"

He nodded, swallowing. "I don't want you to

leave ever again. You understand?"

She laughed, throwing an arm around his shoulders. "I understand."

Her heart warmed at the irony. Here she had spent two years thinking Dakota couldn't make it without her there to protect him, and last night he had been the one to rescue her. A shiver passed through her at the thought of what would have happened to her if he hadn't been hiding in the trees, keeping watch over her. God had given her an unlikely guardian, that was for sure.

The French doors clicked open, and Jessica stepped out onto the deck, followed by a disheveled Stuart, who reminded Kate of a wounded puppy with his arm held awkwardly in a sling.

Kate was surprised to see them up so early. "How are you feeling, Stuart?"

Before he could answer, Jessica rolled her eyes and crossed to the table to pour a cup of coffee. "He's fine. Only my lamebrain brother would go and get himself stabbed in the shoulder."

Stuart plunked himself down in the chair next to Dakota. "Thanks for coming to my rescue, dear sister."

"Humph." Jessica moved to the railing to look down at the dock while she stirred her coffee. "I knew I'd have to post bail for you someday, but I always thought it would be for a DUI, not a robbery." Tipping her head toward Kate, Jessica gave Stuart a stern look.

He cleared his throat. "My sister seems to think I owe you an apology."

Kate pulled in a breath. "I'm sure you had your reasons for taking the money."

"Not just for that. For something I did the night before."

"Oh?"

"See," he squinted, as if the memory added to an already-present headache. "I was upset about that fight I had with my dad. I went out to the yacht to talk to Sam, but when I got there, I overheard her telling somebody on the phone that you had taken his quarter mil and that he should come take you away and get the money back. I figured I needed the money, and that you must have stashed it in the guesthouse."

Kate stared at him. "You mean *you're* the one who ransacked the guesthouse?"

He lifted a shoulder. "I don't make the best decisions under the influence of drink."

"Wait." She reached into her purse—thankful that it had been retrieved from the yacht—and took out the note. "Do you know anything about this?"

As Stuart narrowed his reddened eyes, Jessica peered over his shoulder. She snickered. "Where on earth did you find *that?*"

Taken aback by her amusement, Kate stammered. "I...I found it on my bed in the guesthouse. Any idea whose handwriting it is?"

"Sure." Jessica shrugged. "It's mine."

"Yours?" Kate gaped at Jessica. "You mean, this note is from you?"

"Well, yes, in a way. See, Friday afternoon before you arrived, the bunch of us were playing *Consequences* out here on the deck. Stuart was on the phone with one of his girlfriends—"

"Ahem." Stuart raised his eyebrows.

"—and his turn was coming up. He wouldn't listen to me, so I wrote him a note and flashed it in front of his face." She snapped it from Kate and waved it at Stuart. "He was *next*."

Kate couldn't help a smile spawned by relief. Then confusion crowded out the comfort. "But, how did it wind up on my pillow?"

"I put...put it there." Dakota ran a finger around his now-empty bowl to retrieve the last remnants of oatmeal.

Kate stared at him. "*You* did?"

"Sure. I found it on the ground by your house and I thought it...it was yours. I walked all the way around looking for a place to put it where you'd see it."

She smiled at her 'Sasquatch'. "You walked around the outside of the guesthouse?"

"Uh huh." He licked his fingers. "Then when I saw you run out, I went in and put it where I knew you'd see it."

She shook her head. "But why didn't you let

me know you were there?"

"I was a…afraid you'd make me go back."

"Oh, Dakota—"

Again, the click of the French doors interrupted Kate. This time, it was Chase who appeared in the doorway, stealing the air from her lungs. The last time she had seen him, she'd been convinced he was a wife killer who wanted to add her to his list. Now, she knew how wrong she'd been.

"Daddy." Jessica practically dropped her coffee in her haste to throw her arms around him. "Did you hear about Sam? It's so horrible."

"She's not who we thought she was." Chase gave her a reassuring hug, then smiled at Kate. "Katie. Thank goodness you're all right."

She swung her leg—which now sported a brace to accommodate the healing of her knee—to the floor, then stood. "I'm sorry I ran…or should I say 'drove'…drove away. I seriously thought you were responsible for…" She cast Jessica an apologetic glance, then tipped her head toward the divers down below. "You know. For *that*."

Closing his eyes, he nodded gently. "I hope you understand now that I only came back last night so I could take you away before Joe could harm you."

"But…" Kate slanted him a confused look. "I never *told* you about Joe."

"You didn't have to. I already knew."

"You did? But how…?"

"Let me start at the beginning." He gestured for them to sit, then started to pace as if he were about to give a business presentation.

"When we met in San Francisco, I thought you were a nice young woman, but I would never have thought to pursue a relationship with you."

Kate lowered her chin, not sure how to take that.

"Until," Chase went on, "I believe it was the third night of my business trip. I sat down at the bar and the man next to me started to boast that he was a detective and that he'd tracked you from San Diego."

Kate's face went cold. "You talked to Detective Johnson?"

"Yes…or rather, he talked to me. He told me about Joe Malone and the clinic, and that he intended to threaten to arrest you to get information. So I did what I felt I had to do. I helped you get away."

"But why? I mean, you didn't even know me."

"No, but I felt like I did. You see, you reminded me of the two women I had loved and lost."

"You helped me because I reminded you of Emily and Trina?"

"I'm sorry Katie." His look of remorse seemed genuine. "I realize now that I was trying to protect you because I failed, or *thought* I had failed, to

337

protect my wives. I thought I could somehow make up for that by saving you. I hope you can forgive me."

"Forgive you?" Her throat tightened around the words. "I don't know what would have happened to me if you hadn't stepped in."

Chase let his gaze linger on Kate for a moment before he went on. "I was prepared to go through with the wedding up until yesterday when things...changed. Sam called me in a panic. She said that you had found Trina's body and that the two of us—she and I—had to leave the country before one or the other of us got arrested."

Jessica's eyes widened. "Did you know she had done it?"

"Not until that moment did I even suspect. I had no idea she'd been pining for me all these years, or that she was responsible for Emily's drowning." He gave Stuart a sympathetic look. "I'm sorry, son. I should have paid more attention to your version of the events of that night."

A corner of Stuart's mouth lifted at the long-overdue apology.

Chase continued. "I said I couldn't leave the country because of my impending wedding," he looked at Kate, "and she told me about her plan to eliminate you."

"'Eliminate'?" Kate shuddered. "That's harsh."

"She said she had found out about Joe and that she intended to turn you over to him, so I hurried back from Vegas. I wanted to get you away from here before Joe got to you."

"But…" Kate gave him a questioning look. "Why didn't you just tell me that?"

"I wanted to get away first. I was afraid that the appearance of the body was all the police needed to build a case against me. I would have explained everything that Stuart told you."

"So, explain it now." Stuart perked up. "I saw you skulking around in the woods the night Trina vanished."

"You saw me." Chase tipped his head. "So I have no choice but to admit that I'm guilty."

The comment instantly won him everyone's full attention.

"Guilty," he added, "of being a jealous husband. After Trina and I fought about her attraction to one of the island's summer residents, I left, then snuck back to see if she'd go to him. So you see my motive for 'skulking' wasn't exactly innocent, but it was far from homicidal."

"Sorry, Dad." Stuart sounded surprisingly contrite. "I never should have doubted you."

"No, you were right to doubt me, just wrong about the reasons. I've long enjoyed the advantages to financial solvency, but the time has come for justice to be served."

Jessica's finely-plucked brows arched. "What do you mean, Daddy?"

"I mean that while I'm innocent of the crimes

of which I was unofficially accused, it's time I faced up to my other offences. I haven't exactly been upfront in my business dealings. I'm willing to pay the price for all the payoffs I've doled out over the years."

"Payoffs?" The word felt heavy as it rolled off Kate's tongue. "Is that what you were talking about when you said you could go to prison?"

He nodded. "It's a considerably less serious crime than spousicide, and not nearly as newsworthy."

The doors opened again and Kate's heart went into an immediate flutter at the sight of Josh. He also had his arm in a sling and Kate knew he was wrapped like *The Mummy's Uncle* under his shirt.

She tried to spring to her feet, but the brace reminded her to take it slowly. As she limped toward him, she realized that he hadn't arrived alone. She slowed to acknowledge the woman standing next to him. It was a nun.

Josh smiled at Kate as he addressed the group. "Good morning, everyone. This is Sister Marie Agnes from the monastery on the island. She picked me up from the hospital this morning."

As a round of confused greetings worked through the group, Kate recognized her as the same nun they'd spoken to at the general store a few days before.

Dakota lifted a wave. "Hello!"

As Sister Marie noticed him, her smile relaxed.

"Oh, hello."

Kate gave him a puzzled look. "You've met?"

"When I got off the...*ferry*...I asked her where I could find you. She told me."

Kate looked at the nun. "He's the 'nice young man' who asked about me?"

She nodded, clearly unaware of the alarms she had set off in Kate's head.

Just then, Jessica shrieked and leapt to her feet, commanding everyone's attention.

Kate turned to see the sheriff standing at the top of the stairs, and nearly choked. He was carrying a skeleton.

Chapter 31

Kate stumbled backward, and Josh placed a steadying hand on her shoulder.

The sheriff held up a hand to silence the group. "Sorry to alarm you, but I think you should see what our divers brought up."

Turning away, Kate noticed a slight smile playing across Chase's lips. She steeled herself, then forced a brave look.

The skeleton, which had appeared so gruesome through the murky water, now looked more like something you'd see in a classroom or a chiropractor's office.

She spurted out a chuckle. The thing wasn't real.

"Is that what I saw under the dock?"

"Yes ma'am." The sheriff gave it a shake, and it made a light clacking sound. "We figure it's been there a little while, but it's probably not much worse for the wear than when it took the plunge."

"You idiot!" Jessica cuffed Stuart on his good shoulder.

"Ow." He winced. "What are you hitting me

for?"

"You said you got all those things out of the woods the day after the Halloween party."

"So, I missed one. Obviously, it fell out of the tree it was hanging in. I wasn't in the best shape that day, if you remember."

"No different than any other day, *if I remember*." She cuffed him again. "Look at all the trouble you caused."

"Jessica, you're forgetting something." Kate crossed to the sheriff so she could get a better look at the wayward party decoration. "If this isn't your mom, that means there's still hope."

Jessica's face lit up.

Kate looked at Josh, who gave her a wink as he put a hand on Sister Marie's shoulder. "Just tell them what you told me, Sister."

She dipped her chin, as if she wasn't used to getting so much attention. "Last night, I was over at the general store when the ten o'clock ferry came in. I saw this young man..." she gestured toward Josh, "...having car trouble. He seemed frantic, so I offered him a ride in my van."

Josh picked up the story. "She drove me here, and I explained why I was in such a hurry to get back. That I thought Kate might be in trouble, because my roommate had called to tell me that Trina's body had been found and that it looked like Mr. Cole might be guilty—"

"And I told him to stop right there because I

knew for a fact that Mr. Cole hadn't murdered Trina Cole."

Clutching her elbows, Jessica stepped toward her. "How did you know that?"

Sister Marie put her hands to her face. "I promised I wouldn't tell. I even sent the seahorse sculpture…" She gestured toward Josh. "I told this young man about that. I wanted Marion to get the message so I wouldn't have to break my promise."

Josh put a hand on her shoulder. "Some promises need to be broken. Let's not keep everyone in suspense, okay?"

She nodded. "I knew Mr. Cole hadn't killed Trina Cole, because I knew she wasn't dead."

In the next moment, a stunning blonde wearing a pale blue sundress and a hesitant smile appeared in the doorway. Silence fell over the group.

Kate pulled in a sharp breath. It was Trina. Flesh and bones…real ones.

"M…" Jessica's voice came out in a crackly whisper. "Mom!" She ran to her, and the two women held onto each other. Stuart joined them, wrapping his one good arm around them both.

Chase held back, his hands folded. From the look on his face, Kate got the impression that Trina's appearance had come as no surprise to him.

"I don't understand." Jessica spoke through a tear-filled voice. "What are you doing here?"

"Well," Trina wiped her cheeks. "When I read last evening's paper and found out that my body had been found, I just about died."

Everyone laughed, breaking the last bit of tension in the air.

"Then dear Sister Marie Agnes returned to the monastery with a surprise."

"Wait." Stuart frowned. "You mean, you were staying on Shaw this whole time?"

She nodded. "If you'll remember a year ago, I was pretty upset. I wasn't being a very good wife or mother, and I think I had announced once or twice that I was ready to just leave all of you."

"I remember." Chase looked askance. "The sailor."

Trina looked distraught. "There was nothing between me and 'the sailor'."

Chase looked at her sideways. "No?"

"No."

"But what happened?" Jessica clung to her mother's arm as if fearful she'd vanish if she let go.

"As you all know, I had lived with the press hounding us for years about Emily's death. There were always the rumors, whispers behind our backs that Chase had killed his first wife. Over the years, I saw how easily Chase's anger could flare up, and I have to admit that I had my doubts. I knew he was involved in some shady business dealings and frankly, I had stopped trusting him."

Kate eased back into her chair, and Josh

moved to stand next to her.

"Then when Stuart told me he had his suspicions about his mother's death, I started to get scared." Trina looked at Chase. "And you got so angry with me when I tried to talk to you about it. Remember, you turned it into a fight about Bruce."

"Bruce?" Jessica asked.

"The 'sailor'," Trina explained.

"I hope you can forgive me." Chase folded his hands in front of him. "I'd been falsely accused for twenty years, and when I thought you were turning against me, I didn't handle it as well as I should have."

"So you stormed off, leaving me with no one to turn to but Sam...my *friend*." Trina's emphasis on that word imbued it with an added touch of irony.

Stuart raised a hand. "But Dad came back that next night to spy on you."

Trina raised a brow at Chase.

He lifted his hands in defense. "I wanted to see if you went to meet the sailor—"

"Bruce."

"Yes. *Bruce*. I was relieved to see you leave with Sam."

"I didn't know who else to turn to. She suggested we go out on the yacht, like we always did. Only this time, she started to act strange." She regarded Chase narrowly. "She told me that she was in love with you. Did you know that?"

"Not until yesterday."

"Well, she got a little hysterical. She told me that if the authorities found out about the payoffs you'd been making to FDA officials, I would be the one to go to prison. She convinced me that the two of you would make it look like it was all my doing, and I know how persuasive you can be when you start throwing money around."

Chase shook his head. "You might be considered legally culpable as my spouse, but you wouldn't go to prison."

Trina pinched the bridge of her nose. "Anyway, it was a terrible, stormy night, and she went to the bow of the boat and said she was going to jump off and kill herself."

Kate shook her head. "That's not the way she tells it."

"Sam is not to be trusted. Well, of course, I tried to stop her, but she fought me off. The boat tipped and I lost my balance."

A chill traveled through Kate at the reminder of her own ordeal. "What did you do?"

"I just started swimming. I decided to get myself to the dock behind the general store where Bruce kept his boat."

"Bruce," Chase repeated dryly. "The *sailor*."

"Please forgive me, Chase. But I honestly thought you had killed Emily, and that Sam meant what she said about making me pay the price for your crimes. I was afraid to go home. Anyway, once I got to the dock, I discovered that Bruce's boat was gone."

Sister Marie spoke. "That's where I came in. Trina stumbled out onto the road, looking like the Creature from the Black Lagoon. She told me her story and asked if she could stay with us until she sorted out what to do. She asked me not to let on that she was there, and I agreed, of course not realizing what a stir her disappearance would cause."

"At the monastery," Trina said, "I was surprised to find some of my glass pieces."

"We love to collect local art." Sister Marie explained.

"I was so upset about everything in my life, that I shattered them. Sister Marie swept up all the pieces, and over the next months helped me to heal and to find peace and God. When she presented me with the broken glass, I literally put the pieces back together by creating mosaics from the artwork I had destroyed."

Kate smiled. "The seahorse."

"That was one of them, yes." Trina gave her a gentle smile.

Sister Marie kneaded her hands together. "And when I finally started to realize what a problem this was, I sent the seahorse sculpture to Marion. I thought she'd pick up on the clue. I guess I should have been a little more direct."

Chase cleared his throat. "Then last night, as I was panicking, thinking I had killed that poor deputy, the sister and Josh suddenly appeared in her van. I told Josh where to find you," he gestured toward Kate, "and the sister and I took care of the deputy. I told her my situation and she drove me to the monastery before the sheriff came. Imagine my surprise at finding my 'dead' wife there." Chase closed the gap between himself and Trina. "We've been up most of the night negotiating the terms of a second chance."

For a long moment, the group encased the two of them in a collective hopeful gaze, until Stuart broke the spell.

"Hey Dad. I've been thinking about our conversation. You know, about me getting a job?"

Chase gave Trina's hand a squeeze before turning his attention to his son. "Yes?"

"I think I might like to become a ski instructor."

Dakota's eyes lit up. "You sk...ski? Will you teach me?"

"Sure, bro." Stuart gave Dakota's arm a friendly flick. "Anybody can ski with the right teacher."

As the boys' conversation hopscotched from skiing to snowboarding to skateboarding, Chase moved to the chair on Kate's other side. "I think I speak for both of us when I say it's best we call off the engagement."

"I'd have to agree." She smiled, then glanced at Trina. "Besides, I have a feeling the second Mrs. Cole is going to be happy she gave you that second chance."

"I'm banking on that." He winked at Kate, then again at Josh as he stood.

Claiming the seat Chase had just vacated, Josh cleared his throat. "If you're up to it later, maybe we could go grab some burgers and take in a movie."

"Sounds good." Her cheeks heated a little at the thought of going on an actual date with the *actual* man of her dreams.

"Or…" His eyes seemed to catch a glint off the sparkling water below. "We could go kayaking."

"Kayaking?"

"Sure. I'm an old hand at it now."

Kate felt her jaw literally drop. "You mean, that's how you got out to the yacht last night?"

He nodded in triumph. "I had no other choice. Mr. Cole had told me you were out there and that you were probably in trouble."

"But you said you'd rather die than get into a small boat like that."

"I didn't say I'd rather see *you* die, which seemed like a distinct possibility."

"You're right about that." She smiled lightly. "And I was right too. About fate bringing Chase into my life. That was one of the best things that ever happened to me."

"Yeah?" He raised a brow.

"Uh huh. Because that's what brought me to you."

As they shared a smile, she glanced out at Blind Bay, where her life had almost ended the night before, but had instead only just begun.

Epilogue

One year later.

"Do you trust me?"

"Well…" Glancing down at the gorgeous vintage dress that Audrey Hepburn herself would have loved, Kate pretended to ponder. "Promise not to get any frosting on the lace?"

"Cross my heart." Josh made an X over his chest with his finger. "Now do you trust me?"

Her grin blossomed. "With my life."

Grinning, he placed a bite of cake gently in her mouth while she did the same. He flicked a dollop of frosting onto her nose. "Good thing."

The friends and family surrounding them laughed and applauded as cameras clicked. Kate didn't even mind that a few of them belonged to members of the media.

As the cake was served and their guests returned to mingling, Kate and Josh scanned the beautifully manicured front lawn of what had once been the Cole home but now served as the headquarters of the Safe Harbor Foundation,

Kate's non-profit organization which housed teenage runaways. Standing at the center of the enormous front porch, she felt like a princess surveying her kingdom.

"There you two are." They looked down as Marion mounted the stairs carrying a large box wrapped with what was, knowing Marion, hand-stamped paper.

"I'm setting this on the gift table, but I want you know that it's fragile."

"Let me." Josh reached out and took the box as Marion hit the top step. He turned and disappeared into the house.

"Thank you so much." Kate smiled at Marion, who had definitely lightened up since her best friend's resurrection. "It will look beautiful on the mantle of the guesthouse."

Marion gave her a wry look. "Why Kate. You talk as if you already know what it is."

Kate feigned innocence. "Well, Jocelyn hinted that you had finally decided what to do with the seahorse. When she said 'no' to both my guesses—keeping it or selling it—I kind of assumed..."

Marion smiled. "Jocelyn never could keep a secret."

As Marion slipped into the line for cake, Josh returned. He stood behind Kate and put his arms around her waist. "That gift table is now officially overflowing."

"Everyone's been so generous. Especially

Chase and Trina." Glancing over the heads of their friends—his from Seattle and hers from Sacramento and San Diego—she leaned into his embrace. "I still can't get used to thinking that we're actually going to be living in the guesthouse."

Josh kissed the side of her head, just below where the baby's breath clung to her brunette chignon. "It's perfect. And with Dakota living over here with the Safe Harbor kids—"

"Are you sure he can handle the job?"

"He's the maintenance man, not the CEO. He can handle it. Besides, we'll be right next door."

"Excuse me, you two."

They turned to see Jessica, looking downright demure in her lavender bridesmaid dress, balancing two small plates of food. Tad followed, carrying two cups of punch.

"As my last official duty as maid of honor, I'm making sure the two of you eat." With a satisfied grin, she handed each of them a plate.

"Thanks. I'm starved." Kate smiled at Jessica, who still had the occasional diva moment, but had undergone a lot of changes since her mother's return. She'd gotten her own place—a cute little house in Friday Harbor, conveniently located just a few blocks from Tad's apartment—and a job at Marion's art gallery.

Tad set the drinks down on the porch rail and addressed Josh. "I didn't get a chance to tell you I loved your documentary. The one about the artist. What are you doing next?"

Josh picked up an egg roll. "After we get back from our honeymoon, I'm going to the penitentiary in Atwater, California to interview Joe Malone."

Jessica shuddered. "Isn't that a little scary?"

"I've already faced my biggest fear." He gave Kate a wink. "After that, nothing seems to faze me."

Kate picked up a chicken skewer. "Josh is making a documentary about scam artists, and how people like Joe take advantage of teenage runaways."

Jessica's face lit up as she turned to Tad. "They got Shania Hane to narrate the documentary. Isn't that awesome?"

"My son-in-law has some impressive connections."

"Mom." Kate turned to see her mom approach, along with Trina. Both of them carried plates of cake. "You look like you're having a good time."

"I am." Her mom brushed the last bit of frosting off Kate's nose. "Trina is trying to convince me to go back to Seattle with her to spend a couple of days in her condo."

Trina nodded. "I promised I'd give her some glass-making lessons, right Ellen?"

Kate's mom smiled. "She has her own studio

right in her condo, did you know that?"

Kate grinned. It was good to see her mom feeling so happy and free. She had confided in Kate that her running away had opened her eyes to how abusive Kate's stepfather was. It had been a blessing when the marriage had dissolved soon after.

"I'd appreciate the company." Trina slid her fork across the creamy white frosting. "It's going to be lonely in that big condo for the next year until Chase gets released."

"I can't wait to meet him." Kate's mom gave Kate a side hug. "I want to thank him in person for everything he's done for you and Josh. Letting you use this house. Funding your movie."

"He really has turned a corner." Trina beamed. "He's like a new man."

"Speaking of new men." Kate gestured with her plate toward the edge of the driveway, where Stuart and Dakota balanced on a log, as if in the middle of a snowless snowboarding lesson. "If you had told me a year ago that Stuart would be teaching skiing at Whistler and coming up on his one year anniversary of sobriety, I don't think I would have believed it."

"They're going to get their tuxes dirty." Trina tsked. "Come on, Ellen. We're going to ask them to dance."

"Oooh. Sounds like fun." Jessica took Tad's arm. "Come on, Deputy. Let's dance."

"Excuse me, Mr. and Mrs. Collins." The photographer who had chased her down in Friday Harbor all those months ago looked like a different person with his nice suit and fresh haircut. "I'd love to get a shot of the two of you here with the bay in the background. *People* needs their cover shot."

Smiling, they situated themselves next to the porch railing and gazed at each other. They had agreed to a cover story for the magazine, on the condition that it focus more on Kate's foundation and Josh's film than on the scandal of the Cole family.

"Let's get one of you kissing the bride."

"How about it, Mrs. Collins?" Josh smiled. "Every good movie ends with a kiss." He took her in his arms and lowered her in an elaborate dip. "Even the one about the swamp monster."

She giggled. As his lips touched hers, her amusement gave way to something else. She returned the kiss with the joy that came from finally finding what she'd been looking for. Not just passion or protection, but something more. She clung to him, giving over control of her fate to God, and the only man who'd ever made her feel truly safe.

"That's perfect." The photographer called out between shots. "Just like that."

As his camera clicked and whirred, Kate smiled up at Josh and counted her blessings. It had been a long journey, but this runaway had finally found her way home.

The End

Coming Summer 2015…

by Janalyn Voigt

Chapter 1

Piper closed her eyes and tilted her face toward the morning sun, letting herself think of nothing at all. There was only the sway of the pier and the wind fingering her hair as it left the kiss of salt on her lips. A stray tear cooled the corner of one eye, and her throat thickened.

When had she stopped letting herself feel the joy of the moment?

Harsh cries rose above the beat of a motor, and with a sigh she opened her eyes. Seagulls wheeled above a small speedboat arrowing toward a small fleet of pleasure craft anchored beyond the marina's fuel dock. With the tranquility shattered, she turned away just as light flashed in her peripheral vision.

What was that?

The small mystery held her. Perhaps on one of the boats riding at anchor something metallic had caught the sun. The vessels gleamed pristine white, yielding no answers. The engine cut out, and in sudden silence the speedboat slid through the blue waters.

There it was again.

Light flashed from one of the boats as a figure at the helm lowered an arm. Someone had been using binoculars. How ridiculous to feel they'd been trained on her, but she couldn't help the uncanny awareness crawling up her spine.

An anchor glinted, and the speedboat dragged to a stop. The wash from its wake kept coming.

Piper braced as water sloshed beneath the weathered boards at her feet and buffeted the dock. The vessels in the marina creaked and groaned against their moorings. She balanced on the balls of her feet until the water smoothed over, but for some reason the dock was still pitching.

"Prince!" A girl's voice called as claws scrabbled on wood.

Piper turned to see what was wrong. Massive paws thudded into her shoulders. A hairy monster filled her vision. She flailed, and the dock slammed into her. The monster stood over her with fanged mouth gaping and paws planted on her shoulders.

"*Prince!* Stop that."

Ignoring this suggestion, Prince slathered Piper's face with his tongue.

"Ooomph! You…great big…oaf. *Get off!*"

Prince, seemingly impervious to the yanking of his studded collar, whined deep in his throat.

"I mean it, Prince. Sit!"

Prince whined again but removed his paws from Piper's shoulders and withdrew to crouch on his haunches nearby. Rolling to her side with cautious movements, Piper watched her adversary for any sign of a renewed attack.

A young girl captured Prince's leash, her blond hair swinging in a ponytail. Dressed in faded jeans, a pale blue sweatshirt, and sneakers, she looked about twelve and far too light to manage such a brute. "I *am* sorry. Prince is a good dog. He just doesn't know his size."

"Dog? I took him for a small bear, although I wondered where he came by those whiskers." Piper pushed into a sitting position, doing her best to smile.

The girl returned the effort, her smile transforming her face. "You're all right, aren't you?" She extended the hand not clutching the dog's leash.

"I'll be okay." Hesitant to touch her with Prince on guard, Piper scrambled to her feet without help and smoothed her fleece jacket with shaking hands.

"I'm glad you're not hurt. My aunt almost didn't let me bring my dog on vacation, saying he was bound to be a problem. If I can't keep him out of trouble, he'll have to go to a kennel." She said the last part in an indignant tone.

The girl's aunt probably had a point, although Piper kept her opinion to herself.

"My name's Lindy Carlisle, by the way. That's our yacht, the *Lady Gray*." She waved a nonchalant hand at the yacht moored alongside the t-head dock where they stood. "This is my first visit to the San Juans."

"I'm Piper Harrington, and it's my first visit here, too."

"Are you a boater?"

Piper shook her head. "No, I came out for a walk and stopped to admire the boats. The *Lady Gray* is beautiful. I'm renting a condo here at Rosario Resort."

"We're neighbors, then. My aunt and I are staying at one of the condos, too. Behave yourself!"

Lindy's last words were for Prince, now thumping the pier with repeated blows from his tail as he wiggled ever closer. At his mistress's reprimand, he plopped down and divided mournful glances between them.

Piper laughed. "Prince doesn't look so scary as when we first met."

"He's still a puppy, but being an Irish

wolfhound, he's already big. My aunt doesn't like him much."

So far the girl had spoken of her aunt only by title and not by name. Perhaps they weren't close. Why, then, were they traveling together? Such things were none of Piper's business, of course. "Have you been here long?"

"Only a couple of days."

"Are you planning to visit Mount Constitution? It's the highest peak in the San Juan Islands, and the view is supposed to be miraculous."

Lindy's brow furrowed. "My aunt doesn't care for sightseeing." She flicked Prince's leash. "Come on, boy." The dog lumbered to his feet, his back coming almost to Piper's waist. "I'd better get back before she sends the police after me."

Such a dramatic remark from a pre-teen might have passed Piper by if it hadn't been for the girl's look of bewildered pain. During their marriage Able had teased Piper about her tendency to take in stray animals, champion lost causes, and rush in where angels feared to tread. He'd listed all the reasons she shouldn't interfere in other people's lives. And yet...a young girl should never have to look like that. Piper drew a breath. "What about your parents? Will they be joining you and your aunt?"

Lindy's eyes widened. "My mother died six months ago, and my father—well he—you see, he..."

"Forgive me. I shouldn't have asked. I'm sorry about your loss." Able had been right, as usual.

"Lindy!" A red-headed woman wearing sunglasses and what looked like an expensive black pantsuit called from the end of the dock. "How long does it take to walk a dog?" Something in the tilt of the woman's head gave Piper the impression she was watching her rather than her niece.

Lindy rolled her eyes. "I have to go." Holding Prince on a short leash, she started down the pier with a hesitant step. After a moment's conversation, the pair moved off toward the condos with the dog pulling at his leash, tail wagging like a flag.

Light reflecting from the water made rippling patterns up the side of the yacht. Piper tilted her head to gaze at the majestic vessel as a familiar yearning stirred. Her dream of cutting loose and sailing the seven seas with her husband had remained unfulfilled. Able had loved the idea, and they'd had the means to carry off such a trip, but he had been too entrenched in New York's literary scene to break away for long.

Hugging herself, Piper looked out across Cascade Bay to Eastsound. Beyond the shifting waters of the inlet that divided Orcas Island nearly in two, the emerald swells of Blakely Island cupped the water as if with gentle hands.

If they'd gone, he'd be alive today.

Piper caught her breath and blinked away sudden moisture. In the nearly two years since Able's car crash, she'd laid far too many tears at the altar of memory. For sanity's sake, it was time to free herself of grief.

Her thoughts weren't helping her mood any. A distraction was in order.

At her condo, Piper pulled off her fleece jacket, which smelled a lot like dog, and dropped it into the hamper. An inspection in the bathroom mirror revealed a pale woman with eyes nearly as dark as her tousled shoulder-length hair. Although she'd showered before going out, the smell of dog still clung to her…

As she stepped into the shower, the spray instantly warmed her. Lifting her face, she scrubbed away the dried saliva from her encounter with Prince, then let the water thrum against the back of her neck to ease her knotted muscles.

The morning hadn't started well, but if she wore her favorite jeans and sloppiest sweatshirt any day could be improved. With the worn fabric comfortable against her skin and her hair dried and pulled into a simple ponytail at the back of her head, Piper felt ready for an adventure. She filled her water bottle and threw a bag of potato chips, some cheese, and an apple into a satchel. A bungee cord would easily secure the satchel to the back of the serviceable bicycle that had come with the condo.

It had been five years or more since her last bike ride, but it was supposed to be something you never forgot how to do. Going the eight miles to Doe Bay might be more than she could manage, but it would be fun to try. According to the Orcas Island visitor's guide, the Doe Bay resort boasted soaking tubs and a sauna. After today's two showers, she'd pass on both, but dining at the restaurant would be a nice reward, although eating alone in public still cost her a small effort.

Of course, all of that depended on her making it up the hill to Olga Road, also known as the Horseshoe Highway because it formed that shape as it curved around Orcas Island. It had seemed so much less steep when she'd driven it yesterday in the rental car. At least this part would be *downhill* when she came back. She made slow progress and had to climb off and walk the bike now and again, each time vowing to visit the gym more regularly. Since it was midweek and barely summer the traffic was light. Thankfully, that meant fewer witnesses to her humiliation.

Piper reached the highway and stopped to drink from her water bottle. The day had warmed, making her wish she'd layered her clothing. She perched on the bike, undecided. Going back to the condo would be an easy ride, but the road didn't seem too bad now. The guidebook claimed the ride to Doe Bay wasn't difficult.

A deer stepped from the forest across the highway. Piper held her breath and went motionless. The deer glanced backward, and then dipped her head to graze alongside the road as two spotted fawns with ears twitching emerged behind her. Piper waited until the gentle creatures ranged northward along the road before sending her bike south toward Doe Bay. The unexpected sight had enticed her with possibilities. What other discoveries might today bring?

The forgotten freedom of riding a bike on a summer day sent a shaft of pure joy through her. She had left her bike at her mother's house in Stockton without a backward glance after marrying Able. What had Mom done with it? It hadn't been there when she and her brother, Paul, had gone through her mother's things after her funeral. Perhaps Mom had held onto it for a while before giving it away, remembering the daughter who had grown and gone.

Piper rode on amid the scents of road dust and evergreen needles until reaching Cascade Lake, where the cooling breeze off the water came as welcome. At the day-use area she refilled her water bottle and slipped into the shade of the charming stone picnic shelter. It was crowded, but she found a spot a little apart from the families gathered there.

The apple in her satchel was crisp and sweet, not surprising since Washington was famous for this particular fruit. She pulled her cell phone out of her bag. Her phone advised her there was no signal, so she switched it off. Checking her emails was a ploy that helped her feel less awkward when eating alone, anyway. One of the families packed up and another took its place. Voices echoed from the trail around the lake and boats dotted the blue waters. Cascade Lake was obviously well loved.

Piper ripped the bag of potato chips open, then looked up into a pair of light eyes that were a cross between green and brown, made all the more striking by their owner's tanned skin and dark hair. He wore a white button-down shirt and dark blue jeans and carried a day pack. "May I join you? The other tables are full."

A glance around the shelter told her this was true. "Yes, of course." She could hardly refuse without seeming selfish, but now she really felt awkward.

"Thanks."

The smile that lit his face nudged a memory. Had they met before? He slung his day pack onto the bench and sat across from her. She realized she was staring and dragged her gaze away as heat rose into her cheeks. Hopefully, he wouldn't mistake her interest, although he *was* attractive. In fact, maybe she noticed him a little more than felt comfortable. Piper's stomach clenched, and she stood up without looking at her table mate. This situation wasn't something she could handle. "I was just leaving." She fled the picnic shelter.

"Wait!" He called after her, causing several heads to turn her direction. After catching up to her, he held up her satchel. "You left this."

"Oh. Thank you." She reached for the satchel, but he didn't release it.

"I didn't mean to drive you away. Please. Go back and finish your lunch. I feel bad for upsetting you."

Piper opened her mouth to deny being upset but couldn't quite make that claim, although not for the reasons he'd named. She tugged the satchel out of his grasp. "No, it's all right. Really. I needed to come out and stretch a bit. My legs were cramping. It's been years since I rode a bike."

He smiled that familiar smile. "How far have you come today?"

"Just from Rosario." She bent to strap the satchel onto the bike.

"Do you think you can you make it back?"

"Oh, yes. I'm doing so well I may go on to Doe Bay." There was no need to add that last part, but his question had stung her pride a little.

His eyes widened. "That's quite a distance. Look, I hate to nip ambition in the bud, but maybe you should choose a closer destination. You might not do so well on the return trip, and then you'd be stuck."

She frowned. "I hadn't thought of it in that light."

He smiled. "Olga is worth seeing and only a couple of miles more. It's a historic town with a café and art gallery."

She straddled her bike and fastened her helmet. "Thanks for the suggestion."

He looked past her to the lake. "I know we've only just met, but would you be interested in having coffee with me?" The tips of his ears turned pink, as if he'd embarrassed himself.

"Thanks for the offer, but I'm not really ready for something like that." Regret tinged her voice, but she had to be honest.

"Thought I'd try." The glance he sent her almost had her changing her mind. "Have fun today."

"I will." Piper pushed the bike into motion but stopped at the road and looked back. He was standing where she'd left him, looking oddly forlorn. He must be very lonely. For that matter, she had to be, too. Why else would she feel such a wrench at parting from a stranger? After returning his wave, Piper turned away to follow the road as it skirted the lake.

Something was nagging at her, but she couldn't say what. The encounter had unsettled her so much it was hard to pay attention on the mechanics of shifting gears. The forest closed in, and she slipped through light and shadow, giving herself to the journey.

A silver Mazda was parked alongside the road

with its nose facing south, its windows so darkly tinted she couldn't tell if anyone was inside. Maybe the driver had stopped to eat lunch. Just past the car, she came to a one-lane bridge lined by concrete rails topped by moss. A cliff rose on one side of the vintage structure and a drop fell away on the other. The curve of the road made it impossible to see if anything was coming. She strained to hear the sound of an approaching vehicle. In a car crossing would have seemed considerably less intimidating, but it wasn't far and she couldn't hear anything coming. Her tires swished onto the bridge.

An engine roared to life, and as she glanced back, the silver Mazda hurtled toward her.

ACKNOWLEDGMENTS

To the lovely people of Shaw Island and Friday Harbor. Thanks for letting me bring a little mayhem to your community.

Michael Berry from
Underwater Criminal Investigators, LLC. Thanks for teaching me everything I could ever want to know about underwater body recovery.

My brother, Jeff Even, for giving me the right legal terminology. It's good to have a lawyer in the family.

Lynnette Bonner. Thanks for the fabulous formatting!

ABOUT THE AUTHOR

Born in Missoula, Montana, Lesley earned a degree in acting at Willamette University in Salem, Oregon. She fell in love with theatrical costuming, and pursued that as a career while nurturing her passion for writing on the side.

Between working as a homeschooling mom and a professional theatre costumer, Lesley has completed several novels. She would have done more by now if she didn't occasionally stop to clean the house. Fortunately, she loves to cook, so no one in her family has starved yet.

Lesley now resides in the Seattle area with her husband, two daughters, three cats and a big loud dog. She is a member of the Northwest Christian Writers Association.

In her spare time (ha!) she chips away at her goal of reading every book ever written.

Please visit her website at:
www.lesleyannmcdaniel.com

11754875R00225

Made in the USA
San Bernardino, CA
28 May 2014